Advance P...

Lost & Found in Lunenburg

"With her latest novel, Jane Doucet brings us a whip-smart, sweet (and salty) tale of love, loss, and starting over. Brimming with heart, humour, and hope, *Lost & Found in Lunenburg* is charm defined and a pure delight from beginning to end."

BOBBI FRENCH
Raddall-shortlisted author of
The Good Women of Safe Harbour

"Every time I open a Jane Doucet novel, I know I am going to find a world full of characters who feel like friends, and *Lost & Found in Lunenburg* is no exception. But while this novel has the cheekiness, wit, and heart you expect from Doucet, it is also a startlingly poignant meditation on grief and resilience. Above all, Doucet writes with a joyfulness that you can't help but get swept up in."

AMY JONES
Leacock finalist and author of *Pebble & Dove*

"Big-hearted, playful, and chock-full of truths, *Lost & Found in Lunenburg* explores midlife love, loss, and second chances with warmth and wit. With a quirky cast and rollicking prose, Doucet reminds us of the healing power of community to help us live and love again."

ALI BRYAN
Leacock-shortlisted author of *Coq* and *The Figgs*

Lost & Found in Lunenburg

Jane Doucet

Vagrant PRESS

Vagrant Press is an imprint of
Nimbus Publishing Limited
3660 Strawberry Hill St, Halifax, NS, B3K 5A9
(902) 455-4286 nimbus.ca

Printed and bound in Canada. Vagrant Press is based in Kjipuktuk, Mi'km'aki, the traditional territory of the Mi'kmaq People.

Editor: Whitney Moran
Cover design: Jenn Embree
Typesetting: Rudi Tusek
NB1667

This story is a work of fiction. Names, characters, incidents, and places, including organizations and institutions, are used fictitiously.

Library and Archives Canada Cataloguing in Publication
Title: Lost & found in Lunenburg / Jane Doucet.
Other titles: Lost and found in Lunenburg
Names: Doucet, Jane, 1968- author.
Identifiers: Canadiana (print) 20230217842 | Canadiana (ebook) 20230217850 | ISBN 9781774712252
  (softcover) | ISBN 9781774712269 (EPUB)
Classification: LCC PS8607.O9143 L67 2023 | DDC C813/.6—dc23

Nimbus Publishing acknowledges the financial support for its publishing activities from the Government of Canada, the Canada Council for the Arts, and from the Province of Nova Scotia. We are pleased to work in partnership with the Province of Nova Scotia to develop and promote our creative industries for the benefit of all Nova Scotians.

For Craig, and fresh starts

❧

In memory of Cheryl Lamerson

Prologue

SHORTLY AFTER ROSE AINSWORTH'S FIFTIETH birthday everything went to shit. A catastrophic collision at a busy downtown street corner would change the course of the rest of her life.

On a sunny Friday morning in mid-November, a delivery van struck Rose's husband, Jim, on his bike ride to work. The police officer who rang the front doorbell was impossibly kind, and wise beyond her years, as she broke the news to Rose. And strong, Rose noted weakly, when the young woman's uniformed arms wrapped around hers as her own knees buckled.

In that moment, Rose managed to absorb only big-picture details. The distraught driver had called 911, sobbing. *Sunblindness* was a factor. It was deemed an *unavoidable collision.*

The driver was devastated. So was Rose.

The rest of that day passed by in a blur.

It was some comfort to later learn from the medical examiner's report that Jim had died instantly from the impact. Unfortunately, that detail did nothing to lessen Rose's shock and grief.

In the days following the accident, Rose operated on autopilot. She called the funeral home and made the necessary arrangements. Wrote an obituary and a eulogy. Dug out a demure black dress from the depths of her closet. Delivered the eulogy dry-eyed. Received and responded to an outpouring of condolences and sympathy. Performed a dizzying number of administrative death duties. Fed and walked their two dogs. She was efficient, if nothing else.

In the weeks following the memorial service, Rose lost count of the number of times well-meaning relatives and friends told her *you shouldn't make any big changes in your life until at least one year after a loved one's death.*

It was sensible advice. And Rose considered herself to be a sensible person. Which is why she couldn't explain how, just three months later, she found herself signing the paperwork that would make her the sole proprietor of a sex shop in Lunenburg, a tiny coastal Nova Scotia town an hour's drive away. Ignoring the little voice in her head that kept whispering, *Don't do it.*

One

TWO WEEKS BEFORE THAT FATEFUL DAY, JIM MERCER had managed to pull off a mind-blowing surprise party for his wife's milestone birthday. It fell on the first of November, a cold, grey Saturday. Once, in the early years of their marriage, Rose had hidden friends in their tiny Toronto apartment to shout "Happy birthday!" at her husband on his special day, but he had never planned anything like that for her. In fact, their lives had been fairly quiet since moving to Halifax thirteen years earlier. They had been drawn there mainly by Jim's ad-agency promotion, but also by the slower pace of life and affordable house prices in the small capital city of Rose's home province. And to be closer to her family.

Three years after moving to the East Coast, when Rose was forty and Jim thirty-five, they handed in the keys to their south end apartment. They had become the proud homeowners of a charming red-brick house on Drummond Court, a curving street in the north end's historic Hydrostone District. When Rose first viewed the post–World War II home, it reminded her of the childhood dollhouse her father had built for her. Sold! Just a few years before the Halifax housing market burned red-hot. She and Jim felt at home right away.

At twelve hundred square feet, the place was just the right size for them, plus a pair of one-year-old mutts they adopted from an animal shelter soon after the last piece of furniture was in place. The dogs were siblings, and Rose and Jim couldn't bear to break them up. They decided to change their names, however—Bonnie and Clyde they were not. Of questionable breeds, the friendly female was christened Molly, the scruffy male Relic. Both loved to stick their snouts into smelly seaweed on beach walks, and the names stuck. Beachcombers, they were.

On Rose's fiftieth, they had supper and a cake aflame with candles with her older sister, Daisy, her brother-in-law, Steve, and the four Turner kids in suburban Bedford. Rose could barely believe her nieces and nephew had grown so big, so fast. Athletic Ella was twenty and living at home while studying kinesiology at Dalhousie University. Katie was eighteen and in her final year of high school, with plans to submit her photography portfolio to art college. Awkward, serious, fifteen-year-old Ryan loved showing Jim the newest additions to his extensive comic-book collection. Lulu Rose, a thirteen-year-old piano prodigy, was studying at the Maritime Conservatory and was every bit as sweet as the day she was born.

Rose squeezed each of them in turn before she and Jim readied to leave, laden with gift bags.

"How's it feel to hit the half-century mark?" asked Daisy as she watched Rose and Jim button their coats in the messy front entryway littered with boots.

"Old as dirt," said Rose, wrapping a red scarf snugly around her neck.

"You're literally middle-aged," said Ryan. "If you live to be a hundred."

"That's what he told me when I turned fifty, too," said Daisy, ruffling her son's shaggy brown hair.

"Thanks, pal," said Rose, hugging her nephew again as punishment. Except it wasn't. He loved his aunt. In fact, his sensitive, caring nature had gotten him bullied in school. Until he started doing jiu-jitsu and taking kids twice his size down to the mat.

Jim and Rose waved as they pulled out of the driveway. When he opened their front door on Drummond, her heart skipped several beats as a chorus of "Surprise!" lit up the living room. Rose blinked several times before she was able to trust her eyes.

In front of her stood the smiling faces of some of her favourite people on the planet. Neighbourhood friends. Sharon, her best friend from childhood, who still lived an hour away in their hometown of Wolfville. But most surprising were two women who had flown in from Toronto: Rima and Yuki, Rose's longtime colleagues at *Dash*.

When Rose lived in Toronto, she had been the national fitness magazine's health editor. Now, she worked remotely as its executive editor. Over the years, the small team had stuck by each other and had been rewarded with promotions for their loyalty and hard work. They had grown professionally, and personally, together. Deputy editor Rima was forty-one. She had married Rose and Jim's former plumber after an arranged engagement to a man in India fell apart when Rima learned he didn't want children. Associate editor Yuki was thirty-six, single, and still playing the field. Fifty-year-old Alison, the magazine's creative director, was sidelined at home recovering from a double mastectomy. Editorial director Kelly, in her mid-fifties, who remained steadfast in her "no socializing with staff outside the office" policy, had sent Rose an enormous floral arrangement and a generous gift card to a spa.

"I can't believe you came!" said Rose, bursting into tears while wrapping her coworkers in a warm group hug. Six times a year she flew to Toronto to work with them at the office, but they conducted the rest of their business over emails and video calls. After so many years with a single employer, Rose would admit only to herself that she was tiring of the routine.

"Christ, you're as big a mush-bag as ever, even though you're ancient and decrepit," said Yuki, kissing Rose's tear-stained cheek. "And probably still as square." (Yuki found it laughable that while Rose's parents had once been hippies, their younger daughter had never even smoked pot.) The women held each other tightly. Yuki had never forgotten her older coworker's kindness when she had found herself unexpectedly pregnant at twenty-three. Since she couldn't tell her strict, traditional Japanese parents, she had turned to Rose for support.

Molly and Relic, now eleven, were lapping up the attention being lavished upon them by the guests, delirious that someone had discovered their treat jar on the kitchen counter.

"Make them sit and shake a paw," said Jim sternly, likely aware that no one was paying attention to him. He laughed at how fast the dogs' tails were wagging. *Best decision ever, adopting those two*, Rose thought each time she looked at them curled up together on the couch.

෴

Late that night, after everyone had gone home or to a hotel, Rose lay in bed with Jim spooning her. Jim's right hand cupped her left breast under her T-shirt, while the fingers of his left hand ran through her hair.

Rose thought wistfully about a long-ago birthday that had been far less fun. Her thirty-seventh. How full of angst she had been in the year leading up to it. Back then, she had tied herself tightly into knots of indecision about whether she wanted to have a baby. Not long after that birthday, she had needed surgery to fix a painful twisted ovary. The surgeon had also removed two ovarian cysts, cautioning her that there would probably be more in the future. Then he had suggested that she start trying to conceive sooner rather than later.

At that time in their lives, Rose had been undecided about parenthood. Jim? A firm "not right now." The night Rose was discharged home from the hospital, she had brought up the surgeon's words. And shared her feelings about them.

"Don't you know what kind of pressure that puts on me?" Rose had said. "You have the luxury of having lots of time to make up your mind. I don't. What if we wait too long and then it's too late?"

Jim's heated reply: "Do you know what kind of pressure having you constantly bring up this topic puts on *me*? You're just out of the hospital, you're tired and emotional, and now isn't the right time to have this conversation."

"I get the impression that as far as you're concerned, it will never be the right time to have this conversation," Rose had shot back. "If I had known you didn't want children, I would never have married you. We even had a conversation about having kids before we got engaged, but you don't *remember it*."

Rose distinctly recalled that Jim had rolled his eyes. "That was years ago. I can't remember what I had for dinner last week. I just wish you'd stop asking me to predict how I'm going to feel in a year or two, because I don't know."

And so, Rose had stopped asking. Looking back now, she was sorry she had been so self-absorbed. And that she had been so hard on Jim. And, on herself.

In the end, the universe had decided for her. Or her body had, anyway. At forty-one, a total hysterectomy to relieve unbearable ovary and fibroid pain had launched her into full-blown menopause.

Adoption was never discussed. If pressed, Rose would have admitted that, even before the surgery, she'd made her peace with not having children. She and Jim had enjoyed babysitting Daisy's kids when they were young. Now, they loved their home, their dogs, and their neighbours. They had fulfilling careers. They travelled to places like Cornwall and Copenhagen, eager to share one adventure after another.

Rose and Jim had each other. They were enough.

THE MORNING AFTER HER BIRTHDAY PARTY, ROSE
met Rima and Yuki for brunch at a trendy north end restaurant.
The clouds that had been hanging around for days finally lifted,
beaming sunshine on the old friends. Jim stayed home to clean
the house and walk the dogs.

"You should have seen the look on your face when Jim
opened the door," said Yuki, chuckling as she tucked into ricotta
pancakes. "Priceless! And on social media now for all the world
to see."

"Did you have any idea he was planning something?" asked
Rima, poking at her lobster eggs benedict.

Rose took a break between bites of French toast. "Not a
clue. Long-range planning isn't his strong suit. Or surprises."
She took a sip of her mimosa. "After seventeen years of marriage, this is definitely a first."

Yuki picked up her coffee cup. "Any milestone goals? Don't
you want to write the Great Canadian Novel?"

Rose laughed. "Not a novel, no...but I'm thinking about
joining the provincial writers' federation, maybe taking a
workshop. Memoir writing, or creative non-fiction. I think the
story of my childhood—you know, being raised by hippies on
a commune—could be compelling." Wondering how much to
reveal, she decided to be honest. "Professionally, I'm kinda in a
writing rut. I thought something like that would help."

It was then that Rose noticed Rima wasn't eating much.
Sensing something was up, she asked, "How's Harry?"

Long ago, Rose had fantasized about the hunky plumber. But because she was already married, and she knew that both Rima and Harry wanted to get hitched and have kids, Rose had introduced them at her and Jim's farewell-to-Toronto party. Rima had decided to overlook the fact that he wasn't Muslim. Sparks had flown. Rose had been a bridesmaid.

"He's great," said Rima quickly. "It's just…"

Rose raised her eyebrows, encouraging her friend to continue.

"Our last round of IVF didn't work," said Rima, lowering her head to avoid eye contact. She and Harry had been trying for years to have a baby.

Rima's fertility issues often sent her into a depression. To make matters even more stressful, she had cashed out most of her investments to afford the treatments.

"I feel like such a failure," said Rima, absentmindedly tapping her fork on her plate. "And now I'm…old."

Rose and Yuki watched wordlessly as their friend's eyes filled with tears and her lower lip trembled.

Rose reached across the table to grasp Rima's hand. "I'm sorry," she said. "I know how much you and Harry want a baby." Yuki stayed silent, shifting uncomfortably in her chair.

Rima blew her nose in her napkin with one hand and held Rose's hand with the other. "No, *I'm* sorry. I don't mean to be a downer. We're supposed to be celebrating you."

Rose squeezed Rima's hand. "Don't fret. That's what friends are for. I'm just so happy you're here."

"To Rose!" said Yuki, raising her mug.

The rest of brunch went by in a blur of laughter, gossip, and promises to stay in touch—outside of work hours. Just as they were getting the bills, Rose was surprised with a question that none of them had ever asked her.

"Do you miss living in Toronto?" asked Rima, moving her napkin from her lap to the cleared table.

Rose paused for a moment, considering the question. "Toronto will always be my 'second home. I miss working with you guys in person every day. But I wouldn't trade the quality of life I have now to move back."

"I wouldn't last five seconds in this one-horse town," said Yuki, snorting. "The dating pool would be too small…and, I'm guessing, conservative."

Rose laughed. "I'm lucky I landed my guy before I got here. But you might be surprised. I'd guess there are at least *two* single male horses with potential in Halifax."

"Doubt it," said Yuki. The women laughed. Then they put on their coats, picked up their purses, and walked out into the sunlight.

☙

After brunch, Rose, Jim, and the dogs drove an hour northwest to Wolfville, the charming university town where her parents lived, and where Rose and Daisy had grown up. Both seventy-eight, John and Joanne Ainsworth had fully stepped away from their business, J&J Organic Enterprises, before their seventieth birthdays. Joanne hadn't wanted to, but when John was sixty-five, he'd suffered a mild heart attack. It was a wake-up call for both of them that they were working too hard. The eventual sale of the organic-food company they had launched in the 1970s had given them an extremely comfortable retirement.

"Happy birthday, dear," said Joanne, greeting them at the door of their seniors' condo and hugging Rose lightly. Not the most demonstrative of mothers, Joanne's embraces were a quick catch-and-release, with light butterfly pats on the back. John, on the other hand, wrapped his daughter in a big bear hug.

"I can't believe our Rosie's fifty!" John boomed. Rose's father was one of only two people allowed to call her that. The other was her Toronto tailor, Vincente, who texted her regularly. The chatty fifty-nine-year-old loved sending updates on the twenty-year-old daughter he and his Puerto Rican husband, Paulo, had adopted a decade earlier after becoming her foster parents. In return, Rose texted him cute photos of Molly and Relic.

Jim and Rose accepted Joanne's offer of tea and cake, even though Rose was still stuffed from brunch. Lanky, lean Jim, who had the metabolism of a greyhound, would happily polish off her dessert if she couldn't finish it. When her mother thought Rose wasn't looking, she slipped Molly and Relic salmon-flavoured treats after asking each dog to shake a paw. Rose smiled at the sweet scene. The dogs had brought out a softer side of her mother.

"How's work, you two?" asked John while they had coffee in the living room, a dog curling up on either side of him on the couch. Before the Ainsworths had retired, they'd handed over J&J Organic's marketing copywriting to Rose, who juggled it with her *Dash* duties.

"It's good," said Rose. "I like the variety. There's nothing like assigning stories about how to make your biceps burn in the morning, then writing a brochure about the benefits of barley in the afternoon."

"Nice alliteration," said Joanne, nodding her approval.

"Thanks," said Rose wryly. "I don't even have to try; it just comes out."

"A copywriter's curse," said Joanne, sighing.

"All good at my end, too," said Jim. He had worked his way up to managing partner at the advertising agency that had transferred him to Halifax from Toronto. Between the two of them, they were grossing six figures annually.

After passing a pleasant afternoon with the Ainsworths, it was time to head home. Molly, Relic, and Rose napped on the drive, waking when Jim pulled into their driveway.

Rose unbuckled her seat belt, turned to Jim, and kissed him. "This has been a great birthday and a wonderful weekend. Thank you."

"You're welcome," said Jim. "Just don't expect a party for your sixtieth."

"You're off the hook," said Rose, smiling. "It can't get any better than this."

Three

ROSE WANTED TO PUNCH NOVEMBER IN THE FACE. At the end of the month, she still couldn't sleep more than four consecutive hours. Since Jim's memorial service, she had been tossing and turning while Molly and Relic snored softly at the foot of the bed. For two weeks, they had been looking everywhere for Jim. So had she.

So many things reminded Rose of him. Of their shared interests and loves. Certain sounds were especially evocative. They had called them the city's "symphony." Warning toots from trains. Ambulance, fire engine, and police sirens. Ferry horns in the harbour on foggy nights. The roar of revolving air ambulance rotor blades on their way to a hospital's rooftop helipad. The family next door's labradoodle barking, and their kids giggling as they bounced on their trampoline.

Rose caught glimpses of Jim everywhere. Especially when she saw tall, middle-aged men on bikes. Except they weren't Jim. Which brought her painful reality back.

For several days after Jim died, Rose kept catching herself performing familiar, ordinary tasks that had revolved around him throughout their workdays. Picking up her phone when she took a mid-morning tea break to text him. Putting his beer glass in the freezer with two ice cubes after lunch, so it would be chilled by suppertime. Setting the table for two. Glancing at her watch to see if it was time for him to cycle up the driveway. Lifting his dirty laundry out of the hamper. Inhaling his scent. Then washing, folding, and putting it away for the last time.

Jim had been in one other bike accident. In Toronto, when he was thirty-one. A jerk in an SUV had sideswiped him at a red light. He hadn't been hurt seriously enough to stop cycling, but after the shock of that first accident had worn off, Rose had thought about what she would do if she lost Jim.

She'd be alone.

Sure, she'd still have Daisy's family, but it wouldn't be the same. They had their own busy lives.

Rose had occasionally tried to imagine what a life without children would be like for her and Jim when they were older. Would they feel like something was missing? How would she feel when she looked at the Ainsworth family tree with its extended branches—especially Daisy's long one—and saw only her and Jim's names, with nothing below them?

Rose hadn't considered what her life would be like without kids *or* Jim. She had only considered them growing old together. Passing away in old age, within months of each other, as his parents had done a few years before.

This torturous ruminating was getting Rose nowhere, except to dark places she wasn't fully prepared to go. She reached over to her bedside table. Without disturbing the dogs, she popped the lid off a small plastic bottle and slipped a sleeping pill under her tongue.

ɔ⤳o

The next morning, Rose woke up groggy. The pill had left a metallic taste in her mouth, like she had sucked a stainless-steel lozenge. Molly and Relic needed to do their business. Her personal leave from work was over, and she had to try and get back in the groove. Sipping water from the glass on her bedside table, she wrapped herself in Jim's cozy terry-cloth robe and made her way to the back door, which opened onto the fenced backyard.

After, Rose fed her pups. Thank goodness for them. They gave her a reason to get up in the morning. She tried swallowing a spoonful of oatmeal, but it wouldn't move past the lump in her throat. After composting it, she went back to their bedroom— she still thought of everything as "theirs"—to get dressed.

On Jim's bedside table sat an unassuming, eco-friendly envelope. The one-hundred-and-eighty pounds of her in-the-flesh husband now fit into a two-hundred-cubic-inch biodegradable container the funeral home's marketing depart- ment misleadingly called an *urn*. Instead, it resembled the packaging for a massive McDonald's Baked Apple Pie. Minus the logo. And in "natural white."

The wording on the paper wrapped around the middle of the urn was simple: Jim's full name and birth and death dates, followed by *Loving husband and son* and *He will be missed*. There was something comforting about the container. And Jim's presence. Each night, Rose barely stopped herself from placing the package on his pillow. She couldn't bear to consider where its final resting place would be.

"What would you like done with your remains?" Rose had asked him when they were drafting their wills. They'd just bought the house, and Rose had done her research; she was insistent they have all their paperwork in order.

"Doesn't matter to me," said Jim, shrugging. "I'll be dead. You decide."

So, they'd left it open. Because they assumed they had lots of time to discuss those details.

But now she was a widow. At fifty. Long before they were ready to retire. She hadn't even begun to process that yet. Weren't widows meant to be seniors?

"Hi, honey," said Rose, touching the envelope with her fingertips. "I miss you. So do Molly and Relic."

Sitting on the bed, Rose breathed in her husband's scent from his robe. Molly and Relic climbed up on the bed to lick their human's salty, tear-stained cheeks. Rose put her arms around them and held on tight.

Four

CHRISTMAS. FUCK.

That was Rose's first thought when she woke up on December first.

Freezing rain pinged off the windowpanes. One of the dogs farted. Rose wrinkled her nose, and not just at the rank smell. Normally she loved Christmas. Not this year.

Why?

Because her husband had died. Two short, yet interminably long, weeks ago.

I am a widow. With practice, the sentence might one day roll more easily off her tongue, but she still hadn't been able to even say it out loud. It was an unwelcome badge of honour she felt should be glued to her forehead.

Christmas. Fuck.

Joyful family-themed holidays weren't designed for the newly bereaved.

Fuck Christmas.

⁓

In a misguided attempt to be helpful, Daisy had handed her sister a book called *The Hot Young Widows Club*. The author's husband had died of a brain tumour at thirty-five, leaving her a widowed single mother to a toddler at thirty-one. A few weeks before that, the author's father had died of cancer. And if that weren't enough pain for one person to bear, at around the same time she'd had a miscarriage.

Did Daisy hope this book would make me feel better? Rose wondered. *Was it supposed to help me realize that as much as I'm suffering, other people have it worse?* Grief didn't work that way, she was learning. Although she had to admit that Nora McInerny's sad story *was* a sad story. And yet, her tightly written, emotion-packed paragraphs peppered with humour made Rose laugh. In spite of herself. It just didn't make her feel her own loss any less.

What *was* helping was that Rose had started journalling about her feelings. To help process them. Also, she figured her notes might be useful if she took a writing workshop someday.

Anyway, Rose couldn't relate completely to the hot, young American widow. She was hardly a hot young widow herself. A lukewarm, middle-aged widow, more like. Nora had hoped to find love again—and she did, only a year later. The author had tall, blond, pink-lipsticked youth on her side. At her age, Rose couldn't imagine finding someone new to love. That would have to involve dating. Most likely online. No way.

Giving a widow a book about a widow is redundant, Rose thought as she finished the final page. She would have preferred a collection of David Sedaris essays. His neuroses very nearly matched her own, and he never failed to make her roar with laughter. Even at the dark side of life. *Especially* at the dark side of life.

Escapism. That's what Rose needed. Not reality sucker-punching her in the gut.

That was it! Rose would escape. Their house, and the memories it contained. Constant reminders of what was missing. *Who* was missing. As she got up to let the dogs out, she wondered where she should go.

She closed her eyes and, as much as it hurt, she thought about Jim.

She saw ocean. She saw old, brightly painted buildings. Laughing over ice cream cones. A picnic on the beach.

Lunenburg. Some of her best memories with Jim were from their jaunts to the seaside town. It was only an hour's drive away. Just for a weekend. To clear her head. Give her some perspective. Do some journalling. Tourist season was over, so the town should be pretty quiet. She'd drop the dogs off at Daisy's on Friday after work, then pick them up Sunday on her way home.

Rose would book a vacation rental and visit her friend Wendy, who owned the sex shop in town. Rose had met her at the grand opening a decade earlier where they'd had a short, but pleasant, chat. Then Rose's ballot had been drawn to receive a gift card. When she had returned to use it, she and Wendy had resumed their conversation. They had kept in touch ever since.

At the grand opening, Jim had bought a sexy fishnet body stocking for Rose. He had loved looking at her in it—and then helping her take it off. *Maybe there are too many memories in Lunenburg*, Rose worried. But Wendy was older, and wise, and a good listener. She and her husband, Paul, had attended Jim's memorial service. At the reception, Wendy had held her friend's hands, looked in her eyes, and said, "If you need to talk, I'm here for you. Day or night. I mean it."

Rose knew Wendy had been sincere, but she hadn't reached out. Now she was ready.

⁂

Rose's weekend in Lunenburg was already feeling bittersweet. The vacation rental on Lawrence Street was modern and spacious, but she pined for her travel partner. Maybe she shouldn't have come. Since she was there, she'd have to make the best of it.

On Saturday morning, Rose walked around town, stopping to look at the fishing boats moored in Front Harbour. The sloping golf-course greens across the bay were closed for the season. Trudging up the hill toward the bandstand, her lungs and heart pumping, she pulled her knitted hat lower with gloved hands to shield her ears from the wind.

Next stop, the stately three-storey Lunenburg Academy atop Gallows Hill. Built in the nineteenth century, its white wood, black trim, and red roof were majestic. Inside, she scanned the public library's bookshelves in rooms that were more than a hundred years old.

Leaving the Academy, Rose hesitated. Normally, she enjoyed wandering around the adjacent Hillcrest Cemetery. When Jim was with her, they would walk hand in hand among the gravestones. Reading names and dates. Wondering aloud who the souls were resting there from centuries past. What kind of lives they had led. And if any of their descendants visited them now.

Today, Rose turned away from the dead and toward Fishnets & Fantasies Adult Emporium, and Wendy.

The women exchanged hugs and greetings. Sitting on a well-worn, comfortable loveseat near the fitting room, they sipped tea and nibbled Wendy's homemade banana bread. Rose loved the shop's décor. Hanging on the soft grey walls was framed artwork by local painters for sale. White ceramic pots containing green succulents added pops of colour here and there.

Wendy didn't wait long to check in with her friend.

"So, how are you doing, really?"

Before replying, Rose lifted her mug to her lips, wincing as she burned the tip of her tongue on the hot liquid. "I'm struggling. I don't like change. And the more I try to escape my memories of Jim, the more they seem to find me."

Wendy nodded, choosing her next words carefully. "I understand that change can be hard...but it can be healthy, too. In fact, I'm about to make a big change myself." Blowing on her tea, she said, "I'm putting the shop up for sale."

Rose's mug paused on its way to her mouth. "Wait, what? Why? Isn't it doing well?"

"It's doing very well, and that's exactly the right time to sell," said Wendy. "I'll be seventy soon. I've put a decade of hard work into growing this business. I accomplished what I set out to do. Now it's time for someone else to take the reins."

"I didn't think you sold reins," said Rose, a hint of her old playfulness surfacing.

"Ha, no. And no whips, either. It isn't *that* kind of sex shop. Well, you'd know—you're one of its best customers!" Wendy paused, swallowing a bite of loaf. "And in fact...you should think about buying it."

Rose choked on her tea. "What, me? No."

Wendy shrugged. "Why not? Might be just what you need."

"What exactly do you think I need? Besides for Jim to be alive," said Rose. Voice trembling, eyes growing moist. "I can't stop thinking that I didn't get to say goodbye to him."

Wendy took a sip of tea. "Do you think it would have been easier if Jim had been terminally ill? You'd have had time to say goodbye then."

"I guess so," said Rose hesitantly. "But I wouldn't have wanted him to suffer just so I could have goodbye closure."

"Goodbye closure?" Wendy raised an eyebrow.

Rose smiled. "Every morning before Jim left for work, he'd kiss me goodbye in the hallway. Then, after he was outside, he'd turn around at the door, kiss me again, and say he loved me. I'd say it back. He needed that ritual before he left for the day."

Wendy asked her next question gently. "Did he give you those two kisses and say he loved you on the morning he died?"

Rose's eyes filled again. Not trusting herself to speak, she nodded.

"And did you say it back?"

"Yes." Tears slid down Rose's cheeks.

"Then, my dear, you got your goodbye closure," said Wendy, reaching over to squeeze her friend's hand.

Rose lowered her head. Her shoulders shook slightly. Wendy passed her a tissue.

"Taking over the shop could be a good challenge for you, Rose. Something new to focus on. A change of scenery, perspective."

"It's too soon," Rose protested, wiping her eyes and blowing her nose. But her curiosity was piqued. "Besides, I have a job. Two jobs, actually."

"And how long have you been doing those jobs?" asked Wendy.

Rose did the mental math. "A long time. Years."

"Aren't you bored?"

Rose sighed. "Yeah, kinda. But it's…comfortable. Change is hard. And I'm staring enough of it in the face right now."

Wendy nodded. "That you are, my dear." She took a sip of her tea, then turned back to her friend. "What if I sold you the shop in the next couple of months but stayed on to help run it for a while?"

"I think you've lost your mind," said Rose, walking over to the teapot to top up her mug.

"That's what Paul said to me when I suggested *opening* this place," said Wendy.

Rose winced at the memory. Wendy had told her all about how the shop had put a strain on her marriage. "It hasn't always been easy, though, has it?"

"Nothing worth pursuing is."

"I've never thought about being an entrepreneur," mused Rose, returning to the loveseat.

"It's really no different than what you are now, being self-employed. You have two clients to please. With the shop, you'll have customers to please. Customer service is half the battle."

"You make it sound so simple. We both know it wouldn't be."

Wendy tried again. "But what if I stayed on part-time for a year to show you the business? To train and mentor you?"

Rose had always admired her friend's ambition and drive. And persistence. "Hmmm," she said, noncommittally. "I'd have to move here."

"Well, yes, you would. But you like Lunenburg. Don't you have a relative who lives in the county?"

In fact, Rose did. Her first cousin May. Mid-fifties, or thereabouts. A kooky character, according to family lore. Rose thought she worked for the local SPCA. Rumour was she had several rescue dogs and cats. No partner or kids.

Apparently, May had a tender heart when it came to needy creatures. Once she had waited patiently for hours in the woods trying to capture three rogue roosters that had escaped their pen. In December. During a heavy snowfall. John Ainsworth had read about his niece's successful rescue in an online news story and shared it with his daughters. There was a clear photo of the roosters, but none of May.

"I do, but I don't know her," said Rose.

"Maybe this would be an opportunity to get to know her," Wendy pressed.

Rose ignored her suggestion. "I'd have to be a landlord." The heritage building housing the shop had an upstairs flat.

"On paper only. Paul would continue acting as property manager."

Rose was perplexed. "Why me? Wouldn't you rather stay on as owner and hire a manager?"

"That isn't a smart succession plan," said Wendy. "And Ellen has no interest in taking over."

The Hebbs' only child, in her mid-forties now, was a tenured professor in the gender, sexuality, and women's studies master's program at a university in British Columbia, clear across the country. The year before, she had married a fellow professor named Fay. They all knew Ellen had no plans to return to the East Coast.

"When you met me that very first time, you said you thought what I was doing was brave," said Wendy.

"I still think that," said Rose, smiling.

"Well, then. Now it's your turn. Be brave."

"I'm not brave. I'm scared and weak and sad."

"You won't be forever," said Wendy, the corners of her lips turning up in a reassuring smile. "At least think about it."

"No," said Rose, firmly. Paused. Tilted her head to one side. Chewed her bottom lip. "Maybe."

"Fresh start," said Wendy. Then, standing up as an older couple entered the shop, she added, "Watch and learn, hungry grasshopper."

❦

"You've lost your mind," said Daisy, eyebrows raised in disbelief.

Rose had just explained Wendy's proposal over tea and warm-from-the-oven blueberry muffins at the Turner house. It wasn't so much that Daisy thought the proposal was insane, but rather that Rose appeared to be actually considering it.

Molly and Relic were asleep on dog beds on either side of Rose's chair. While they liked staying with their Aunt Daisy, they were overjoyed to have their favourite human back. Especially since their other favourite human didn't appear to be returning.

"Maybe I have," Rose replied, shrugging her shoulders. "But what if the universe is sending me to Lunenburg to find it?"

Daisy sighed, then took a sip of tea. "I guess there's only one way to find out. Shouldn't you wait at least a year before making a big move like this?

"I love you, but please don't *should* me right now," said Rose. "There aren't any handbooks for what I'm going through."

"Actually, there are," said Daisy slowly. "Lots of them, in fact. And grief counselling. If you move to Lunenburg, I'll worry that you'll be running away."

"Would not," said Rose, pouting, reverting to her five-year-old self.

"Would too," said Daisy, only slightly more mature at six and a half. "It wouldn't work, you know. You can't run away from yourself."

"Did I ask for your advice?" said Rose tersely, tearing her muffin wrapper into tiny pieces.

"Nope. But someone has to look out for you. I'm assuming you're fixed all right for money?"

"I'm fine. Jim's life insurance would cover the cost of buying the business."

In fact, Rose had more money than she knew what to do with. Jim had inherited a bundle from his parents. Although he had bequeathed some to charity, he had left the bulk of his estate to his wife. Plus, she had her own savings and investments.

Rose Ainsworth was a multi-millionaire.

Their conversation was interrupted when Ella popped in to grab an apple from a bowl of fruit on the counter. Molly and Relic got up to get pats and give kisses.

"Hi, Aunt Rose. Mom, could I borrow the van to go to volleyball practice?"

"See if Dad needs it first," said Daisy.

"Okay, thanks," she said, heading out to the garage, where Steve was untangling the Christmas lights. Every so often, the sisters could hear what sounded like muttered cursing.

"Polite kid ya got there," said Rose, nodding her approval as Ella retreated.

Ignoring the compliment, Daisy returned to her interrogation. "What if the shop loses money with you in charge?"

"Thanks for the vote of confidence," said Rose, shooting Daisy a hard stare. "Now I know how Wendy felt when Paul wouldn't support *her* in the beginning."

"I'm sure he had legitimate concerns," replied Daisy, palms raised. "As do I. Plus, it was Wendy's dream. It isn't yours. What do you know about running a business, anyway?"

"I've been self-employed for thirteen years," Rose pointed out. "I'm fifty, not a kid, and not the dullest blade in the drawer. Wendy would stay on part-time for a year to show me the ropes. Mom and Dad would be amazing resources. If I hate it, I'll sell." Rose mindfully chewed her muffin. "Besides, I'm ready for a career change. I'm tired of writing and editing the same old shit. It's like never-ending homework. I've been on autopilot for years."

"Do I need to point out that you've only been widowed for one month?" said Daisy, nervously folding her muffin wrapper into a tiny square. Unfolding it. Then folding it again.

Rose took the wrapper away and put her hand over Daisy's. "No, you don't. Trust me, I do the math. Daily."

Just then Ryan stuck his head in the kitchen door. "Hey, Aunt Rose, how's it goin'? Mom, can I have twenty bucks?" Molly and Relic got up to get pats and give kisses.

"For what?"

"Dues for comic book club."

"Sure," said Daisy, "just grab it from my wallet."

"What will you do with your house?" asked Daisy after Ryan had run back upstairs, drumming her fingers on the table. She seemed to be throwing up as many obstacles as she could think of.

"Rent it. Sell it. Burn it to the ground and collect the insurance money."

"You won't get any if it's arson," Daisy pointed out.

"I know people," said Rose mysteriously.

"No, you don't."

"No, I don't," Rose admitted.

Suddenly, the soothing sound of "O Holy Night" coming from the piano in the den filled the air. Lulu was practicing for a Christmas concert at the conservatory. Seconds later, Katie charged into the kitchen. Molly and Relic looked up from their beds. Too tired to greet another person, they went back to sleep.

"If I have to hear that song *one more time*, I'm going to chop her hands off!" said Katie, waving her arms dramatically. "Oh, hi, Aunt Rose, nice to see ya." She turned on her heel and walked out.

"You have far too many children," said Rose dryly.

"There are days when I would agree with you," said Daisy. "This being one of them."

To halt Daisy's inquiries, Rose asked, "What do you know about our cousin May?"

"She's a kook," said Daisy.

"Yeah, that's what I thought," said Rose.

"Why do you ask?"

"No reason, really. Just that she lives in Lunenburg."

"She's Uncle Andy's middle daughter." Daisy smiled conspiratorially and glanced out the window at the light snowfall. "I remember Dad saying that Andy named his daughters April, May, and June, even though they were all born in the winter."

Rose laughed. "Baby-name weirdness runs in the family, I guess," she said, sipping her tea.

Daisy nodded. "Bunch of hippies. Anyway, I think May works for the SPCA. She's some kind of wildlife-rescue activist, too. Bit older than me. Are you planning to look her up?"

"Nah, just curious."

Standing up to put their mugs in the dishwasher, Daisy steered the conversation back to her sister. "I know you won't be feeling festive this year, but what are your Christmas plans? Because we'd like for you to come stay with us."

Rose bit her tongue. In stressful situations, gallows humour was her go-to response. But she worried that Daisy might take *I'm planning to do a forward dive in the pike position off the MacDonald Bridge* the wrong way. Besides, some do-gooder had put up nine-foot safety barriers along it several years earlier.

"I've decided to convert to Judaism," Rose said instead.

Daisy laughed. "No, you haven't."

"Buddhism, then. Or atheism."

"Nice try. You're a lapsed Catholic, so your version of Christmas isn't even about religion."

"This year I've decided that Christmas *is* about Jesus, and that I don't believe in him."

"You're so full of shit," said Daisy, lightly slapping Rose's arm. "Christmas is about fighting with family, overeating, and overspending. Crass commercialism, especially when it comes to my kids. Stay with us. We want you to." Daisy placed a hand on Rose's shoulder and squeezed.

At that moment, Steve wandered into the kitchen, sweaty and appearing defeated by the tangled lights in his grip. "Honey, I think we need new lights… Hey, is she at you to come for Christmas?" The tall, lanky sexagenarian who addressed Rose was like a fun older brother who loved to tease. "No one asked me," he added, throwing his hands up in mock despair, hoisting the lights along with them. "For the record, I don't want you here. Nope. Stay home and mope. Doctor's orders."

"I'm not a toddler, so reverse psychology won't work," said Rose, shaking her head. "Appreciate the effort, though."

"Can't blame a guy for trying," said Steve. Then he frowned. "You're not gonna do anything dumb, are you?"

"Depends on your definition of dumb, I guess," said Rose, shrugging.

"I dunno…like take a snooze spread-eagled across the train tracks right as the four o'clock from Moncton pulls in?"

"Steve!" said Daisy, aghast.

Rose snorted. Steve shared her dark sense of humour. He was a radiologist, so she supposed it came with the territory.

"Nah, too messy. What else ya got?"

Steve cocked his head. Rubbed his chin thoughtfully. "Pills and booze are cliché. You don't own a gun. And you're a klutz with sharp objects. How did Sylvia Plath kill herself, again?"

"Head in a gas oven," said Rose quickly.

"Yours is electric, so that's out. What about Virginia Woolf?"

"Drowned herself in a river with stones in her pocket."

"Stones, like pebbles?" said Steve, intrigued. "Would that even work?"

"Yeah, I've always wondered about that," said Rose, pursing her lips. "Maybe *boulders* wasn't poetic enough."

"I hear drowning is a pretty peaceful way to go," said Steve.

"There's that," said Rose, nodding. "Fast, too."

"Knock it off, you guys," said Daisy sternly.

"Sorry," said Steve sheepishly, winking at Rose. Winking back, she suppressed a smile.

Steve set the lights on a chair, kissed both women on the cheek, and swiped a muffin from the plate on the table on his way out.

"Where are you headed?" asked Daisy.

"To the basement. For some peace, quiet, and Sunday-afternoon football."

Daisy looked at Rose. "Will you at least think about staying here for Christmas? You know it's what Jim would want you to do."

Rose sighed. "Fine, I'll think about it." There was a lot to consider over the next few weeks.

Five

ON THE TWENTY-FIFTH OF DECEMBER, ROSE WOKE up early in the Turners' spare room in their finished basement. Two dog beds lay empty on the floor. Molly and Relic were asleep near their human's feet.

The house was silent. The double bed felt too big, even with the dogs on it.

The alarm clock on the bedside table said six o'clock. The perfect time to cry. Before Rose had to drag herself out of bed to put on clothes and a brave face.

"Merry Christmas, honey," whispered Rose. The envelope with Jim's ashes was propped up on the bedside table. Next to it was a framed photo of the two of them as newlyweds cutting their wedding cake. Reaching over to the table, she picked up her journal and a pen. Opening to a blank page, she wrote: *My first Christmas without you. I am so lonely my whole body aches. My heart, especially. I love you. I miss you. I hope wherever you are, you're okay. At peace. Be nice if you sent me a sign. Because it's Christmas.*

Rose waited for a tap on the wall. Or for the photo to move an inch to the left. Or to the right. For Relic to bark and Jim's voice to come out.

Silence.

Rose remembered a long-ago Christmas morning when she and Jim had woken up together in this very same bed. They had flown down from Toronto for the holidays, something they couldn't afford to do every year. Ella had been seven, Katie five, and Ryan two. Sweetness personified. Shortly after they arrived,

Daisy had blindsided Rose with the news that she and Steve were expecting their fourth child.

At six-thirty on Christmas morning, the kids had barged into Rose and Jim's bedroom and jumped on their bed. Ella had grabbed Jim's hand while Katie and Ryan took Rose's, hauling them out of bed and upstairs to the living room where Daisy and Steve were waiting. The multicoloured tree lights had twinkled, filling the space with a soft glow.

Rose had taken her time opening her gifts. She wanted to drink in the image of her nieces and nephew unwrapping their presents while they still believed in Santa Claus. As corny as the Norman Rockwell-esque scene had seemed, it had been magical. John and Joanne had arrived later that morning to help Daisy and Rose prepare the turkey dinner. After feasting at one o'clock, they spent the rest of the afternoon sitting around the living room, watching the kids play with their new toys.

Things were different now.

There was no more Santa.

And no more Jim.

To try to put her family at ease, Rose did her best to go through the motions. She opened gifts. Helped make dinner. Pushed her food around on her plate to make it look like she had eaten. Helped clean up. Pretended not to overhear Daisy ask Ella and Katie to accompany their aunt when she walked the dogs.

"How *are* you?" asked Daisy as her sister took off her boots in the back entryway. In the living room, Steve chatted with John and Joanne, who had driven in for the day.

"Fine," said Rose, hanging the leashes and her coat on a hook.

"Fine as in coping? Or fine as in trying hard not to break down in front of your family?"

"A little from column A, a little from column B," said Rose, lifting one hand and then the other as though they were weighing scales.

Daisy hugged Rose. "You can break down if you want to. I've got broad shoulders. There's been a lot of snot and spit-up on them over the years."

Rose squeezed Daisy tightly. She fully expected the first year without Jim to be hard. People kept warning her that all the "firsts" would be the worst. His birthday. Her birthday. The anniversaries of their first date and wedding. Valentine's Day. Every over-hyped family-themed holiday. Including this one.

The first anniversary of Jim's death would fall six weeks before the following Christmas. And every Christmas after. Rose didn't know how she'd bear it. A *deathaversary*, it was called. As an editor, Rose didn't care much for catchy made-up words. Another one she disliked was *cremains*. Were people too lazy to say *cremated remains*? Or—even easier and less creepy—*ashes*? Had the funeral industry's marketing machine gone mad?

Rose imagined a team of hip ad-agency creative types sitting around a boardroom table, tossing out death-themed jargon to the tune of two hundred dollars an hour. *Casketing* and *cosmetizing* must have been popular picks, Rose thought wryly. Much to her great relief, Jim hadn't wanted either of those.

∽

Boxing Day brought a light snowfall and a return to Drummond Court. There was still New Year's Eve to get through. Rose had decided to stay home that night. Alone, with Molly and Relic. And Jim.

Opening the front door to the house that used to be her home, hers and Jim's, Rose was awash in a wave of sorrow. She couldn't catch her breath. The house was squeezing the oxygen from her lungs and her heart. Suffocating her. It dawned on her that she would never be able to outrun Jim's memory if she continued to live here.

Then, clarity cracked through her sadness, like a ray of sunshine illuminating a cloudy day: she didn't have to live here. After the holidays were over, Rose would call Wendy Hebb. To find out how her Christmas had been. To ask how Ellen and Fay's visit was. To say Happy New Year.

And to accept her friend's business proposal.

Six

THE HEBBS' HOLIDAY WITH THEIR DAUGHTER AND daughter-in-law had been a gift. Paul and Wendy wished they weren't so far away. Or so career-minded. Ellen had been clear: neither she nor Fay planned to get pregnant.

Which meant there would be no grandchildren for Wendy and Paul to spoil. No pawing through the tables for baby clothes at Frenchy's. No helping tiny hands to decorate gingerbread cookies at Christmas. No reading bedtime stories from the books Wendy had saved from her daughter's childhood.

The day before Ellen and Fay flew back to Victoria, Wendy sat on their double bed, watching her only child put clean laundry in her suitcase.

"Fay and I saw Allan at the Banker yesterday," said Ellen, rolling a pair of socks. "He's aging well. Is he seeing anyone?"

The last summer Ellen had worked at the Banker, she and Allan had dated for a few months. When she started applying for teaching jobs out west, she broke it off. It was an amicable parting. No hurt feelings. For Ellen, anyway. She'd made no secret that a life in Lunenburg had never been part of her master plan.

"Not that we know of," said Wendy, stretching her legs out and flexing her feet.

"That's too bad," said Ellen, carefully folding an almost threadbare purple sweatshirt with *MSVU* in white on the front. "He has such a lovely heart. He deserves a good life partner. Someone should find him a kind divorcée, someone who will stick with him. He's been stood up so many times."

Or a widow, mused Wendy silently. Tucking that thought away to explore later.

⸙

The first two weeks of January were quiet at the Hebbs' bungalow on Oxner Drive. Ellen and Fay had flown back to Vancouver two days after Christmas, eager to bring their cat home from the sitter's. The house felt empty without them. There were only a few centimetres of snow left over from what had fallen during the holidays and the decidedly un-magical reality of the new year was in full effect.

At least Fred and Laura lived nearby. Ten years ago, Paul had met the son he didn't know he had for the very first time, under the saddest of circumstances. Fred was forty then, and his mother was dying.

When Paul was nineteen, Wendy had split up with him. During the month between the breakup and getting back together, Paul had a drunken one-night stand—with Wendy's best friend, Betty Zinck. A seamstress who had long been quietly in love with Paul. Betty had always maintained that Fred's father was Mark Richardson, a young lobster fisherman on Paul's father's boat. Sadly, Mark was only nineteen when he died in a tragic accident while aboard the *Lucky Haul*.

At the time, Betty had been three months pregnant. No one knew that she and Mark had been seeing each other until she said so after he drowned. When her parents found out she was expecting, they disowned her. Mark's family didn't want anything to do with her—or Fred either—so the two lived with a friend's family for a year, until Betty started earning enough to rent a cheap apartment.

Betty had confessed her secret to Fred, Wendy, and Paul as she lay in Fishermen's Memorial Hospital dying of cancer. Not able to take her lie to the grave.

On a clear, cold October morning a few days later, Betty took her last breath. Her son, his father, and her best friend were by her side. Slowly, over time, Fred had forged a comfortable relationship with the Hebbs, although he would always call them Paul and Wendy.

Not long after his mother's funeral, Fred had met a veterinarian named Laura Richardson at the animal hospital when his beloved dog, Buddy, was a patient. Buddy had since died of old age, but Laura's own rescued dogs and cats helped fill the hole in Fred's heart.

Today, however, Wendy didn't want to dwell on the past. Hanging up her cellphone, she looked at her husband. Paul was sitting next to her on the sofa watching football.

"Rose said yes," said Wendy, her voice laced with surprise.

"Yes to what?" said Paul, eyes glued to the TV. The Super Bowl was four weeks away. He had tuned out Wendy's call.

Paul had retired from lobster fishing a decade earlier, a few months before Wendy opened Fishnets & Fantasies. A silent partner in the business, he'd let his wife take the lead, none too eager to participate publicly. To pass the time, carpentry jobs around the county kept his hands and mind busy.

In Paul's right hand was a pager, so he wouldn't miss an alert. Fit and strong at sixty-nine, he was one of the oldest members of the local volunteer fire department. He had recently celebrated his tenth year serving his community with a cake and balloons at the fire hall. On call this weekend, he hoped he'd be able to catch the end of the game. But there was no question—his firefighting family, and their duty, came first.

"Yes to buying the shop," said Wendy, waiting for her husband to register the news.

"No shit!" said Paul. Pressing mute just as a commercial came on, he added, "She's as crazy as you are."

Wendy laughed. "Somewhat less so. I've built a strong business. I even steered it through a global pandemic." Much to her surprise and relief, sales had never been stronger than when the province had locked down and lovers were forced to stay home, alone, for months on end. "All Rose has to do is maintain the status quo."

"Well, that's great news. What's your plan?" If there was one thing Paul knew for sure, it was that his wife of forty-eight years always had one.

"I'll get the legal documents drafted next month," said Wendy, ticking boxes off in her head. "I agreed to stay on part-time for a year, to teach her the business and introduce her to regular customers. They're comfortable with me, but they may be shy with a stranger. You know what people here can be like with outsiders."

Paul's gaze returned to the TV as the game resumed, but he left the sound muted. "Do you think she should be makin' a move like this so soon after Jim died?"

"I didn't pressure her," said Wendy quickly.

Paul raised his eyebrows.

"Really, I didn't," Wendy insisted. "I just pointed out that a fresh start might be a good idea."

"I'm not sure who you're tryin' to convince," said Paul, chuckling. "Why do you want her to take over, anyway?"

"I could see that she was interested from the get-go, it just never occurred to her that the business might be hers one day," said Wendy, stretching her legs and putting her feet on the coffee table. "She's curious by nature and always asking me questions about what it's like to run a sex shop in a small town. I think I've subconsciously been grooming her to take over."

"What *did* you tell her about what it's like to run a sex shop here?" said Paul, giving up the game to give his full attention to his wife.

Wendy smiled. "I told her the best part is the people. Earning their trust. Learning about them and hearing their stories. Sharing the excitement of a new romance, or the rekindling of an old one. Taking their money."

Paul laughed. "Fair enough."

In the months leading up to Fishnets & Fantasies's grand opening, and even in the year that had followed, Paul had doubted that Wendy could make a go of it. It was on the tip of his tongue to say, "If I was a betting man, I'd have lost that coin toss," but he thought better of it. The last thing he wanted to do was remind his wife of the old gambling habit that had cost them their retirement savings.

Just then Paul's pager buzzed. The dispatcher was reporting a massive structure fire on the waterfront. Trucks were coming from Dayspring and New Germany to help.

"Gotta go?" said Wendy, frowning. Her stomach clenched and her pulse quickened.

"Yup," said Paul, sprinting to put on his coat and boots. "I'll be a while."

"Be careful," said Wendy, hugging and kissing him at the door. "I've been having that nightmare again."

"Don't worry, you know I'm always careful," said Paul, kissing her back. "Love you." Then he was gone.

Every time Paul raced toward danger, Wendy worried. Knowing he was well trained and experienced didn't loosen the knot in her gut. She had spent forty years with that same knot while he was lobster fishing. Especially when he was on the icy, angry North Atlantic in January and February, when the swells threatened to capsize the boat and its crew. None of whom could swim. Survival suits wouldn't save them.

Nightmares had plagued Wendy for decades. First, of Paul drowning in stormy seas. And over the past decade, of him perishing in a fiery building. She'd wake in a cold sweat. Heart racing. Gasping for air. Only reassured when she saw him sleeping next to her.

There were times when Wendy wished she had married an accountant or a lawyer. Someone with a nine-to-five desk job in town. Boring, but safe. Not a man who didn't feel fully alive unless he was putting his life at risk.

A newlywed at twenty-two, Wendy hadn't considered any of that when she'd accepted Paul's marriage proposal. She just knew she was in love. And that she didn't want to lose him.

Seven

SONYA KING WAS OBLIVIOUS TO THE FLAMES THAT were hungrily licking three historic wooden buildings near the town's wharf. Even though they were straight down the hill from her house at the top of Kempt Street.

So focused on her laptop screen she hadn't heard the sirens, Sonya was firmly in the zone. Perfectly pink-manicured fingernails flew across the keyboard. A retired physician, she kept herself busy. Today's assignment required total concentration.

Was she drafting an article for the *Canadian Journal of Anesthesia* about transversus abdominis plane block compared with wound infiltration for postoperative analgesia following Caesarean delivery?

No, she was not.

Sonya was writing her tenth romance novel in as many years.

However, because it was her first attempt at historical fiction for her Toronto publisher, Romantic Escapes, she had swapped her pen name, S. R. Kingsbury, for Silke Solange. Simply because she liked its musicality, and an online search didn't turn up anyone else.

Her main character was a strapping young lumberjack in early nineteenth-century northern New Brunswick. This was also a departure for Sonya, whose previous protagonists had been middle-aged or older women.

Like the fire raging on the waterfront, Sonya's lumberjack was hungrily licking the earlobes of a buxom logging-camp cook.

The sound of the front door opening roused Sonya from her story. *Booth*. Home from a golf club board meeting. Later, she planned to put on a new sheer slip she'd bought from Wendy's shop, where she still worked part-time—and got a tempting discount (and a lot of her ideas). Removing her computer glasses, she rubbed her eyes and smiled. Imagining what her husband of forty years would do when he saw her in it.

The Kings had both gone to school with Wendy and Paul. In grade eleven, Sonya and Paul had dated briefly. While Sonya and Booth had worked for decades in Toronto—she as an anesthesiologist, he as a corporate lawyer—and summered in Lunenburg, they were the first to admit there was little love lost between the two couples back then.

That had changed after the Kings had moved home permanently a decade ago. During that time, Sonya and Booth had worked hard to repair their fractured marriage, as well as their reputation in town as socialites. Booth's face still burned whenever he recalled his feeble attempt to stop Fishnets & Fantasies from opening. *Bygones*, he'd reassure himself. Wendy had accepted his apology and moved on.

Booth had been equally surprised by, and then proud of, his wife's success as an author. Since publishing her first book, she had become involved with the town's annual literary festival. First as a volunteer, then as a featured author and a committee member.

Sonya smiled when she heard her husband's footsteps on the stairs. Seconds later, he strode into the office.

"What's happening in the backwoods of New Brunswick?" Dropping his briefcase on the armchair, he bent to kiss his wife.

Sonya kissed him back, then put her glasses back on and peered at her laptop. "Alphonse and Lisette just made mad, passionate love in a ramshackle sugar shack."

"Yum," said Booth, licking his lips. "Now I want sex *and* pancakes. Did you hear the sirens?"

Sonya looked confused. "No. What's up?"

"Wow, you must really have been concentrating. There's a big fire on the waterfront."

"What?" Sonya stood up and walked briskly to the window overlooking Front Harbour. Smoke and flames filled in the sky. "Oh, no. Any injuries reported?"

"Nothing yet," said Booth, putting an arm around her waist.

"Well, we'll hope for the best," said Sonya, her gaze on the flames. "Those volunteer firefighters take so many risks. Just because they used to battle the seas in their lobster boats doesn't mean they know how to stay safe in a fire. All those wooden buildings with big beams. It's a catastrophe waiting to happen."

Booth squeezed his wife. "You and Wendy worry too much. They're well trained." Adding, in an attempt to change the subject, "What's next for the New Brunswick lovebirds?"

Before Sonya could brief him, her cellphone rang. Wendy's number lit up the call display.

"It's me," said Wendy, her voice strained. "Paul's at the wharf, and it looks like it's gonna be a long night. Could you take my shift tomorrow?"

Sonya gripped the phone tighter. "Of course. Try to get some rest, okay? And keep me posted."

"Well?" asked Booth anxiously.

Frowning, Sonya placed her phone on the windowsill, ensuring its volume setting was high. "Wendy doesn't expect to get much sleep, so she asked if I could fill in for her tomorrow."

Sonya had been working as a part-time sales clerk at Fishnets & Fantasies since it opened. She certainly didn't need the money. When Wendy hired her, she had been lonely and bored. Locked in a loveless, sexless marriage. The job had gotten her out of the house and meeting new people. Before she was hired, however, Sonya and Wendy had had to mend fences. Resolve old grudges, and even older insecurities. Slowly, their relationship had matured into one of mutual admiration and respect.

After the success of her first book, Sonya had reduced her hours at the shop to two days a week so she could focus on her writing. Booth didn't understand why she didn't quit outright. "Because I still enjoy it," Sonya explained. Then she winked. "And sometimes it gives me ideas for my novels."

Booth laughed. He loved it when Sonya bounced ideas off him. Sometimes they acted out a romantic scene she had written. *To test its authenticity*, she teased. If he was lucky, she'd surprise him by wearing the black-leather chaps, corset, and cowboy hat she had bought years ago in a desperate attempt to heal his wounded heart.

It had worked.

໐ᣐໆ

The next day, Sonya was expecting a return call from a supplier that was going out of business when the phone rang. Glancing at the call display, she recognized Wendy's number. Reaching quickly for the phone, she prayed that everything was okay.

Everything was not okay.

Eight

ROSE MANAGED TO SURVIVE HER FIRST VALENTINE'S Day as a widow. She and Jim hadn't been overly sentimental about the holiday, but they'd always exchanged cards. Over the years, she had saved them in a special keepsake box. This year, she lay on the sofa with a tissue box next to her and read each one. All twenty. And bawled.

When is this going to get easier? Rose wrote in her tear-stained journal. *Is this going to get easier?*

Molly and Relic didn't budge from their beds. They had grown used to their human's weepy outbursts.

During the day, Rose had stayed away from social media so she wouldn't have to face sappy tributes to living, breathing loved ones. She wasn't a masochist. Jim had been private, so she'd never posted anything mushy about him.

Daisy and Joanne had texted their love, letting her know they were thinking of her. So had Yuki, which was unexpected and thoughtful.

Otherwise? Radio silence.

When Rose woke the next day, with a dozen crumpled tissues strewn on the floor next to her side of the bed, relief washed over her. Another painful first was behind her. How more of them were left? She wondered which would be the most difficult.

Jim's birthday in May?

Summer, when they took their vacations and travelled?

Their July wedding anniversary?

Thanksgiving, because he had been her family?

Her birthday in November?

Could she count Christmas again, even though she'd already experienced her first without him?

Yes, Rose decided, she could. She could count whatever she damn well wanted to.

⁂

"Can you do a day trip to Lunenburg with me next Wednesday?" Rose asked Daisy as she backed her car into a space in Halifax Central Library's underground lot. They were running late for a beginner meditation session in one of the community rooms. Thinking it would be good for Rose, Daisy had steamrolled her sister's objections.

"Should be able to," said Daisy. "Why?"

"Wendy wants me to sign the business sale agreement sooner rather than later. I wouldn't mind some company on the drive. I'll treat you to lunch."

Rose pressed the remote to lock the wagon's doors as they walked toward the elevator.

"What's the rush?" asked Daisy, hitting the up button.

"You know that big fire in Lunenburg last week?"

"Yeah, I saw it on the news," said Daisy. "Terrible. Was the shop damaged?"

"The shop is fine, but Paul isn't," said Rose. "He tripped on a firehose and fell. He's all right, except for a sprained ankle. From what Wendy told me, his pride is hurt more than anything else."

"The poor guy. Lucky it wasn't more serious. And bad timing for Wendy. Will this affect the sale?"

"No, she's going ahead with it. If anything, she wants to speed things up."

"Will she still be able to work with you? To show you the ropes?" Daisy's list of reservations was growing longer by the minute.

"She will. Paul's recuperating at home," said Rose as the elevator doors opened on the third floor. Making their way to a meeting room, they took two empty seats near the back.

"My next step is to list our house and find somewhere to live in Lunenburg," whispered Rose. A bald, bearded instructor wearing Birkenstocks took his place at the front of the room.

Daisy nodded. Noting the use of the word *our*. As the session began, conversation ceased.

Rose wasn't worried about offloading their house. It was a seller's market, with bidding wars for residential properties on the peninsula. Plus, she didn't need to hold out for the top offer.

Rose and Daisy closed their eyes, according to the instructor's directions. From the depths of their diaphragms, they took a deep breath in, then slowly exhaled through their open mouths. Soon after, Rose fell asleep, her head resting on her sister's shoulder. Daisy didn't have the heart to wake her.

⁂

"I have a lead on a small, furnished, one-bedroom apartment in town," said Wendy. Wearing a wireless earpiece, she was talking to Rose while restocking the shelves.

"Hit me," said Rose, her own earpiece in place. Smiling, she watched Molly and Relic playfully scamper around their favourite park, poop bags at the ready in her pocket. The harbour views were breathtaking from the hilltop. A dusting of snow had fallen overnight, turning the dirty snowbanks along the sidewalks white again.

"It's actually a condo in my Aunt Margot's building in town. The owner is renting it for a year while he visits family in Germany," said Wendy. "Ground floor, so no stairs for the dogs. Stunning view of Back Harbour from the small fenced-in backyard. Mostly seniors, so nice and quiet. Want me to connect you?"

"Sounds great, but there's a problem," said Rose, stooping to scoop after Molly made a deposit, which was easy to spot in the snow. "I have a three-bedroom-house-worth of stuff."

"Sell and donate what you don't need, and put the rest in storage," said Wendy, who had never met a problem she couldn't solve...eventually. "Or rent it furnished."

"I was planning to sell the house, but maybe I'll hold off for a year," mused Rose. "I like that this wouldn't be as big of a commitment as buying."

"In case things go south and you bail after a year, you mean?" said Wendy, forcing a chuckle. But not finding the thought terribly funny.

Rose laughed, too. "Yeah, something like that."

"You still on for Wednesday at my lawyer's office?"

"I'll be there," said Rose.

"No cold feet?" Wendy prayed Rose wouldn't back out at the last minute.

"Are you kidding? My feet are frozen blocks of ice! But maybe I just need warmer socks," said Rose, stomping the snow underfoot. "Listen, the truth is I'm terrified. But I'm going to miss Jim wherever I live. I'll have Molly and Relic for company, and you for support. Daisy will only be an hour away. I think this opportunity is a gift, Wendy."

"Atta girl!" said Wendy. "See, you *are* brave. See you in two days."

"See you then," said Rose, hanging up. She called her dogs, took off her gloves, and clipped their leashes onto their collars. The trio slowly made their way back down the hill toward home.

Rose hadn't been exaggerating. She *was* terrified. But not of buying the business. That would work out or it wouldn't. She didn't need a job. Or the money.

Rose was terrified that her broken heart would never heal.

Nine

IN A SMALL BOARDROOM AT A LUNENBURG LAW firm on King Street, while Daisy killed time in the coffee shop down the street, Rose and Wendy signed the paperwork that would make Rose the owner of Fishnets & Fantasies. Smiling as they put their pens on the table, they shook hands. Wendy's lawyer took the documents to make copies.

"How do you feel?" asked Wendy, glancing at her watch. Although Paul's injury was healing, she didn't like leaving him alone for long. He disliked her hovering, but she wasn't taking any chances. A fall at this stage of his recovery could be disastrous. Restless and bored from taking it easy for so long, he was anxious to get the all-clear from his doctor so he could return to the fire hall.

"I'm excited!" said Rose, whose heart was racing. "And scared. But mostly excited."

"Jim would be proud of you," said Wendy.

"I think so, too," said Rose, dabbing her eyes with a tissue. "He wouldn't want me to be afraid to try new things. New adventures."

"How do your parents feel about all of this?" Wendy hadn't thought to ask her before now.

"I can hardly believe it, but Mom has been super supportive. I knew Dad would be. They both miss running their business, so I think they're going to live vicariously through me. They've offered to help in any way they can."

"That's great," said Wendy. "And don't forget, you'll have

a website designer and an accountant who'll be working for you remotely."

The town's head librarian, Will Tanner, had retired two years earlier but continued his web design freelance business from Calgary. He and his spouse, Fishnets & Fantasies's accountant, Megan Bailey, had moved west to be closer to her family. Wendy smiled at the memory of introducing the awkward, middle-aged, never-married singletons at a business meeting a decade ago. They were now the parents of twins.

The lawyer returned with the copies. Thanking her, Wendy and Rose put on their coats and picked up their purses.

"I have to run home, but why don't you come see me in a couple of weeks and we'll discuss next steps," said Wendy.

"Sounds good, text me a date. I've resigned from *Dash*, and one of my freelancers is taking over J&J Organic's copywriting. I'm ticking off my to-do boxes. Next on my list is to rent my house for April first."

It didn't escape Wendy that Rose had said *my* house. She hoped it was a sign that her friend—and now, her new boss— was healing.

"Have you sorted out the rental here?" asked Wendy.

"Done," said Rose, nodding. "It's a cute little place. You were right about the view."

"Margot is looking forward to meeting you," said Wendy. Her widowed aunt, who had been married to Wendy's late uncle Eric for sixty-one years, would be good company for Rose... and vice versa.

"I'm looking forward to meeting her, too," said Rose as they walked down the hall side by side. "You know what? I'm a terrible friend. I haven't even asked what your retirement plans are."

Wendy smiled. "Actually, I'm not retiring. I'm pivoting. I'm planning to train as an end-of-life doula."

Rose stopped walking and faced her. "A what?"

"A death doula. It's like a birth doula, only I'll be offering emotional and practical support to dying people and their families. There's a growing demand for those services, you know. And I feel like I'm being called toward it."

Rose shook her head, then hugged her friend. "You are amazing. Truly."

Wendy held Rose tightly. "Oh, I don't think so. I'm just following my heart. I hope that by helping people understand and prepare for death, they can embrace it as a natural transition. Margot has offered to be my first volunteer."

Rose looked startled. "Oh, dear...is she dying?"

Wendy laughed. "No, she's fit as a fiddle. She's just being supportive."

Rose held the front door open and the two women stepped onto the sidewalk, blinded by sunshine sparkling on snow. Donning sunglasses, they hugged again, then parted ways: Wendy for home, Rose to meet Daisy for lunch at the Grand Banker.

❧

As Rose watched the sunlight sparkle on the harbour, she remembered stepping out onto a Toronto sidewalk soon after she turned thirty-seven. After her final session with her therapist. And how she had felt right before she and Jim had moved to Halifax. Saying farewell to the familiar. Embracing the unknown. The familiar tingle of fear and excitement a big change brings.

Leaving her therapist's office on that late-September day, Rose had felt a lightness radiate throughout her body. Then, she had felt ready for the changes that lay ahead. With Jim at her side. Now, she wasn't so confident. Wendy was the only one who had offered her a life raft, and she had to take it, or drown.

❧

At the Grand Banker, Rose and Daisy sat at a table overlooking Front Harbour, waiting for their lunch to arrive. Daisy scanned the room, noting the other diners. "It's busy in here," she said. As her gaze landed on the bar, she whistled softly. "Who's that tall drink of water over there?" she said, nodding to her left.

Rose glanced in that direction. She spotted a man with short, curly, salt-and-pepper hair. Around their age. Even from several few feet away, she saw dimples flashing and green eyes glinting with mischief.

"He isn't *that* tall. Five nine, maybe. Jim's six two." *Dammit.* Rose kept forgetting to use the past tense.

"Don't be such a killjoy. I'm focusing more on the drink-of-water part," said Daisy, trying not to stare. "I mean, *look* at him. He's hot!"

"May I remind you that you're a happily married woman?" said Rose, sipping her water. In high school, Daisy had gone through several boyfriends...some at the same time. Occasionally, she'd tried to steal Rose's, just to see if she could. Both sisters had been gymnasts, and in spite of their closeness, they could never fight their competitive natures.

"I'm married, not dead," said Daisy indignantly. Then she blushed, "Sorry, that was insensitive."

"That's okay," said Rose, mindlessly moving her white-gold engagement and wedding rings back and forth with the opposite thumb and index finger. "I'd prefer to not tiptoe around the fact that my husband died recently."

"No tiptoeing—got it," said Daisy, relieved. "But back to me for a minute. I may be married, but I'm allowed to look. Steve thinks Helen Mirren is hot. Especially when she's dressed to the nines and firing a machine gun."

"Helen Mirren firing a machine gun *is* hot," admitted Rose.

"I wonder who he's talking to," mused Daisy. "A relative, maybe? If so, that guy got the short end of the family's good-looks stick."

The person who was engaged in conversation with the bartender was short and stout. His short, straight, grey hair was badly in need of a shampoo. A plaid lumberjack coat had seen better days. Just then, he turned around to signal a server.

"Oops," said Daisy, surprise written all over her face.

"What?"

"My mistake. It's a woman."

"Are you sure?" said Rose, trying to spy inconspicuously. "If you're right, she looks like that character Mary Walsh played in drag on *This Hour Has 22 Minutes*. What was his name?"

Daisy went to pull out her phone.

"Don't google it!" said Rose, slapping her sister's hand. "Remembering things on your own is supposed to help stave off dementia."

Grunting, Daisy put her phone down. They thought for a few seconds, then said in unison: "Dakey Dunn!"

"At least she doesn't have a mustache," said Rose.

Daisy squinted. "She kind of does."

"Stop it!" said Rose, kicking Daisy's shin under the table. "If it weren't for laser treatment, I'd have one too."

The sisters started laughing. Rose felt a case of the giggles coming on. The sensation felt foreign. And wonderful. Effervescent. Bubbly and light, like champagne. Tears streamed down her cheeks. She couldn't remember the last time she had laughed so hard.

"We'll get thrown out of here," said Rose, when she was able to talk. Reaching into her purse for a tissue, she wiped her eyes and blew her nose. "Besides, I don't get what's so funny. She's a bit mannish—what's the big deal? Androgyny is trending again."

Daisy grinned broadly. "It's funny because that, dear sister, is Cousin May Ainsworth."

Rose's jaw dropped. "You're shitting me. How do you know?"

Daisy smiled. "After you mentioned her the other day, I searched for her on social media. Her photo is all over wildlife-rescue sites, and she's been in the news. She's famous in these parts."

Their server interrupted them, handing the fish cakes to Daisy and a house salad to Rose.

"You should eat more," said Daisy, placing her napkin on her lap. "You've lost weight."

"I've lost my appetite," said Rose, picking at her plate. "I'm fairly certain it's a side effect of losing my husband." Not even chocolate could tempt her, and that was saying a lot.

"No doubt," said Daisy gently, "but you can't stop looking after yourself. Your dogs need you."

"Not my family?" said Rose, raising an eyebrow.

"Nope. We'd manage without you. Molly and Relic would be sad, though, and I'm not taking them. My house is too full as it is."

"Piss off," said Rose, laughing. To appease her sister, she lifted a forkful of salad into her mouth. Chewing dramatically with her mouth open, she swallowed and said, "Happy now?"

"You're worse than a toddler," said Daisy, spooning green-tomato chow on top of a fish cake. "When we're done, we're going to introduce ourselves to May."

"Why?" said Rose, sneaking a peek at her cousin, who was also eating.

"Because you share DNA. You both have rescue animals. And if you're moving here, you could use a friend."

"Just because we're related and love dogs with hard-luck backstories doesn't mean we'll be friends," said Rose, pushing a leaf of lettuce around her plate.

"You never know," said Daisy, taking a big bite of fish cake. Rose watched her sister savour every last morsel of her meal. Unable to finish her salad, Rose passed on tea and dessert.

After Rose paid the bill, Daisy said, "Come on." Slinging her coat and purse over her arm, she strode purposefully toward the bar. Rose followed a few steps behind.

May was laughing at something the bartender had said. Daisy tapped the woman's shoulder.

"Excuse me, sorry to interrupt, but my sister and I want to say hello. We're your uncle John Ainsworth's daughters. I'm Daisy, and this is Rose."

May blinked. Looked them up and down. Titled her head and frowned, as though English wasn't her first language. Then she stood up, wrapped her arms around both women, squeezed hard, and shouted, "Holy shitballs! Howdy, cousins!"

Not expecting such an enthusiastic response, Daisy and Rose had no choice but to hug her back. When May released her grip, Daisy and Rose exchanged a look that said, *Kookiness factor: high.*

"Great to see ya. Been what, thirty, forty years? Long time, anyhoo."

May turned to the bartender, who looked amused. "Allan, these here are my first cousins...what'd ya say your names were?"

"I'm Daisy, and this is my *younger sister*, Rose," said Daisy pointedly, purposely not looking at Allan. "Her husband died three months ago."

"Jesus," said Rose under her breath. Daisy would pay later for lobbing that emotional grenade at these unsuspecting strangers.

That piece of information prompted May to hug Rose tightly again. "Sorry to hear that. So sad. My heart breaks every time one of my animals dies. Gets me right here." She pounded the left side of her chest with a fist. "Bleeds for ages. No expiration date for grief." May's big, blue eyes filled with tears. Looking at Rose, she asked, "You heartbroken?"

Rose didn't miss a beat. "Yes."

"Ah, girlie. Rough stuff. Got any animals for company?"

"Two rescue dogs," said Rose, grateful to move the conversation in another direction.

"Names?"

"Molly and Relic."

"Cute! Loved that show. Ages? Breeds?"

"They're eleven. Siblings. Not sure about the mix."

"You let me take a peek at 'em and I'll tell ya," said May. "When can I meet them? Are they here?" May looked around the restaurant as if the dogs might be seated at a table nearby.

"Actually, Rose is moving to Lunenburg in April," said Daisy.

May looked at Rose. "No way, little lady! What for?"

"I'm buying a friend's business," said Rose, hoping Daisy would stop volunteering information about her. She'd always been a busybody.

"Fishnets & Fantasies?" asked Allan, looking at Rose. Daisy watched his eyes drop briefly to her sister's wedding rings, then move back to her face.

"How'd you know?" said Rose, frowning.

Allan smiled, dimples flashing. Daisy almost passed out. "It's a small town. And Wendy's a friend."

"Where's my manners at?" shouted May. "This here's Allan Conrad. He owns this joint and helps me out on rescues from time to time. Heart as big as a prairie sky."

"Nice to meet you," said Daisy, extending a hand to shake Allan's, fully prepared to never wash it again. "We really enjoyed our lunch."

Shameless suck-up, thought Rose.

"Nice to meet you, too," said Allan. Rose hid her hands in her coat pockets.

"Rose, you aren't the only lonesome dove here," said May. "Allan got his heart broken ten years ago and hasn't been with a woman since."

Used to his friend's directness, Allan threw his head back and hooted. Then he looked serious. "You know it's only because you won't have me, May."

"Aw, g'wan, ya big ole teddy bear," said May, punching him in the arm. "You know I love ya like a brother, but the buck stops there."

"How are April and June?" asked Rose, trying to steer the conversation away from heartbreak.

"Those two slags? Dead to me. Next question."

But not like Jim, who is actually dead, thought Rose. Feeling anxious, she decided it was time to bow out.

"It was nice to reconnect with you, but we'd better get back to the city," said Rose, looking at her watch. "The dogs will need a walk and their supper."

May's phone buzzed. Glancing at it, she said, "I gotta go too. Duck in distress in Mader's Cove. Nice to see you gals. Get home to your pups and give them a big hug and a smooch from their cousin May. Can't wait to meet 'em. Look me up when you land, Rose. Allan here knows how to reach me."

"Will do," said Rose, who had no intention of contacting her.

"She's...entertaining," said Daisy as they walked toward the waterfront parking lot, hoods pulled up to shield themselves from the freezing rain. A Maritime winter ran the whole weather spectrum—snow, hail, freezing rain, rain. Sometimes all in one day. Or one hour. Freeze, thaw, freeze, thaw. Boot crampons on icy sidewalks of death to prevent falling. Waterproof thermal outerwear.

"*Entertaining* is charitable," said Rose. "I would have chosen *exhausting*. I have a headache."

"She's kooky, all right, but I can tell she's kind," said Daisy. "And she has a cute, *single* friend."

"Don't even go there," said Rose, unlocking their doors. "It's too soon."

"Not for you, dummy. I'm starting divorce proceedings as soon as we get home."

Rose laughed. "Shut up, you love Steve."

"Who?" said Daisy.

As Rose pulled out of the parking space, wondering how she could possibly share DNA with May, she noticed Allan looking intently out of the window.

Ten

ROSE WASN'T SURPRISED BY HOW QUICKLY SHE WAS able to rent her house. Whether you were buying or renting, the peninsula was a coveted location. She chose a young couple with a toddler who were moving to Halifax on a one-year military posting. Steve, who had cut back to three days a week in the city hospital's radiology department, had agreed to act as property manager.

Packing boxes were stacked in every room. Molly and Relic sensed something strange was happening. Daisy was helping Rose pack when she could and had kindly volunteered her kids' services. Rose would leave some of the furniture and had rented a storage unit for the rest of her things.

On this morning's agenda: tackle Jim's closet.

Taking a deep breath, Rose opened the door. Hanging on the rack were her husband's shirts, pants, and suits. On the shelves, sweaters and hoodies. On the floor, dress shoes and sneakers. She knew she had to do something with them but couldn't decide what. Donate them? Store them? Take some of them with her? It seemed too...soon. He had only been dead for four months. Pressing her face into a stack of sweaters, Rose could still smell his sandalwood soap.

The back pocket of her jeans buzzed. Decision delayed by a text. From Rima. Rose sat on Jim's side of the bed to read it.

Just checking in. Hope the packing's going okay.
Wanted to share some good news. Our adoption is going

ahead...and I'M PREGNANT! Three months, so I can finally share our happy news!

Several emojis with heart eyes followed.

Rose was stunned. Her friend was adopting a baby. *And* having a baby. At forty-one.

The same age Rose had been when she'd had a hysterectomy.

"Molly! Relic! Come!" Rose called out. Seconds later, her loyal canine companions trotted into the bedroom.

"Good dogs," said Rose, kissing each one on the head. "I have news. Our friend Rima is adopting a baby *and* having a baby. But we aren't going to be jealous of her, are we? Even though her husband is alive and she's expanding her family, while ours is shrinking."

Molly and Relic wagged their tails. They looked at Rose as if to say, *We came when you called. Are we getting treats, or what?*

"No, we're going to tell her we're happy for her and Harry. Just because we're in the depths of despair doesn't mean we can't support someone else's good fortune. Does it?"

Molly and Relic sat without being asked. Each held up a paw.

Rose laughed and stood up. "All right, time for treats." The dogs' ears perked up at the magic word, and they made their way to the kitchen.

Screwing the lid back on the biscuit jar after doling out several, Rose returned it to its spot on the kitchen counter, then sat on a stool at the island to compose her reply.

Congrats! Amazing news! So happy for you both. Call me with the details.

Rose hesitated, then added a heart.

Her phone buzzed again. Another text. This one from Yuki.

I feel like a shit-ass friend because I haven't checked in on u in a while. How's tricks?

Rose laughed. Yuki was always a breath of fresh air.

Tricks are good when the johns comply. My pimp's on my ass, tho.

Yuki shot back: *Aren't you a little old for hooking?*

Rose typed furiously: *I prefer the term 'sex work.' And the market for mature women has never been hotter.* Rose hesitated before adding: *Did you hear Rima's news?*

Yeah. Happy for them. It's all she can talk about at work. But enough about her. How the hell are u?

Rose sighed. She never knew how to answer that question. However, she appreciated that some friends occasionally asked. Since Jim died, several had disappeared. Probably worried about saying the wrong thing. Making Rose feel uncomfortable. Feeling uncomfortable themselves.

Rose typed: *Thanks for asking. Keeping busy. Good and bad days. Miss him. Grateful for the dogs. And Daisy. And the move. Good distractions. How are you?*

Pretty good. I met someone…

Rose couldn't type fast enough: *Whaaaat?!? Dish!*

Don't laugh. Blind date. Hedge fund manager. As square as you. Sweet and kind, tho. Guess I'm ready for that. And oh yeah…HOT AF! Just posted a pic on IG.

Rose laughed, then looked at Yuki's feed. She wasn't exaggerating.

I wouldn't kick him outta bed for eating crackers! Invite me to the wedding. I'll be flower girl. So happy for you xoxo.

Yuki signed off with: *Lol. Thanks hunny. Catch u later xx.*

Rose put her phone face down on the island counter. Crossed her arms. Lay her head on them. And cried.

Jim's closet would have to wait.

Eleven

WENDY WAS STILL LAUGHING AT THE PHONE CALL she'd just had at work.

"Fishnets & Fantasies, Wendy speaking. How may I help you?" is how it began.

"Well—well—well, n-now, missy, I'm not too sure you can."

Wendy smiled. The caller was an older, soft-spoken man with a stutter. He reminded her of a Bob Newhart character.

"Are you interested in buying something that we sell, Mr. ...?" Wendy hoped to make this as easy for the gentleman as possible.

"Shupe. And yes—yes, that might be just the t-ticket."

Stanley Shupe, thought Wendy. *Retired postal worker. Confirmed bachelor. Early eighties.*

"Do you know what you're looking for?" It wasn't the shop's first exploratory inquiry from a senior. Wendy was certain it wouldn't be the last.

"I'll—I'll tell you what happened this morning. Now, I live up on Blockhouse Hill Road."

The nursing home. It had a good reputation, but after Eric's death ten years ago, Margot had chosen not to move there. Instead, with her children's help, she bought a two-bedroom condo with the proceeds from the sale of their Linden Avenue bungalow. Close to her church, the grocery store, and the hospital.

"This morning, I got up like usual. When I went to shave, I saw a small packet on the side of the sink. I—I—I don't see too good, what with the glaucoma, so I thought the nurse had

60

left me some of that pain-relieving gel for my knuckles. Full of arthritis, they are. Years of delivering mail in the c-cold, you know. Frostbite and such."

"Oh, dear," said Wendy patiently, waiting for Stanley to get to the point. "That must be painful."

"Yes, 'tis…'tis. So I opened the packet, rubbed the ointment on my hands and—and—I swear, it's a miracle cure! Heated my hands up right some good so as I didn't feel the pain no more. When I asked the n-nurse about it, she said I should call you."

Wendy was curious. "Do you still have the packet?"

"Yes—y-yes, it's right here."

"What does it say on it?" Wendy looked up and waved hello as two millennials walked in.

"Now, let me get my—my magnifying glass. Can't read a d-dang thing without it. There, that's better…it says…*K-Y. Warming. Liquid.* Do you sell that at your store?"

Wendy stopped herself from laughing out loud, wondering if the nurse had really left the packet by mistake. Although she knew that seniors were sexually active, and after a decade in business, nothing surprised her anymore.

"I do, Mr. Shupe. But I have to tell you, K-Y isn't meant to relieve arthritis."

"No? What's it f-for, then?" Mr. Shupe sounded genuinely confused.

"It's to keep things warm…down there…during sex."
Silence.

"Well—well—now that *is* a surprise, I must say. I wouldn't need it for…*that* purpose—but I sure wouldn't mind having more for my knuckles. That ointment they give us here isn't near—near as good, that's for dang sure."

"A pack of two tubes costs about thirty dollars, with tax. Is that in your budget?"

"Yes—yes…I got a good pension."

"Shall I take your order over the phone, then?" Wendy hoped he had a credit card.

"The thing—the thing is, I told a few of my friends here about it—and well, we'd like to place a group order, if that isn't too much bother."

"How many people are interested?" Wendy waved goodbye to the young couple who had been browsing. Some customers liked to be left alone, while others wanted to interact. She could usually tell one group from the other immediately.

"Let me see...there's me. Noreen. Sally. Jack. Geraldine. Doris. Henry. St-Stuart. And Edith. Hang on, now...I almost—I almost forgot Arty."

Ten! Wendy was amused.

"That'll be about three hundred dollars all together, Mr. Shupe. Will you be putting the total sale on one credit card?"

"Yes—yes, dear, I've offered to use my card. My friends are trustworthy. Plus, I know where they li—live." Stanley chuckled.

After taking his card details, Wendy thanked Stanley for his business and told him she'd drop the box off at the nursing home's reception desk after work.

She couldn't wait to tell Paul about the call. *Arthritis, my ass! You can't fool me, Stanley Shupe.*

⁂

Sonya had written almost twenty thousand words of her manuscript. Working title: *Love in the Sugar Bush*. Nineteen-year-old lumberjack Alphonse, a potato farmer in northern New Brunswick, had succumbed once to the wiles of the raven-haired, violet-eyed camp cook with an hourglass figure, Lisette, the foreman's eighteen-year-old daughter. When he was near her, he completely forgot he was engaged to plain but kind Gisèle back home. *There's trouble brewing*, thought Sonya. She had imagined Lisette as a teenaged Elizabeth Taylor.

At the camp, the lumberjacks worked from sunrise to sunset six days a week. When they weren't thawing ice, logs often jammed, forcing them to jump from log to log with a pole to locate the source of the trouble. At times, the river could be too strong, and in removing the jam the men risked getting swept away with the current.

Sonya scanned the last paragraph she had written.

Life in the camp wasn't all work and no play, however. Alphonse and the other loggers spent their Saturday nights dancing, singing, playing the fiddle, and telling stories. Sundays were their day off, and they could afford to sleep in. On this particular Saturday night, Lisette was there. As her father's fingers caressed his fiddle into a slow, mournful ballad, she sang sweetly, her breasts lifting and falling hypnotically with each verse.

Leaning back in her chair, Sonya rolled her shoulders. She was pleased with her progress. This book was a nod to Longfellow's epic poem *Evangeline*, about an Acadian girl who searches for her lost love during the time of the Acadian expulsion in 1755.

Early on, it had dawned on Sonya that Evangeline's story was also the story of many traditional South Shore families, where fishing and farming accidents left the breadwinner of the household seriously injured, with their wives and children caring for them. She knew from Wendy how relieved she'd been when Paul had stopped fishing.

Sonya glanced at her watch. Ten o'clock. She had been working since eight, right after breakfast. It would soon be time for a coffee and brain break.

"I hate to do this to you, Alphonse, but you're going to get badly hurt in a logjam," said Sonya, removing her glasses. "I won't kill you, though. And Lisette will have to nurse you back to health, so you'll end up thanking me."

Sonya often spoke aloud to her characters while she was writing. Booth had gotten used to her mumbling, recognizing that she wasn't talking to him. Just then, he appeared in the doorway.

"Want coffee?"

"Love one, thanks," said Sonya gratefully. "Be down in a minute."

"Can I run something by you first?" Booth sounded serious.

"Of course." Sonya nodded at the armchair on the other side of the desk.

Booth sat down. Crossed his arms, then his legs. Uncrossed them. "I'm thinking about running for town council."

"That's wonderful! What brought this on?" Sonya had fallen in love with her husband's ambitious nature in high school. She was pleased to discover that at almost seventy, there were still things he wanted to accomplish.

"You know I'm not happy with the mayor."

"That is *not* a newsflash," said Sonya, putting her elbows on the desk and placing her chin on her clasped hands. Giving Booth her full attention, even though she was waiting for an important text from her editor.

"He doesn't listen to his constituents, he's slow to adapt, and his lack of transparency is, quite frankly, embarrassing," said Booth, ticking off each transgression on his fingers.

"Well, in his defense—and you know I didn't vote for him, either—he's young and has a lot to learn," said Sonya.

"I wish Derek Young would offer, but he's still on leave from council," said Booth. "If he did, I'd campaign for him. I'm going to call him to ask what his plans are."

"Good idea," said Sonya. "It's a shame what he and Cathy are going through."

A popular local politician in his mid-sixties, Derek had been bitten by a blacklegged tick carrying Lyme disease the previous fall. Long after completing treatment, he was still experiencing some fatigue, joint pain, and weakness in his arms and legs. Derek's wife, Cathy, had retired as minister of Central United Church to care for him full-time.

"I think I can help move Lunenburg forward if I'm on council," said Booth. "The election's in mid-October. I'll have six months to campaign. That should be plenty of time." He paused. "I was wondering how you'd feel about being a politician's wife. If I get elected, that is."

Sonya smiled. "I don't think it'll be as demanding a role as First Lady. I'll support you however you need me to. The bigger question is, how would the politician feel about having a romance author for a wife?"

Booth grinned. "Pretty damn proud of that...*and* of the fact that she had an illustrious career as an anesthesiologist first."

"Then go for it!" said Sonya, walking around the desk to kiss Booth on the lips. "Let me know how I can help."

"Thanks, honey. I'll spend some time strategizing today. But first, coffee. You coming?"

"Give me five minutes. I just had a thought about Alphonse I want to get down." Booth left for the kitchen while Sonya put her glasses back on, then typed quickly. She had learned the hard way that if she didn't make a note about an idea when it popped into her head, it would be gone when she tried to retrieve it later.

When Sonya had finished, she picked up her phone and followed after Booth. At the top of the stairs, her cellphone chimed. An incoming-text alert. Too impatient to wait until she reached the kitchen to read it, she began descending the stairs holding her phone close to her eyes, her reading glasses left behind on her desk.

Terrific! Sonya thought while scanning the message. Her

editor loved the idea for her next novel and planned to draft the contract next week.

"Booth, guess what?" shouted Sonya, skipping down the stairs to tell him the good news.

In her excitement, Sonya's feet missed a step. The next thing she knew, she was lying in a crumpled heap at the bottom of the staircase. Pain pulsed from her right wrist. Her writing hand.

Twelve

IN FLOWER BEDS ACROSS NOVA SCOTIA, SPRING WAS announcing its arrival. White snowdrops and yellow winter aconite had pushed up through the last couple of centimetres of snow, eager to embrace the sun.

On April first, Rose woke up in Daisy's spare room. From a nightmare. In it, she had been cycling toward Drummond Court. On her way home from…no clue where. She knew she had been on her way to meet Jim and their dogs. Excited to see them. Pedalling faster and faster. Legs, lungs, heart pumping. Approaching the driveway, she could see Jim in the living room window. Waving. First, normally. Then, frantically. Was he warning her to slow down? Stay away? Was she in danger? Had she forgotten her helmet?

As her brain fog dissipated, reality dawned. Jim was propped up on the bedside table. In his eco-friendly urn. On either side of her legs, Molly and Relic were snoring.

It's April Fool's Day, but this is no prank, thought Rose. Lifting the neck of the T-shirt of Jim's she had been sleeping in, she peered at her left breast. Above her heart was a colourful dragonfly tattoo. An impulse, after reading in *The Hot Young Widows Club* that some grief-stricken widows got inked. Rose hadn't wanted anything as clichéd as Jim's name encircled by a broken heart. As a child, she had loved the beauty and grace of dragonflies. As an adult, she discovered they symbolized change and transformation.

Rose had read that getting a tattoo would feel like someone was scratching a hot needle across her skin. In fact, it had felt like a thousand angry hornets were stinging her chest. It had felt good—in that, for the first time since Jim died, she'd channelled her psychic pain into physical pain. It was a release of sorts. For a few days afterward, her skin was swollen, red, and tender, forcing her to sleep on her back.

Rousing herself from her reverie, Rose reminded herself that later that day, she was moving to Lunenburg. Most of her possessions were in storage. Daisy had agreed to put her fall and winter clothes in the spare room closet, to save her having to access the commercial storage unit when she needed them.

Rose was taking only the things she really needed. The essentials. Clothes. Dogs. Laptop. Sleeping pills. *The Hot Young Widows Club*. Cremated husband. Even still, her wagon was crammed with suitcases, boxes, and dog gear. There was barely enough room for Molly and Relic.

Daisy had wanted to help, but Rose had politely declined her offer.

"Thanks, but I hardly have anything to unpack," said Rose, struggling to close a bulging knapsack.

"You might want company," said Daisy, taking the knapsack and deftly zipping it.

"I won't," said Rose, facing her sister. "This is something I want to do alone. Besides, I'll have the dogs. And Wendy invited me over for supper. I'll text you as soon as I'm settled."

"Did you say yes to supper at Wendy's?" asked Daisy, hands on hips. The nurse in her couldn't seem to help nurturing. "And how's Paul?"

"I said yes, so quit fussing. Paul has fully recovered. I'll unpack a few things and buy groceries, then head over with the dogs. I'll take them to work with me, too. There's a storeroom all tricked out for when Fred's dogs visit. If a customer is allergic or afraid, I'll pop them in there."

"Sounds like you've got it all figured out," said Daisy, voice pinched. But Rose knew when her sister was lying. Daisy was worried sick.

❧

After lunch, Rose hugged and kissed the Turners, then hit the highway. An hour later, she pulled into the parking spot of her new, temporary home.

"We're here, pups," said Rose. Clipping on their leashes, she led Molly and Relic out of the car and to a grassy area that still had small patches of snow so they could pee.

Behind them, a dirty blue pickup truck peeled into the parking lot.

Slow down, Cowboy, this ain't the autobahn, thought Rose. *Rednecks and their big trucks. Jim would have said he probably has a tiny penis.*

When the driver got out, Rose rolled her eyes.

It was May.

"Hey, cuz! Welcome to Lunenburg! Could those two precious nuggets be Molly and Relic?"

The dogs' ears perked up at their names. May lowered herself carefully onto the ground, even though it was half frozen, to sit cross-legged. Rose let go of the leashes. Usually when meeting new people, they were timid. What happened next surprised her.

Staring straight ahead, May stayed silent. Her hands rested on her knees, palms facing up, Buddha-like. Molly and Relic approached her cautiously. Each sniffed a palm, then licked it.

"Good pups," said May softly.

At the sound of May's voice, first Molly, then Relic, stepped onto her legs, lowered their heads, and pushed them into her chest.

May closed her eyes. Smiled. Inhaled. Exhaled. Wrapped an arm around each dog. Kissing each furry head, she sighed. Rose could tell she was in her element.

"You done a good thing here," said May, opening her eyes to look at Rose. A grin split her face. "This is love. Unconditional. Now, let me have a look at these cutie pies."

May peered at each dog. Tilted her head from side to side. Pursed her lips.

"Father was a beagle." Pause. "Mother was a basset hound–cocker spaniel mix."

"How do you know?" Rose was pleasantly surprised. She had detected beagle in them right away but couldn't pinpoint the rest.

May shrugged. "It's a gift."

"What are you doing here?" Rose was curious about May's timing. And irritated. She had wanted to do this alone.

"Heard this was moving day and thought I'd lend a hand," said May, standing up. "That's what family's for." The dogs wouldn't leave her side, even though their new best friend didn't appear to have any treats.

"But how did you know when I was coming? Did Daisy call you?"

"Nope. Small town is all. People peer out windows and got cell-phones. You'll soon get used to having everyone up in your business."

Rose sighed, attempting to keep her annoyance in check. She suspected that spending time with May would feel like being nibbled to death by ducks.

"Well, it was kind of you to come, but I don't need help. It's a furnished apartment, so I just brought a few personal things."

May looked into the jam-packed Subaru. "Got it. Let's pop this sucker and have at 'er."

It was obvious that May was determined. Her vocation was rescuing and rehabilitating needy creatures. Rose hoped she wasn't going to be one of them.

"All right, come on then," said Rose, raising the hatchback.

May hoisted a box under each arm, while Rose pulled out a suitcase with wheels.

"Let's go, doggos!" said May, falling in step behind Rose. Molly and Relic trotted along behind them.

Inside the apartment, May looked around and whistled. "Wow. Looks like an old-timer lives here."

Rose laughed. "An old-timer does live here, but he's away for a year."

A large leather recliner had pride of place in the living room, in front of an old TV with rabbit ears. There was a lot of dark-wood furniture: dining room table and chairs, coffee table, cabinet.

"Might as well get started," said May, pulling a utility knife out of her coat pocket, preparing to unseal a box.

"Not that one," said Rose hurriedly, stepping over to take it from her.

"Why not? Whatcha hiding in there?" asked May.

"Jim's ashes," said Rose, her voice nearly a whisper. Underneath his urn lay her journal.

May fell silent. Rose could tell that her cousin was more comfortable interacting with furry four-legged creatures than her fellow humans.

A tentative knocking interrupted the awkwardness. The dogs made a beeline for the door. Rose opened it to find a petite older woman with silver hair pulled neatly into a bun at the nape of her neck. She was holding a purple African violet in a pretty ceramic pot.

"Welcome to Lunenburg, dear," the visitor said kindly. "I'm Wendy's aunt Margot."

Rose had wanted to be alone with her thoughts while she unpacked. May and Margot had quashed that plan. But they meant well, so she mustn't be rude.

"Thank you," said Rose, taking the plant in one hand and shaking Margot's hand with the other, then showing her in. "It's lovely to meet you. I hope you like dogs." Molly and Relic were following Margot's every move, vying for attention.

"I love dogs," said Margot, sitting on the overstuffed love-seat and bending down to pet them. Rose couldn't believe the youthful-looking senior was almost ninety. "And who is this sweet pair?"

May piped up, pointing first at one dog, then the other. "This here's Molly, and that's her brother, Relic."

"And how have you been keeping, May?" said Margot, stroking each dog's head gently.

"Oh, not too bad, thanks." May shifted her weight from one side to the other as she spoke. "The gee-dee gout is at me now and then. It's like someone lit my legs on fire. Otherwise, no real complaints."

"Are you taking any medication for that?" asked Rose, lowering herself into the armchair. Years of working for a women's health magazine had turned her into both a pseudo health expert and a hypochondriac. *A little knowledge is a dangerous thing,* she had always thought.

"Nope, don't trust big pharma. I go the natural route. Coffee, vitamin C, cherries."

"To lower uric acid levels?" asked Rose.

"So they say," said May, shrugging her shoulders. "You don't need to tell me twice to drink more coffee, that's for dang sure."

Margot gave the dogs one last ear scratch, then stood up. "I don't want to interrupt your settling in," she said, smiling at Rose. "I just wanted to introduce myself and tell you how pleased I am that we're going to be neighbours. It'll be nice to have a young person in the building."

"Thanks, Margot," said Rose, walking her to the door.

"I'm looking forward to this next chapter of my life." She had rehearsed the words so often, she almost believed them.

Before Margot left, she held Rose's gaze. "I'm very sorry to hear that your Jim died. I was widowed ten years ago. I still miss my Eric every day."

Margot's easy use of *your Jim* made Rose's eyes moist.

"Thank you," said Rose. "I'm sorry for your loss, too."

Margot smiled knowingly, then called out, "Goodbye, May!"

"Catch ya later, little lady!" hollered May, who had clipped the dogs' leashes onto their collars.

"The three of us need some air," said May. "Back in a jiff."

"Need poop bags?" asked Rose, scanning the boxes.

"Nope, I'm always packin'," said May, patting her coat pocket.

As Rose closed the door behind them, she exhaled loudly. This was far too much mental stimulation on moving day. Then her cellphone buzzed.

Jesus H., thought Rose, *now what?* It was from Rima.

Got our ultrasound results. It's a boy!!!

And so it begins, thought Rose. Remembering when her friends began getting pregnant for the first time, most of them in their thirties. And how all of their messages from that point on had revolved around their pregnancy, childbirth, and baby news.

Rose sighed. Because she was older and wiser now, she typed:

Congratulations! So exciting! Will text more later, I'm unpacking in my Lunenburg apartment xo.

There. That would remind Rima about her own big news. *Sorry, I forgot! Good luck with the move. Hugs xoxo.*

Rose got up and went to the box May had wanted to open. Pried apart the flaps. On the top, wrapped in a star-flower quilt Jim's mother had made not long before she died, were Jim's ashes.

Rose cradled the urn in her arms. "Well, what do you think?" she said, walking slowly through the condo. As though she was showing Jim around. Open-concept living and dining room. Galley kitchen. Bedroom. Bathroom. Everything clean and neat. It was a much smaller space than she and the dogs were used to. But how much room did they really need? Besides, they'd be spending workdays at the shop.

Rose opened the sliding patio glass doors and stood in the yard overlooking Back Harbour. Even though the sunshine was brilliant and she hadn't taken off her coat, she felt chilled. "Pretty nice view. Wish you could see it. Then again, if you *were* still here, I wouldn't be doing this."

Rose heard the apartment door open and close, followed by "Good dogs!" May was back. She, Molly, and Relic joined Rose outside.

"I love these kids!" said May. Rose was taking in the view of the harbour, the evergreen trees, and the road below. "You did a good thing."

"Thanks," said Rose. "Jim and I always said adopting them was the best decision we ever made."

"Are ya giving him the tour?" asked May, eyeing the urn. Rose clutched it tighter.

"Maybe," said Rose hesitantly. She felt protective of him. Bracing herself, she waited for her cousin to say something insensitive.

"That looks like a big McDonald's hot apple pie package," said May, looking at it suspiciously.

"Yeah, I know," said Rose, peering down at it. "It's biodegradable, though. Good for the environment."

May took off her toque and held it awkwardly in front of her, her short hair standing on end with static. Looking at the urn, she said, "Howdy, Jim. Pleased to meet you. Lovely missus you got. And Molly and Relic here are the bee's knees."

Rose was surprised. And touched. Maybe May would grow on her. Slowly but surely. Like a fungus.

May put her hat back on. "You lost your wingman."

"I don't think that's what Jim was, actually," said Rose, frowning. She was pretty sure a wingman was someone who helped a friend attract potential romantic partners or avoid undesirable ones. "At any rate, I don't need someone else."

"Yeah, you do," May said. Thumping her chest, she added, "I'll be your wingman."

Before Rose could reply, May's cellphone buzzed. Glancing at it, she sighed. "Shoot. Gotta skedaddle. Injured raccoon in Gold River. Some idiot left it at the end of his driveway after trying to bash its brains in with a shovel. Didn't do the job properly, so it's still alive."

"The poor thing," said Rose, wincing. "Will it survive?"

"Probably not," said May, pocketing her phone. "But hopefully we can make sure it has a humane death."

Rose's curiosity got the better of her. "What did you do after high school?"

May shrugged. "Didn't finish. Dropped out when I was sixteen. Didn't have too many friends. Wasn't popular like Slags One and Two. Had a hard time reading and writing. Couldn't wait to leave. Mom and Pop were freewheeling hippies and said okay, as long as I paid my own way."

Rose placed Jim gently on the coffee table. "What did you do next?"

"I've always loved animals, so I started a dog-walking business, then expanded to pet-sitting. Got experience and good references that helped me land my job at the SPCA. I volunteer for rescue groups, too."

"How many rescue animals do you have?" Rose had her hands full with Molly and Relic, although they were good as gold.

May's face split into a grin. "A twelve-year-old cat who got returned to the shelter three times. Her future looked grim, so I took her. She's a tyrant and rules the house, but we've learned to tolerate each other. I'd have a houseful of animals, but I'm on the road so much, it wouldn't be fair." She pointed at Rose. "You're coming with me on a rescue sometime."

"Thanks, but no. I'm gonna be really busy with the shop," Rose said. "And I have to look after the dogs. They only have me now."

"No one is too busy to help a fellow sentient creature in need," said May sternly. "Margot or Wendy'll mind the pups. C'mon! It'll be fun. Catching critters is a real adrenaline rush. I'll text ya. What's your number?"

Rose didn't see how she could politely refuse to provide it. Their fingers flew as they put each other's numbers in their phones.

May pocketed her phone. "When we do go, make sure you're packin' pepper spray."

"What for?" asked Rose dubiously.

"Brown bears. Big, mean ones. They're crawling all over the backwoods in these parts." May grinned devilishly. Rose got the impression that her cousin could take a bear down in one fell swoop. Or talk it to death.

"Oh, I don't think I'll be going into the woods. Maybe you could sign me up to help with something in town? Like a cat stuck in a tree. I could stand at the bottom holding a tin of tuna and a bag of treats."

May punched Rose's arm and said, "Gotcha! I'm kidding about the brown bears. There aren't any in Nova Scotia."

"Well, that's good news," said Rose, visibly relieved.

"We got black bears here," said May, winking. "And they're just as big and mean as the grizzlies."

"You aren't helping," said Rose, laughing in spite of herself.

"We'll toughen you up in no time, city girl," May insisted. May planted one last kiss on the dogs' heads and gave Rose a bear hug. Because her arms were pinned to her sides, Rose couldn't return the embrace even if she'd wanted to. Then her cousin was gone as suddenly as she had arrived.

Rose's phone buzzed. It was Daisy.

Everything okay? I can come if you need help. Love you.

Rose sighed. While she appreciated everyone's good intentions, she really just wanted to be left alone.

Thanks, but I've got this. May and Margot dropped by. Will unpack a few things, walk the dogs, then head to Wendy's. Come next weekend. Love you too.

Rose put down her phone. Pressed her palms into her closed eyes. T. S. Eliot once wrote that April is the cruellest month. But since Jim died, every month had been just as cruel as the last.

Thirteen

THE FIRST NIGHT IN HER NEW DIGS, ROSE WAS REST-less. It was after midnight, and she was lying wide awake in a strange bed. Not that she had been able to sleep for more than a handful of hours at home. Here, the mattress was comfortable enough, but she just couldn't settle. Not even a sleeping pill could stop her monkey mind from bouncing from one fretful thought to the next. *What have I done?* kept cycling through her brain on repeat. *How can I get out of this? I want to go home.*

Plus, it was quiet outside. Too quiet. Except for the chiming of church bells on Sunday mornings, which disturbed her peace. It reminded her of the holiday weekends she and Jim had woken to them, lying in bed in their vacation rentals. Turning toward each other to lazily make love.

Used to being lulled to sleep by city noise, Rose tossed and turned. Hoping to hear a siren wailing. A car alarm blaring. A dog barking. Something familiar. She felt homesick. Like she had the first few weeks in her university dorm room.

Her own dogs were quiet, twitching occasionally in their sleep. Blissfully unaware their human was upset. If they woke and needed to pee, she'd let them outside. The postage stamp–sized backyard wasn't ideal, but they all had to adapt. Their lives were different now.

That evening at supper, Wendy's house had been cozy. It felt like a home. It *was* a home, and had been for the forty-five years she and Paul had lived there. They were firmly rooted. In the condo, Rose felt like a squatter. Hopefully that unsettled feeling would pass with time. She wondered if the family spending their first night on Drummond Court was feeling the same way. Displaced. If they missed where they had been before. Comparing. Pining for what they'd left behind.

Rose's tears slipped out quietly, so as not to disturb the dogs. Nights were the hardest. When bad dreams crept into what little sleep she could catch.

Jim on his bike.

The van.

The impact.

Silent screams.

In the mornings, she got up early to tackle her to-do list. In the quiet darkness, she was lost.

Hesitantly, Rose reached for her pill splitter on the night table. She had started cutting her sleeping pills in half. Trying to wean herself off them. It wasn't working. In fact, she suspected the pills were causing rebound insomnia.

My kingdom for a good night's sleep, Rose thought. She wondered what that saying meant. Reaching past her pill splitter, she picked up her phone to search for it. Bad idea, she knew, but waiting till morning to learn the answer would keep her awake even longer. Turned out it was the title of an article about how as baby boomers aged, fewer of them were getting quality sleep. Chronic insomnia was on the rise in that demographic. Causes included disorders such as sleep apnea that begin, or worsen, with age. Menopause-induced, middle-of-the-night hot flashes. Depression. Anxiety. Bad sleep habits.

Thanks to her hysterectomy, Rose was done with menopause. Apart from the last four months, her sleep habits had generally been pretty good.

Anxiety. That was her poison.

Wiping her wet cheeks with the bedsheet, Rose thought about her evening. During supper, Wendy had noticed her friend picking at her small portions of shepherd's pie and garden salad.

Molly and Relic had stuck close to Rose—that is, until Paul started slipping them bits of cheese under the table.

Sonya King, who worked at the shop part-time, had dropped by afterward to join them for tea and banana bread. Sonya had agreed to fill in at Fishnets & Fantasies to help train Rose when Wendy needed a day off. Her broken wrist would still be encased in a plaster cast and supported by a sling for a couple more weeks, so she wouldn't be able to lift anything. But she could answer the phone, and Rose's questions, and help customers.

Sonya explained that her fall had frightened her so much that she no longer looked at her cellphone when she was on the stairs. After trying unsuccessfully to type on her laptop with only her left hand, she had asked her editor for a deadline extension for the first draft of *Love in the Sugar Bush*. In the meantime, she was using speech-to-text software to advance her storylines. It was better than nothing, but not as effective as typing, especially when it came to making revisions.

When Sonya reviewed the transcription, there were so many misspelled words that she was spending far more time trying to decipher them than she wanted to. As they sipped their tea, Sonya looked to Rose.

"How would you feel about helping me with my manuscript?"

Rose's eyes widened in surprised, eyebrows disappearing under her bangs. "What did you have in mind?"

Sonya chuckled. "I'm afraid it isn't a sexy proposal. What I really need is for someone to type while I dictate. And I won't always nail a sentence on the first try, so you'd have to be patient. But maybe you could help me flesh out ideas, too? I've never joined a writers' group, but I know many authors would be lost without theirs. And to be truthful, I could use fresh input from someone younger."

Rose took a bite of banana bread, considering the idea while she chewed. This could be a great opportunity to learn about book publishing from a seasoned author. And while romance wasn't a genre that interested Rose, Sonya was a two-time recipient of the prestigious Romance Writers of Canada's Alward Award. There were rumblings within the industry that with her new book, she was sure to become a newly minted member of the Alward Hall of Fame.

"How often would you need me?" asked Rose.

"I'm close to finishing, so how about two evenings a week for two hours? With a coffee break in between. Just until the cast comes off and I can type pain-free. I'll pay you, of course."

Rose smiled. "I don't need the money, but I appreciate the offer. I'll do it because I'm interested, and I'd like to help. On one condition."

Now it was Sonya's turn to raise her eyebrows. "What is it?"

Rose looked down at Molly and Relic, snoozing contentedly on the rug. The longer Jim was gone and the older they got, the more guilty she felt leaving them alone, even for a short time.

"My assistants, Molly and Relic, have to come, too."

Sonya laughed. "Deal! Let's start next week, after you get settled at the shop. I think I can wrestle with the software for that much longer."

Talk then turned to Paul's ankle. Rose was pleased that it had healed completely. He was back on firefighting duty, although with limitations, including no climbing ladders for another month. After their meal was done, he excused himself to head to their recently renovated basement to watch the first baseball game of the season. The conversation moved to Wendy's death doula training.

"Where did the idea come from?" asked Rose, taking a sip of tea.

Wendy swallowed her tea before answering. "My parents had good end-of-life care in hospital, but they would have preferred to die at home. At the time, the right supports to grant their final wishes weren't in place. Now they are. I couldn't help them plan the deaths they wanted, but I can help others."

"But how did you learn about death doulas in the first place?" asked Rose.

"I read a story about a death doula in Halifax. I was intrigued, so I did some research online," said Wendy, topping up everyone's mugs with hot tea. "Then Paul and I chose a death doula for ourselves, in case we need one suddenly. After we had a consultation with her, I just felt so strongly that this was a service I wanted to offer. Especially to those who are alone at the end of their life's journey."

"Margot has hired you, hasn't she?" asked Sonya, dabbing the corners of her mouth with a napkin.

"Not *hired*, just volunteered, to help me. Even though she isn't ill, she knows she's in her third and final act. She also knows that when her time comes, her children will be too emotional to advocate for her."

"She's a sweetheart," said Rose, smiling. "I met her this afternoon. She dropped by the condo with a plant. Speaking of family, do either of you know my cousin May Ainsworth?"

Sonya and Wendy both grinned.

"Everyone around here knows May," said Sonya. "I didn't make the connection that you two were related, but I should have—Ainsworth, of course!" She shifted on the sofa, slowly rolling her right shoulder to move her arm into a more comfortable position. "When it comes to animals, May's heart is so big it barely fits in her chest. Are you two close?"

"No, not at all," Rose admitted. "I lost track of my Nova Scotia cousins long before I moved to Toronto. I hadn't seen her since we were kids. Then Daisy and I ran into her at the

Grand Banker when I came to sign the legal documents. She's quite a...character."

"She's larger than life, that's for sure," said Wendy. "May has no filter and few social graces, but when she chooses you as a friend—and that's a real compliment, given that she'd rather be around animals—there's nothing she won't do for you. Fred's wife, Laura, has donated countless hours of her veterinary services to May's rescues."

Rose sighed. "I think she's chosen me as her friend."

"She'd love that you have rescue dogs," said Sonya. "I can't tell you how many times she's tried to convince Booth and me to foster a cat. She's hoping we'll be foster failures and end up adopting it."

Rose couldn't imagine herself fostering an animal; she knew she'd give in and adopt it, too. She looked fondly at her dogs now, fast asleep by her feet. "Adopting these two was one of the best things Jim and I ever did," she said, her voice trembling. She felt herself getting close to tears but wouldn't let herself cry. She wouldn't be that sad widow who never gets invited to another dinner party.

Composing herself and stifling a yawn, Rose glanced at her watch and saw that it was nine o'clock. "I've had a lovely time, but I'd better get the dogs back. Thanks for having me, Wendy. And lovely to meet you, Sonya. Could I wash the dishes before I go?"

"Not tonight," said Wendy, "that's what the dishwasher is for. See you tomorrow at ten?"

"See you then," said Rose, putting on her coat and boots in the front entryway, then clipping on the dogs' leashes.

The next day, Rose's new career as the owner of a small-town sex shop would begin.

Fourteen

WHEN WENDY HAD SUGGESTED TO PAUL THAT THEY meet with a death doula, he'd restrained himself from rolling his eyes. In fact, he made a concerted effort to focus on the newspaper he was reading at the kitchen table. An empty coffee cup and a plate with toast crumbs waited to be moved to the dishwasher. It was just like Wendy to suggest something ridiculous when he was barely awake.

Here we go again, he thought. *Another one of her cockamamie ideas.*

Aloud, he said, "A what?"

Wendy explained that Heather Barkhouse's role as an end-of-life doula was to educate and encourage people, and their families, to be involved in making decisions about their death. And to help co-ordinate their funerals and burials.

"Sounds like bad luck if you ask me...which you didn't," said Paul, looking up from the newspaper. "We aren't sick. Won't seeing a death lady jinx us?"

Fishermen were a superstitious lot. Whistling will bring on a storm. Disaster will follow if you step onto a boat with your left foot first. Saying good luck before a fishing trip brings the opposite. Bananas on board are bad luck. So is a fishing boat painted blue. Paul's old Cape Islander, the *Lucky Haul*, had been red and white.

"She's a death *doula*," Wendy corrected. "And no, it won't jinx us. At our age, it's just good planning."

"Jesus, we aren't even seventy," said Paul, shaking his head. "Neither one of us has a foot in the grave. Not even a big friggin' toe! I let the doctor poke and prod me once a year and shit on a stick every two years so you don't hassle me about my health. Isn't that enough?"

"We'll be seventy this year, and our parents died young," said Wendy, making her case as she cleared the table. "I'll feel less anxious knowing you'll have support if I die first."

Now was not the time to mention that she was planning to become a certified death doula herself. She would break the news to him after their meeting.

"Can we not talk about this now?" said Paul, his voice rising in frustration. "Anyway, I'll have Ellen if...you know. Won't need any more support than that."

"Ellen lives clear across the country," Wendy pointed out. "She isn't going to drop everything to move back here to take care of us, nor should she." Once the dishwasher was running, she sat next to her husband and took his hand. "What if Fay is sick at the same time? Or, god forbid, Ellen is? We *have* to talk about this now. Heather will be here in a few minutes."

"What?" said Paul, his jaw dropping. It was just like his wife to move on something weird without his say so. Just like when she told him about wanting to open the sex shop. Like she was doing now, she'd simply steamrolled his concerns.

"I knew if you had too much time to think about it, you'd pull a disappearing act," said Wendy, taking her hand from his to tidy the table.

"Is this a free visit, then?" Paul looked skeptical.

"No, she charges a consultation fee, it's how she earns her living. We can afford it."

Just then the doorbell rang. "There she is," said Wendy, getting up to answer it. "Be nice, please."

"Fuck's sake," Paul muttered, brushing crumbs off his shirt. "A man can't even die in peace without having to pay to talk to a stranger about it beforehand. Fool's errand, if you ask me. Which no one in this house ever does."

An hour and two pots of tea later, Wendy could see that Paul was more relaxed. In her early forties, Heather was pleasant but not pushy. A good listener. Detail oriented and organized. Perfect for this line of work. Her laptop file labelled "Paul and Wendy Hebb" was now full of general information about their end-of-life wishes. Do-not-resuscitate orders. Wills. Hospice care. Service and burial. Another time, she'd speak with them separately to get more details.

"That wasn't so bad, was it?" said Wendy, after seeing Heather out.

"She's nice enough," said Paul, his voice gruff. "I still think it's bad luck."

"You think having a woman on board a fishing boat is bad luck," said Wendy, smiling. "You're just superstitious."

"A woman on a boat *is* bad luck," said Paul, crossing his arms.

"It wasn't bad luck when we were newlyweds, if you know what I mean." Wendy winked.

Paul couldn't help but grin. "The boat was docked, so it doesn't count."

Wendy laughed. "I swear, you make shit up to suit your purposes!" Wrapping her arms around her husband, she lifted her head to meet his eyes. "It might have been docked, but it was rocking…"

"Jesus, woman, there's no winnin' with you, is there?" Paul looked at her, his face flushed. Heat rising. After all these years, she still knew how to press his buttons. All of them.

"We *did* get lucky on that boat," he whispered. "More than a few times." Closing his eyes. Remembering the gentle swell of the tide rising beneath them. And within them.

Then they kissed, and there was only the present.

Fifteen

ROSE'S FIRST WEEK IN THE SHOP WAS A WHIRLWIND.
Wendy showed her the inventory and supplier databases, and
the online-ordering system. Taught her how to use the payment
terminal. Informed her that the holy trinity of top sellers was
vibrators, lube, and lingerie. Set her up so she could access
the social media accounts and e-newsletter template. Arranged
video calls to introduce her to Megan, the store's bookkeeper
in Calgary, and her husband, Will, the website and marketing-
material designer.

The shop's upstairs tenant dropped by to say hello. Rumpled
looking but friendly, Josh was an artist in his mid-twenties doing
a residency at the Lunenburg School of the Arts.

"You'll never hear a peep from that one," Wendy said as
the door closed behind Josh. "And if he likes you, he might just
give you one of his paintings." She gestured to the wall, where
a haunting portrait of an old, weather-beaten fisherman hung.
"That's his great-grandfather, who was lost at sea."

Wendy returned to practical matters. "As a business owner,
you're captain of the ship," she said. "It's really no different
than when Paul was captain of his lobster boat. It's your job to
keep the shop afloat."

"No pressure there," said Rose, taking out her notepad and
pen. Wendy paused to greet two women who looked to be in
their thirties. She was introducing Rose to everyone who came
in, explaining that Rose was the new owner, but that she'd be
staying on part-time to train her. And that Sonya would still be
there now and then.

Eyebrows were raised.

Knowing looks were exchanged.

Rose was from away.

A stranger.

Not a local.

Heard she's a widow, Rose imagined folks whispering. In cafés. After church. At the post office, and in grocery stores. *Husband died young, poor thing. Tragic accident. Maybe give her a chance?*

"Oh, there's daily pressure," said Wendy, chuckling. "You'll be juggling lots of slippery, bouncing balls and trying to keep everyone happy. Customers, staff, subcontractors, suppliers, neighbours. Above all, you want to be a good corporate citizen."

"How can I do that?" asked Rose, furiously scribbling in her notepad.

Wendy started taking packets of warming lube out of a box and passing them to Rose, who dropped her notepad to help arrange them on a shelf. "By getting involved in the community," Wendy began. "People will ask you to donate to their fundraising efforts. Gift certificates are good, or you can put together a small gift basket. It helps increase your brand awareness and improve your reputation."

"What have you done in the past?" asked Rose, peering at a packet: *Warming jelly. Gentle warming sensation. Protects against discomfort. Ideal for spontaneous intimacy.*

Rose and Jim had used regular lube. Personally, she thought "ideal for spontaneous intimacy" was false advertising. There was nothing spontaneous about frantically looking for the misplaced tube while praying your husband could maintain his... interest. That treasure hunt was a spontaneity killer. Jim usually tossed it on the floor after they made love. Later, endorphins clouding their memory, they'd forget to look for it under the bed and return it to a night-table drawer.

Wendy interrupted Rose's reverie. "I'm an active member of the local board of trade, which is a great resource. I'll take you to the next event and introduce you around. But I've also donated gift certificates and baskets to non-profit fundraisers that I feel align with my mission."

"Such as?" asked Rose, standing behind the beautiful reclaimed-wood counter that Paul had built.

"Lunenburg Pride. South Shore Sexual Health. Benefits for people with cancer or whose homes have burned in fires. Seniors' clubs."

"Seniors, eh?" Rose chortled. "How are they aligned with your mission?"

Wendy smiled. "Don't buy into the stereotype that Grandma only spends her time baking cookies and knitting, while Grandpa just listens to the radio and does crossword puzzles. You might be surprised to learn that a large part of the shop's sales come from older couples."

Rose whistled. "I guess I'm a bit surprised...I never thought of my grandparents that way. Or even my parents—or at least, I tried not to," she said, grimacing. Avoiding eye contact with Wendy, she paused before adding, "Maybe there's hope for me. I sometimes wonder if I'll ever have sex again."

Wendy looked at her friend fondly. "I think if you choose to someday, you'll have no shortage of suitors."

"I doubt it," said Rose, snorting. "Given that statistically women live longer than men, it'll be an old boys' club. They'll have their pick of the foxy-broad crop. And aren't later-in-life love stories more about companionship than passion?"

"As my uncle Eric used to say, there may be snow on the roof but there's still a spark in the stove," said Wendy, smiling at the memory.

The cordless phone ringing interrupted them. Wendy reached for it.

"Want me to answer it?" asked Rose, realizing with that one simple movement how hard it was going to be for Wendy to let go of the reins.

Wendy pulled her hand back quickly, as though it had touched a hot burner. Hesitated, as the ringing continued. Then nodded.

Trial by fire, Rose thought as she lifted it off the charger. "Good morning, Fishnets & Fantasies, Rose speaking. Yes, that's right, I'm the new owner. Oh, thank you, that's kind of you to say. It's my first week, and I *have* felt very welcomed here so far. How may I help you? Yes, of course...one moment, please."

Rose frowned as she handed the phone to Wendy. "She wants to speak to you."

Holding out her hand, Wendy couldn't conceal a smile.

Rose knew it would take time for people to get to know her. And to trust her. And for Wendy to cede authority. But she couldn't help but feel a sting of annoyance.

Wendy checked an order for the customer—something Rose could have easily done if Wendy had shown her how—and then put the phone back on its charger.

"Don't worry about that. Customers will need to sniff around you for a while, like dogs getting to know each other."

Wendy always seemed to know what to say to get her out of a funk. Even if her friend was partly the cause of her mood.

"As long as they don't push their noses up my butt, I'm okay with that," said Rose. At lunchtime, she had walked her dogs and witnessed that very action from pooches passing by. Hers had been sleeping in the storeroom ever since. Good as gold.

Wendy smiled, relieved that Rose had a sense of humour about it. "For better or for worse, that's how things work in a small town."

"I know," said Rose, gritting her teeth. "I grew up in Wolfville, remember? A tiny university town full of seniors and students. But I left after high school, and since then I've only lived in cities."

"Well, here's how it'll play out," said Wendy, who had lived her whole life in Lunenburg. "People will talk about you behind your back to get other people's impressions of you before fully forming their own. Then they'll dither. *Do we like her? Do we trust her?* It'll go back and forth for a few months while they make up their minds. It helps that you're related to May, you know. You should tell people that. She's well respected."

"Won't people think I'm..."—Rose stopped herself from saying *kooky*—"...quirky, too?"

"They'll know I wouldn't have sold my business to a whack-a-doodle," said Wendy, laughing. "Besides, we don't think of May as quirky in a bad way. She's just very much her own person, and passionate about rescuing helpless creatures."

"Fair enough," said Rose. "I'm happy to play the relative card if it'll help. Speaking of which, I owe her a text." May had been bugging her cousin to come on a rescue. Rose supposed she should finally give in, especially if associating with May could actually be a good thing. She planned to tell her she'd be free the weekend after Daisy's visit.

"My biggest piece of advice is that it's all about the customer," said Wendy. "Make them comfortable, and never judge anyone for what they want by your personal sexual preference barometer. I'm always just grateful they've chosen to shop here."

Rose glanced at the clock on the wall, next to a framed painting of a red-and-white fishing boat in Bush Island by Josh that was for sale. It looked like Paul's old boat, the *Lucky Haul*. Stretching her arms above her head, she couldn't help but stifle a yawn. In addition to her sleep deprivation, being back out in public was exhausting. She hadn't interacted with so many people since Jim's funeral.

"I think we've covered plenty for today," said Wendy, noticing Rose checking the time. "Why don't you go home, and we'll tackle more tomorrow."

"Sounds good," said Rose, heading to the storeroom. After switching from dress shoes to sneakers and zipping her jacket, she shrugged on her knapsack and clipped on the dogs' leashes. She left her dress shoes there, since she had no social life. Following Wendy's lead, she had adopted a business-casual dress code for work. Nice pants. Blazer. Blouse or sweater. When the weather warmed up, she'd wear dresses.

Rose had decided to keep her tattoo hidden. Not that she thought Wendy would mind if it peeked out of her top. Anyway, Rose was the boss now. But her tattoo was private.

Sonya always dressed to the nines. She was so elegant. Sophisticated. Beautiful. Rose felt like a country mouse around her.

Leaning down to give Molly and Relic a biscuit from the jar under the counter, Wendy asked, "What are you doing tonight?"

"Reviewing today's notes, then having a long, hot soak in the tub," said Rose. "What about you?"

"I've got an online training session for my doula certification," said Wendy. "*The importance of advance care planning.*"

"No rest for the wicked," said Rose, winking.

"Except in the afterlife," replied Wendy, winking back.

"Unless you believe in reincarnation."

"Once around the block is enough for me," said Wendy, chuckling.

Rose loved many things about her friend. One of them was that Wendy didn't try to avoid referring to dying and death around her. Given her new career choice, why would she? It was refreshing. Five months after Jim's death, some people were still uncomfortable making lighthearted death references or jokes that had nothing to do with her husband. Rose sensed that if they could, they'd stuff them back into their mouths and swallow them whole.

What would have been Jim's forty-sixth birthday was looming. Rose was already trying to prepare for what that milestone might bring.

Sixteen

BY FRIDAY OF ROSE'S INAUGURAL WEEK, HER FEET were sore and she was bone weary. Her brain was crammed full of so much new information, she worried her head would explode. At the shop, she and Wendy were doing a delicate dance, trying hard not to step on each other's toes. In spite of all that, she was pleasantly surprised to find she was enjoying the work.

Molly and Relic seemed content too. They had no trouble managing the twenty-minute walk to Pelham Street each morning. When they arrived, the short uphill climb had tired them enough that they were happy to sleep on their beds in the storeroom until Rose took a lunch break. Then, after finishing a peanut-butter-and-banana sandwich, she took them for a short stroll. If the shop was quiet, Rose let them hang out with her. She discovered they were good icebreakers, so she put a sign in the front-door window that read, *Two friendly dogs on deck.* If someone was allergic or afraid (no one had been either, yet), she'd put them in the storeroom. After an afternoon snooze, they had enough pep in their step to walk home.

If the weather was messy, Rose drove and parked in her designated spot beside the building, but she found she looked forward to her on-foot commute. On their walks, Rose was noticing new signs of spring appearing in flower beds. Cheery purple, pink, yellow, and white crocus petals added pops of colour to an otherwise neutral landscape. Daffodils and tulips would turn up next. She hoped her tenants were enjoying Drummond Court's spring flowers. Steve reported that they were no trouble; the husband had only contacted him once to ask about having the bathtub drain snaked.

Rose still said a daily good morning and goodnight aloud to Jim, who remained on her bedside table. She still cried, but less often. She still dreamt of him, but the details were foggy as she awoke. She wished she could share the events of her days with him in person, but she made do with speaking to his spirit.

After Rose got home and fed the dogs, she put a pot of water on the stove to heat spaghetti. When it was ready, she'd stir in some pesto and toss in a few baby tomatoes. Easy. Rose realized her appetite was slowly returning. Good thing. Even she had noticed how loose her pants had become.

While she waited for the burner to bring the pot to a boil, she scanned her texts. There were several. Her mother. Daisy. Yuki. Rima. Her Drummond Court next-door neighbours, saying they missed her. A handful of Halifax friends. All wanting to know how things were going. How she was doing.

Plugging her phone into the charger, she decided to send brief replies on the weekend: *Good. Busy. Interesting. Lots to learn.*

Tomorrow was Saturday. The forecast was calling for a cool, cloudy day. No April showers. Daisy was coming for lunch, then they were taking the dogs for a walk along the Back Harbour Trail. No spare room or sofa bed in the condo meant no overnight guests. Just as well, because Rose didn't have the energy to entertain. What did the hot young widow call it? *Grief fog.* It took all of her brainpower to focus on what Wendy was teaching her. One notebook was already filled with scribbles.

༺✲༻

After finally falling asleep at two in the morning, Rose awoke six hours later to a tingling right leg. Opening her eyes, she figured out why. Molly's head was on her thigh.

"Rise and shine, pups, Aunt Daisy will be here soon," said Rose, running a hand over each of their heads. "Breakfast!"

Relic, the more food-motivated of the pair, didn't have to be told twice. After a big stretch and yawn, he planted a smelly kiss on his human's cheek, then hopped off the bed and trotted to the dining room. The galley kitchen was too small for their bowls, so Rose had set them on a mat on the floor next to it.

Relic's sister liked to laze in bed as long as possible. Rose got up, put on her slippers and Jim's robe over her pyjamas, and went to pee. Not until Molly heard the sound of kibble hitting the bowl did she join her brother.

Switching on the electric kettle while the dogs ate, Rose glanced at her texts. New ones from her mother and Daisy, who planned to arrive at ten. Opening the patio door, she let Molly and Relic into the backyard to do their business. Closing the door after the dogs were done, Rose picked up her phone and typed a brief reply to Joanne:

Good so far. Lots to learn! Have some questions, will call soon. Daisy's coming for lunch. You and Dad should visit soon. Love to you both xo.

There. Dutiful daughter duty done. Then, to Daisy:

Travel safely and see you soon! Text from the parking lot and I'll meet you.

Rose sent quick notes to her Toronto friends, then poured milk over granola. Carrying the cereal bowl to the dining room table, she studied Fishnets & Fantasies's social media posts while she ate. Rose was slowly finding what she needed in kitchen cupboards and drawers. She had the sensation that she was living in a fully equipped vacation rental.

The condo might have been a rental, but this wasn't a vacation. It was real life.

Her new life.

Even by the end of the year, Rose didn't expect the place to feel like home. Already, she missed her Drummond Court clothesline. The small, stackable washer-dryer set in the hall closet here was cute, but her laundry lacked the fresh outdoors scent that has yet to be replicated in a dryer sheet. Those promising a "spring fresh" scent were full of shit.

Without Jim living with her at Drummond Court, Rose knew it would no longer feel like home. Not like it used to. There were too many raw reminders of the life they'd shared. Here, nothing was theirs. The condo was an emotionally sterile cocoon. A protective chrysalis from which she'd emerge in twelve months. Would she be fully formed? Healed? Time would tell.

After breakfast, Rose brushed her teeth, dressed, and walked the dogs around the block. Her good-natured mutts seemed content wherever they landed, as long as she was with them. She wished she could be as adaptable as they were.

The spring air smelled salty, a splash of sea on the breeze. Squinting, Rose paused to pull her sunglasses from her purse. An older woman walking a Jack Russell Terrier on the other side of the street nodded and said good morning. Rose echoed her greeting. Strangers were certainly friendly here.

Rose checked her watch and decided to head back so she wouldn't be late meeting Daisy. As she picked up her pace and they rounded a corner, she almost bumped into a golden retriever.

"Sorry!" said Rose, watching the dog excitedly sniff Molly and Relic, tails wagging a mile a minute. "My fault, I wasn't looking."

"No problem, neither was I," said a familiar voice.

Rose looked up. Into the dazzling green eyes of Allan Conrad.

"Hey," said Rose, startled to see him out of context.

Daisy was right. The Grand Banker's owner *was* good-looking. "I didn't realize it was you," said Rose, flustered. "I always look at the dog before the human. Who's this?"

"This is Taylor Swift, my sister's dog," said Allan, bending down to pat Molly and Relic. "Her oldest daughter named her. Two of her kids have the flu, and her husband's out of town, so I'm pitching in."

"That's nice of you," said Rose. "I thought maybe my cousin had gotten to you."

"She got to my sister," said Allan, laughing. "Taylor's a rescue. I just foster dogs for May now and then."

Rose glanced at her watch. "Speaking of sisters, mine's arriving in a few minutes, so we'd better get going. Nice to see you, and to meet a celebrity."

"Say hi to Daisy for me. Drop by the Banker if you don't have lunch plans. On the house."

He remembered Daisy's name? thought Rose. *She'll swoon when I tell her.*

"Oh, that's kind, but no, we couldn't." Surprised by his generous offer, Rose was certain he was simply being polite. Daisy would be delirious.

"Why not? Consider it a welcome-wagon gift."

With a shy smile, Allan continued on his walk, Taylor Swift leading the way. Rose's phone buzzed. Daisy. Rose typed quickly: *Out with the dogs, on our way.*

ⵙ

Sitting at the dining room table, the sisters warmed their hands around mugs of hot tea. Daisy started in right away.

"Your left eyelid is twitching," she said, leaning forward to take a closer look.

"While I am impressed by your keen power of observation, I am fully aware of that," said Rose, gently pressing on her eyelid with an index finger.

"Eye twitching can be caused by stress and fatigue," said Daisy knowingly.

Rose sighed. "No shit, Sherlock. That's what my official source said, too."

"Your doctor?" Daisy cocked an eyebrow.

Rose shook her head. "Mayo Clinic's website. Trusted source for hypochondriacs around the world."

"Ah." Daisy frowned with concern. "Are you still taking sleeping pills?"

"Yeah, but they aren't helping."

Reaching across the table, Daisy covered Rose's hand with her own. With a catch in her voice, she said, "I miss Jim, too."

Unexpected sympathy pierced Rose's heart like an arrow. And her tear ducts. Pulling a crumpled tissue from her hoodie pocket, she dabbed her eyes.

"Kindness makes me cry," said Rose softly. "Quick, say something mean."

"You're an asshole," Daisy whispered, wiping her nose with the back of her hand.

"No, *you're* an asshole," said Rose, doing her best to smile.

"That's my girl." Daisy composed herself before reverting to no-nonsense nurse mode. "Do you remember when we were in elementary school and we used to tell Mom and Dad we were saying *Gee, sis* when we were mad to get out of trouble for swearing?"

Rose laughed. "Yeah, we thought we were so smart. Where'd that memory come from?"

"No idea, it just popped into my head." Daisy topped up her mug with hot tea while Rose blew her nose. "How's your appetite these days?"

"Starting to come back," said Rose. "Which is good, because my pants are falling off, and you know I hate shopping. How's yours?"

Daisy snorted. "Well, my hormones are all over the place from the menopause. I'm starving all the time, and, unlike you, I can barely zip up my jeans." She sighed, then helped herself to one of the banana-chocolate chip muffins she'd made early that morning. "Got any butter?"

"You're gonna butter that? Gross. Way to ruin a perfectly good muffin. That's as bad as putting liquor in chocolates."

Daisy sat up straighter. "Boozy chocolates—yum! Do you have any?"

Rose laughed. "No, but I'll get the butter."

"So, how'd your first week go?" asked Daisy while Rose was in the kitchen. If she still had concerns about her sister's move, she kept them to herself. It was a done deal. A door had opened, and Rose had chosen to walk through it.

Rose returned to the table and handed the butter, a knife, and a plate to Daisy. She reached for a muffin for herself while considering her sister's question. "I enjoyed it, which made me feel happy. Then I felt guilty for feeling happy. Then I felt weak for feeling guilty."

"If I'm hearing you correctly," said Daisy, slathering a generous portion of creamy yellow deliciousness on half of her muffin, "you're the same neurotic mess you've always been."

"I guess so," said Rose, fiddling with the silver chain around her neck that held Jim's titanium wedding ring.

In that moment, Rose missed her therapist. Since leaving Toronto, she hadn't felt the need to find a new one. Charlotte had given her plenty of helpful resources to pack into her emotional toolbox. Now she felt like not only had she forgotten how to use the tools, she'd misplaced the whole box.

"Lulu wants to visit next time," said Daisy, changing the subject.

"That would be great," said Rose, her face lighting up. "Tell the kids I miss them. Steve, too."

"What are you doing for Easter?" asked Daisy, her mouth full of muffin.

"Wendy invited me over for glazed ham." Rose shrugged. "Ellen and Fay aren't coming home from Victoria. I'll fill an empty chair at their dining room table."

Without saying a word, Daisy pulled a book from her purse and handed it to Rose.

"Oh, no, not another one," Rose groaned, taking in the title: *A Widow's Awakening.* "I know you mean well, but would you please cease and desist?"

"It's good, you'll like it," Daisy insisted. "It's based on the true story of a woman whose police-officer husband died suddenly in a tragic accident."

"I could write my own true story about losing a husband in a tragic accident," said Rose dryly, sipping her tea. Thinking about her mounting journal notes. "How do you know I'll like this one?"

"I read it." Daisy paused before continuing. "I've read all of the books I've given you."

Rose laughed and shook her head. "Why are you reading books about widows, you wingnut?"

"Because Steve keeps saying he's going to die first, statistically speaking," replied Daisy matter-of-factly. "Might as well do some advance prep."

"Steve is one of the healthiest sixty-year-olds I know," Rose pointed out. "He has more energy in his little finger than I have in my entire body. I couldn't run around the block at fifty, never mind do a half marathon at his age. And yet...good health is no guarantee to a long life, is it?"

"You know that he and I are long-range planners," said Daisy, ignoring Rose's rhetorical question. "Just read it, okay? It'll stop me from bugging you to find a new therapist."

Rose ignored the therapy reference. Instead, she filled Daisy in about bumping into Allan, casually mentioning his lunch invitation.

"We aren't going," said Rose firmly, holding a palm up. Even though she knew it wouldn't stop Daisy's protests.

"Are you crazy? Miss a free lunch? Stop thinking about yourself for one hot second. It'll have been worth the drive here alone if I can look at that sweet eye candy again."

"Thanks for nothing," said Rose, snorting. "If I end up marrying him, are you going to be able to control your feral sexual impulses when he's in the same room?"

Daisy's jaw dropped.

It was the first time Rose had mentioned remarrying.

"Calm down, it's a joke," said Rose, interpreting the look on her sister's face. "But it's why we aren't having lunch there. I don't want him to think I'm interested."

"*You* aren't interested in him," said Daisy. "*I* am. All you have to be interested in is a free lunch."

"You're married, so shut up. Here's the non-negotiable plan: we are staying here and having leftover spaghetti with pesto and baby tomatoes. Then we're taking your favourite dogs for a walk. End. Of. Story."

When Molly and Relic heard the magic four-letter word, they lifted their heads and thumped their tails on the floor. Since the humans didn't appear to be moving, though, they stayed put.

"You're such a wet blanket," Daisy pouted.

"We widows often are," said Rose, heading to the kitchen.

"*Your mommy's such a wet blanket, isn't she?*" said Daisy in a baby voice to the dogs, leaning down to pat them. Two tails thumped.

"I can hear you!" Rose hollered from the kitchen.

⚬❧⚬

Between noon and one o'clock, Allan Conrad cast his eyes over the Banker's bustling dining room. It was filled with hungry patrons and nimble servers. Friendly chatter filled the air. At one thirty, he removed the *reserved* sign from the lone empty table, sighing as he put it away.

Seventeen

ROSE WAS SO TIRED SHE COULD BARELY TIE HER shoelaces without falling over. Her left eye was twitching so often that her customers must have thought she was winking at them, from the puzzled looks she was getting. Keeping herself busy at the shop during the days, she'd been enjoying her two weeknight evenings with Sonya in the Kings' beautiful home on Kempt Street.

Their house was located on the highest point on the hill. From an upstairs window, Sonya and Booth could see the sun shimmering on Front Harbour. To the east, the view of Back Harbour below was breathtaking. Seawater surrounded a small peninsula dotted with houses, farmers' fields, trees, and a winding coastal road. Brightly painted pleasure boats were moored here and there.

Rose didn't know how Sonya could concentrate when the scenery was so distracting. She was pretty sure she'd spend her time gazing out the window. Daydreaming. But when it came to the experienced author's characters and what she had planned for them, she was all business. Her mind was a steel trap. Rose could barely type fast enough on her laptop to keep up.

Booth was usually out campaigning or at a golf club board meeting when Rose was over, so the women and the dogs had the house to themselves. Snug in the upstairs office, when Sonya's words flowed, Rose's fingers flew. Now and then, they stopped to discuss a perplexing plot point or conflicting character traits.

"Do you think Gisèle should be more spirited?" asked Sonya during one of their sessions. "Have I painted her as too dull? Too—what's the right word—simple?"

Rose tapped her fingers on Sonya's keyboard. "Well, she *is* a nineteenth-century farm girl in northern New Brunswick. So her life would be pretty simple."

"But would *she* be simple herself?" Sonya mused. "Maybe I've made her too passive, and Lisette too fiery."

"Lisette has to be fiery to be a temptress, doesn't she?" asked Rose, standing up to stretch her shoulders. "As a reader, I like the contrast between the two women. But...."

"But what?" asked Sonya. "Go on, I can handle constructive criticism."

"Well...maybe you could add more about Alphonse's internal struggle. His guilt, if you will. When we're deep into the sugar-bush scenes, they're so dramatic I forget all about sweet Gisèle back home on the farm, pining for him. Does he ever pine for her? Does he still plan to marry her when he goes home? Why did he fall in love with her in the first place? Is he *really* in love with her? Or does he just want a nice Catholic wife to bear a dozen of his babies so they'll grow up to help out on the farm?"

Sonya nodded, drumming the fingers of her good hand on the armrest. "Nuance...yes...I see. Read that last paragraph to me, will you? Then let me know how you'd modify it."

Looking at the screen, Rose began to read:

Alphonse tossed and turned on the narrow wooden cot, throwing off the threadbare wool blanket that barely covered his tall, muscular frame. Sleep wouldn't come. When it did, he knew his dreams would be filled with Lisette.

Rose closed her eyes for a minute. Opening them, she started typing. "Okay," she said a moment later, "how about something like this?"

Alphonse tossed and turned on the narrow wooden cot, throwing off the threadbare wool blanket that barely covered his tall, muscular frame. Sleep was a thief in the night, stealing his peace. When it finally did embrace him, he knew his dreams would be filled with Lisette. And yet, when he woke as dawn's light filtered through the dirty cracked windowpane, it was Gisèle who had appeared to ease his tortured mind and heart. Calling him home.

"I love it!" said Sonya. "You're good at this. But how about we swap *embrace* for *engulf?*"

"Okay, and thanks," said Rose, cheeks turning pink at the praise.

Maybe she *was* good at this.

∽

On Sonya and Rose's last session together, when they went downstairs for a coffee break, Rose summoned her courage.

"Sonya," said Rose, sliding into the cushioned corner banquette in the spacious modern kitchen. "I wonder if I could run something by you."

"Of course," said Sonya. Her back was turned to Rose as she fiddled with the settings on a latte machine.

"Well, I've been thinking," Rose began slowly. "I've been a writer my whole career, but just magazine articles and corporate content. Ever since Jim died, I've been journalling. Mostly to help process my feelings. But also about my unusual childhood, raised by hippies turned capitalists. And...this new chapter of my life."

Sonya turned around to face Rose. "That's wonderful. Journalling is such a healthy outlet. Have you given any thought to writing a memoir?"

Rose sighed, feeling the tension leave her shoulders. Sonya had made it easy for her. To not sound foolish, or self-indulgent.

"It had crossed my mind. I mean, my sister keeps giving me memoirs written by widows. Two of them are by women in their thirties. The other is by Joan Didion."

"Ah, a senior," said Sonya, nodding. "*The Year of Magical Thinking*. So powerful."

"I haven't come across any written by someone in my demographic," said Rose, reaching out to take the coffee cup Sonya was handing her. "Early middle age. Not ready to retire, and still with hopes and dreams for a future together. I wondered if there'd be any interest in that."

Sonya joined Rose at the banquette. Sitting in a chair across from her, she leaned down to slip biscuits to Molly and Relic. "There's a new publisher in town, Liz Penny. Retired judge from Colorado. Buddhist. Lovely lady. I met her at a Lit Fest open house. She's actively seeking writers. You should get in touch. Tell her I suggested it."

"Thanks, I might do that," said Rose, sipping her latte. Butterflies started banging around in her stomach.

Sonya picked up her cup. "You also might consider applying to Pitch the Publisher at the literary festival in September. If you're accepted, you'll have a chance to pitch your book idea to three local publishers."

"I don't think I'm ready for that yet," said Rose.

"When are any of us really ready for anything?" said Sonya, shrugging. "I didn't feel ready when I submitted my first manuscript to Romantic Escapes. In fact, it was rejected, but with a helpful note from an editor with suggestions on how to improve it. The stronger, second draft landed me a contract."

"And the rest, as they say, is history," said Rose with admiration. She envied so much about Sonya. Her success as a doctor, an author, a retail associate. Her loving, long-time partnership with Booth. So fortunate. For the first time, it occurred to Rose that, like her and Jim, the Kings didn't have children. Her curiosity was interrupted by Sonya's hoot of laughter.

"That's right. Fame! Fortune! Glory!" said Sonya, punching the air after each word. "Actually, none of the above. But I'm having fun, improving with each book, and meeting interesting people. You would, too."

"Well, I'll think about it," said Rose. September was five months away. Could she cobble something together in time? She wasn't sure.

"There's something else," said Sonya.

"What?" Rose leaned forward, both hands wrapped around her cup.

"I wrote my first novel in secret, during a rough patch in my marriage," Sonya confessed.

"Really?" Rose squeaked, then cleared her throat. She couldn't picture put-together Sonya ever having a hard time with anything.

"Really. It was therapy. I was reading romance novels to escape my unhappiness, and I decided to try writing one. I thought that if *my* relationship didn't work out, maybe I could write a happy ending for someone else."

"Wow," said Rose softly. "Thanks for sharing that with me." She paused, not wanting to push too far into the personal zone. "I'm glad you and Booth worked things out."

Sonya smiled. "So are we, but it wasn't easy. It took time, and patience. We had to allow ourselves to feel vulnerable and exposed. I transferred all of those emotions into that first book."

Maybe I can use my journal entries in the same way, Rose thought. *As therapy. And to let others know they aren't alone.*

Standing up to put the cups in the sink, Sonya said, "All right, union break is over! Let's get back at it."

Five minutes later, the pair was transported back to the harsh environment of the sugar bush. There, luscious Lisette was tenderly nursing ailing Alphonse, who was recovering from the injuries he had sustained in a logjam. And who had pushed aside guilty thoughts of his betrothed, Gisèle, who was busy back home planning their simple Catholic wedding.

Rose read the last passage aloud.

As Lisette leaned over to press a cloth gently to Alphonse's damp brow, which was feverish from a raging infection, the top of her bronzed, sun-kissed breasts brushed his arm.

"Mon dieu," he mumbled.

Yes, he was in pain, for that arm was broken and crudely set, but Lisette's soft touch was a far more effective pain reliever than whisky.

"Est-ce que ça va?" asked Lisette.

Through a haze, Alphonse saw her beautiful brow wrinkle in worry.

"Oui, ça va," he whispered. "Tu es un ange."

"*You are an angel.*"

An angel.

Like Jim.

Swallowing a lump in her throat, Rose returned her hands to the keyboard. Then Sonya picked up where the story had left off.

~ ⤫ ~

Rose found a new daily rhythm in looking after the dogs, working at Fishnets & Fantasies, and texting her family and old friends. She didn't have the time or energy to try to make new friends. In her spare time, she turtled. Withdrew into herself in the condo. Into her protective shell. Where she could talk aloud to Jim's urn. And journal.

Slowly, thanks to Wendy's introductions and Rose's friendly nature, just like the spring temperatures, customers began warming up to her.

Not all of them, though. The second week, Wendy had left Rose alone in the shop one afternoon. A middle-aged woman who walked in the door stopped when she saw her.

"Is Wendy in?" she asked.

"No, but I'm Rose, the new owner. May I help you with something?"

The woman paused. Took her bottom lip between her teeth. Chewed it nervously. "No, that's okay. Will she be in tomorrow afternoon?"

"She will," said Rose, forcing a smile.

"Okay, thanks." The woman spun around and left.

As the door closed, Rose sighed. It had happened a handful of times. Mostly with customers around her own age. She tried not to take it personally. Wendy had advised her to be patient. She was trying.

Although most of the shoppers in the run of a week were women, some men dropped in to buy anniversary or birthday gifts for their significant others. For the most part, they didn't seem embarrassed to tell her what they were looking for. Sometimes their partners had sent them with a list, which was helpful.

The customers in their twenties often just browsed, or bought condoms, lube, and lingerie. The holy trinity. Maybe a cute box of novelty cards, or a book. Small, inexpensive purchases. Some tittered quietly, pointing at a vibrator here or the shop's signature fishnet body stocking there.

The older women were all business. No pussyfooting around. They knew exactly what their issues were. Dry vaginal walls. Difficulty reaching orgasm. Painful positions due to arthritis. A partner's lack of interest in sex, or his trouble getting, or keeping, an erection. They hoped Rose could help them find something to fix whatever wasn't working. They often arrived at Fishnets & Fantasies at their doctor's suggestion. Money was never an issue.

Sometimes all those women wanted was a feather tickler, or a pretty piece of lingerie. Other times it took more—a vibrator, a book on intimacy, the increasingly popular warming lube. Rose found she loved listening to her customers, then advising them. The first three weeks she was like a sponge, watching Wendy and Sonya. Absorbing. Learning.

Like the seniors, those from the 2SLGBTQIA+ community often weren't afraid to ask for what they wanted. They'd hold hands, peck their partner's cheeks, or pat their bums. Rose admired how comfortable they seemed in their own skin. Envying their togetherness.

Twice in one week, Rose spotted an older woman peering in the front window. A clear plastic rain bonnet covered her curly white hair, even though there was no rain forecast. The second time she saw her staring, Rose smiled and waved. The woman scuttled off like a mouse with a cat in hot pursuit. It was odd, but Rose was so busy she soon forgot about her.

What Rose loved most about the shop was that she never knew who was going to walk through the front door. One afternoon, it was a middle-aged man in firefighting gear.

"Larry Purcell," said the man, gripping Rose's hand tightly. "You must be Rose."

"I am," said Rose. "Nice to meet you."

"My twenty-fifth wedding anniversary's coming up. Paul helped me put together this list."

Larry handed Rose a crumpled piece of notepaper. Reviewing the handwritten scribbles, she said, "Sure, I can pull these together for you. Would you like them gift-wrapped?"

"That'd be great, thanks," said Larry, leaning on the counter. "Paul says you grew up in Wolfville. It's a long shot, but do you know Rob Hennigar?"

Rose did know Rob. In the biblical sense. You don't forget your first, especially when it was a positive experience.

"Rob and I went to high school together," was all Rose revealed while moving around the shop, picking out products. "How do you know him?"

"He's my investment advisor," said Larry. "Good guy. Lives in Yarmouth. Went through a rough divorce last year. Small province, eh?"

"It sure is," agreed Rose.

As she was packaging Larry's purchases, a woman wearing scrubs who looked to be in her early thirties rushed in.

"Hey, Lare, buying something for Sophie?" she asked.

"Yeah, but it's a surprise, so you never saw me," said Larry, winking.

"Saw who?" said the woman, grinning. "I'm late for my shift, but I've got a date with someone new after work, so..." Now it was her turn to wink.

Rose loved watching customers chat and catch up.

Just then, Booth King barged in. "Sorry for interrupting," he apologized. "Oh, hi, Jemma, how's your dad?"

The woman smiled. "Tough as overcooked steak. Stubborn, too. Survived a quadruple bypass, but give up bacon and fried eggs for breakfast? Nope." Jemma sighed and shook her head. "Thanks for asking."

"Old fishermen are made of stern stuff," said Booth. "Glad he's on the mend. Rose, do you mind if I put a campaign sign out front?"

"Fill your boots," said Rose agreeably. "And good luck!"

❧

By the end of April, Rose had filled four notebooks. Her brain was ready to burst. It felt like she was cramming for a business exam. Most days, she enjoyed herself, especially when Wendy wasn't there. Being around elegant, accomplished Sonya still made her self-conscious, although the older woman had only been kind and helpful. Her cast finally off, she was fully mobile again but going to physiotherapy to help strengthen her wrist.

Helping Sonya with her novel had inspired Rose. And motivated her to do even more journalling of her own. That, plus the memoirs Daisy had given her, had planted a seed. One she intended to keep watering.

❧

Wednesdays were trivia night at The Knot Pub over on Dufferin Street. May had somehow convinced Rose to join her team, the SPCA's Wily Whiskers, for a game after a player called in sick. Rose reluctantly agreed.

It would be her first social outing since she'd moved to town. Standing in front of her closet, she looked at Jim's urn and asked, "*What should I wear?*"

Soon, several tops, pants, and dresses were scattered across the bed. Rose stared at herself in the full-length mirror in her conservative choice: blue jeans and a black turtleneck. Hopefully the pub wouldn't be hot.

Applying tinted lip gloss, she studied her reflection in the bathroom mirror, then rubbed it off with a tissue.

Chrissake, it's just trivia with your cousin, she scolded herself. *No need to be nervous.*

Five minutes before the eight o'clock kickoff time, Rose slid into her seat at the table.

"Hey, cuz," said May. "This here's Joe and Connie. They're the brains and brawn behind the mobile spay-and-neuter clinic for feral cats in the county."

The couple, who looked to be in their mid-sixties, smiled and said hello. Joe's arm was slung casually over the back of Connie's chair. Rose noticed their wedding rings. Something she'd started paying attention to since Jim died.

"And this here's my cousin Rose," said May, adding proudly, "I'm her wingman."

Rose couldn't help but laugh and shake her head. "No, you aren't."

"Yes, I am," said May, punching Rose lightly in the arm.

"Nice to meet you," said Rose to her teammates.

At the table next to Wily Whiskers was a rowdy team called Take It to the Banker. Rose's stomach muscles tightened. It was Allan Conrad and three of his staff members. Another team sat nearby.

"You're goin' down, Conrad!" shouted May, pounding her fist on the table.

"In your dreams, Ainsworth!" Allan hollered back. Although he was looking at the other Ainsworth sitting at the table.

Throughout the evening, the "other Ainsworth" kept sneaking glances at Allan. Noticing how cute it was that his hair curled up at his collar. Smiling when he threw his head back each time he laughed.

Only once did they make eye contact. Blushing, Rose looked away. Not noticing Allan's gaze lingering.

Two hours flew by. The teams' conversations were cut short when the host stepped up to the mic to announce the winner.

Wily Whiskers had managed to edge out Take It to the Banker, but Lunenburg Library Literati ended up beating them both.

After the winner was announced, Joe and Connie said goodnight to their teammates. As Rose rooted through her purse for her wallet to pay for her tea and apple crisp, a man approached their table.

"Rose? I thought it was you. Rob Hennigar, from high school. Although you called me Robbie back then."

It had been more than thirty years since Rose had laid eyes on the tall, handsome man with sparkling blue eyes like the Aegean Sea, but he didn't need to introduce himself. As a teenager, he'd looked like a young Daniel Craig in denim overalls driving a tractor around his father's apple orchards. Unforgettable. He'd aged well.

Funny timing that Larry Purcell had just mentioned him. And that he was divorced.

Recovering quickly, Rose replied, "Rob! What a nice surprise. What are you doing here?" She reached out to give him a hug. She could feel Allan watching from the next table.

May stood up to get a better view of the scene unfolding in front of her. As Rose and Rob talked, her head swivelled as though she were watching a tennis match.

"I'm here for a couple of days for work," said Rob, lowering himself into the empty seat next to Rose. Then he put his arm over the back of her chair. Like Joe had done for Connie. Like he had done for Rose in high school. Protectively.

"I'm an investment advisor. My firm is in Yarmouth, but I travel across the province to visit valued clients. What are you doing here?"

When Rose hesitated, May piped up: "Her husband died and she moved here from Halifax to get a fresh start. Now she runs a sex shop. Howdy, Rob, I'm Rose's cousin May."

She stuck out her right hand, almost poking Rose in the eye as she reached across her.

"Nice to meet you, May," said Rob, returning her handshake.

May gave Rose a not-so-subtle wink. "Lookit, I've gotta run. Thanks for pitching in, Rose. Ciao, Rob." As she walked past Allan, she called out, "Later, loser!"

Out of the corner of her eye, Rose caught Allan flip May the bird.

Rob turned back to Rose, covering her hand on the table with his. "I saw your husband's obituary in the newspaper. I'm really sorry. Is there anything I can do for you?"

He sounded sincere. And his hand, soft but firm, sent heat coursing through her veins. In that moment, she knew exactly what Rob could do for her.

All of her life, Rose had done the right thing. Got good grades at school, then a university degree. Worked hard. Donated to charity. Didn't drink much. Never smoked or took drugs. Was faithful to her boyfriends, and to Jim. She had never even wanted to do anything she felt she *shouldn't* do.

Until now. Because what Rose wanted to do felt wrong. But she also knew that nothing would stop her.

"There *is* something, actually," said Rose, sounding more confident than she felt. "I know it's late, but if you have time to come to my condo for a coffee, I'll explain."

"Sure, as long as it's decaf," said Rob, checking his watch. "My first meeting isn't till ten tomorrow morning, so I'm good for a bit. It'll be nice to catch up."

಄

With a sinking feeling, Allan watched the pair walk out of the pub together. A strange man's hand on Rose's back. After a few minutes, he left, too. To drown his disappointment in a beer at home. Where he would scan his phone contact's list, stop at "K," then send a text. Knowing the answer would be yes. No strings attached.

If there was one thing Allan excelled at, it was numbing his emotional pain with occasional casual sex. Half an hour later, as he was still trying to get the image of Rose leaving the pub out of his head, the doorbell rang.

☙

While the coffee brewed at the condo, Rob let Molly and Relic inspect him. Rose slipped into the bedroom—not to put on something more revealing, but to remove the chain around her neck with Jim's wedding ring on it. And to move his urn and photo into the closet. *I'm sorry, but I need this*, she whispered as she shut the door.

An hour later, Rose was relieved to discover that while a piece of her heart had died along with Jim, her body was still very much alive. Surprised by her request, Rob had been receptive and kind. Gentle. A safe, familiar touchstone to her life before Jim.

At the door, Rose hugged her first love goodbye. With no promises to stay in touch that both of them knew they wouldn't keep.

Then, she cried. And slept like the dead.

Eighteen

THE SUNDAY AFTER DAISY'S VISIT, MAY MADE GOOD on her threat to drag her cousin along on a rescue. Rose had been hoping May had forgotten her offer to help out, or that there'd be no creature in distress that day.

No such luck. As she was finishing a peanut butter-and-jam sandwich with a glass of chocolate milk for lunch, Rose's cellphone rang.

"I need your help," said May, who didn't beat around the bush.

"What's up?" said Rose, her mouth still sticky from the peanut butter.

"Otter on the loose in a boat shed."

"Is that...code for something?"

May paused, then said slowly, "There. Is. An. Otter. Loose. In. A. Boat. Shed."

"I'm busy," lied Rose. "And the dogs need walking."

"You aren't busy because you have no life outside work, and I know you aren't working today," said May, calling her bluff. "The dogs will be fine for a couple hours. Margot can let them out."

"Maybe Margot's busy," said Rose, doing her best to stone-wall her cousin.

"She's free. I called her, and I know she has your spare key. Meet me in front of your place in five minutes. Oh, and don't wear a ball gown. You're gonna get down and dirty." May hung up.

Rose shook her head and sighed. May wasn't going to give up, so she might as well get it over with. All she had scheduled for the afternoon was reading *A Widow's Awakening* and a nap. Maybe a change in routine would be good for her. She pulled on a well-worn pair of jeans, one of Jim's ratty sweatshirts, and an old jacket.

Five minutes later, Rose was buckling herself into the passenger seat of her cousin's truck. Before she could sit down, she had to move a cane to the backseat. *Her gout must be really bad*, she thought.

Old fast-food wrappers and takeout coffee cups were strewn on the floor mat, along with jumbo-size bottles of vitamin D and Aleve.

"Sorry about the mess," said May, glancing at it. "Just kick it out of the way. And don't get the wrong idea, the junk food isn't for me. I buy cheeseburgers when I need bait during rescues."

"Are you a vegetarian?" Rose asked. For some reason, the idea surprised her.

"Sure am. Don't know about you, but I don't eat my friends."

You'd eat an otter otherwise? mused Rose. She wasn't sure May would find that funny, so she kept quiet. Instead, she said, "That's noble."

Thinking about chewing a juicy, tender piece of medium-rare steak pan-seared in garlic butter sent Rose's salivary glands into overdrive. Her appetite *was* returning. May probably didn't rescue cows. To be on the safe side, she wouldn't ask.

"Nah, I just don't have the stomach for it after some of the terrible things I've seen," said May. "People can be cruel."

"What do you do at the SPCA?" Rose knew that May worked there but realized she'd never asked her about it.

"Vet tech," said May. "Love it. Pay's crap, though. My folks left me a little something when they died, so I can afford to work part-time. Gives me more time for rescues."

"Are you on call for rescues whenever you aren't working?" Rose wished she shared May's passion and drive for a good cause.

May laughed. "Nope, I'm pretty sure that would kill me. I'm not comfortable driving at night anymore. I won't go out in bad weather. And I don't rescue on Wednesdays."

"Why not?" asked Rose.

May hesitated. "I swim at the public pool in Bridgewater. And sometimes I have…appointments. In the city."

"You swim?" In many ways May was an open book, but Rose was coming to realize that her cousin had secrets, too.

"What, I don't look like a swimmer?" asked May, sitting up straighter to improve her posture.

"It isn't that," Rose stammered. Truthfully, it was exactly that. May did not look like a swimmer. "It's just, I'm not a strong swimmer myself, so I admire anyone who is."

"Gotta stay in shape for this type of work, and I hate the gym," said May. "I got some dumbbells and a treadmill at home for when the weather's bad."

There was something about what May had said that didn't sit well with Rose. "What kind of appointments do you have in the city?" she asked.

"Aren't you a Nosy Nellie?" said May, side-stepping the question.

Rose nudged the bottles on the floor out of her way. "What's the vitamin D for?"

"Gout," said May abruptly.

"I thought you took vitamin C for that?"

"I'd take the whole gee-dee vitamin alphabet if I thought it would help," replied May curtly. Then she sighed. "Sorry to be sharp. I'm tired and cranky. Happens every year during baby season. Don't take it personally."

"Baby season?" asked Rose, reaching for the bottle of painkillers to look for the expiry date. She had a feeling May wouldn't bother checking. It was good, there was one year left.

"In nature, lots of babies are born in the spring," May explained as they headed out of town. "Some get orphaned, then we get calls. Last week I picked up a baby seal on his own in Liverpool. The day before, a fawn. The little critter was lying in the ditch on the side of the highway, within sight of its dead mama. When they're real young, they don't like to leave her."

"The poor things," said Rose sympathetically.

"It's humans' fault," said May hotly, waving at the road in front of them. "We've built our highways through their habitats."

Feeling a rant was imminent, Rose changed the subject. "When's your birthday?"

May snorted. "Don't remember. I'd have to check my driver's licence. All's I know is some days I feel like I'm a hundred years old."

Rose was sure her father would know, or he could find out easily enough.

"Where are we going?" asked Rose, peering out the window.

"Upper LaHave. Guy called it in from his uncle's place. An otter's been camping out in the old man's boat shed. Thinks it might have an infection; there's gunk coming outta its eyes and nose."

"Gross. Can't the guy who called catch him?" *Do otters carry rabies?* Rose wondered.

"Best to leave it to someone with experience. Otters are slippery buggers, like weasels. And they may look cute and cuddly, but don't let 'em fool ya. They're dangerous, wild animals. They have strong teeth and a powerful bite. Can't trust 'em."

"That's reassuring," said Rose. On cue, her left eyelid started to twitch. She couldn't recall when she'd had her last tetanus shot, or a reason she might have needed one. Which surely meant she was overdue.

"Buck up, cuz! It'll be fun. Capturing a critter is a real adrenaline rush. You'll see."

When they pulled into the old man's driveway, Rose's heart skipped a beat when she saw who was standing outside waiting for them.

Allan Conrad.

Rose immediately regretted her clothing choices.

"What's he doing here?" Rose asked, her heart struggling to resume its normal rhythm. She still felt guilty about ghosting his kind offer of a free lunch. And wondered if he'd given a second thought to her leaving the pub with Rob.

"This here is his uncle's place," May said slowly, as though speaking to a simpleton.

"Why didn't you tell me?" Rose tried to hide her anxiety. Although she hadn't told a soul she had slept with Rob, she was worried that word of her night of therapeutic sex had leaked.

For the record, Rose could now testify under oath that the old saying *The best way to get over a man is to get under another one* wasn't true. (She had been mostly on top, anyway.) She suspected that only referred to a bad breakup. Not a death.

May hid a sly smile. "Didn't think to. Just responded to the call and needed an extra hand."

"Couldn't Allan help?" Rose prayed her face wasn't as flushed as it felt.

"You and your jeesly questions!" cried May, turning off the ignition. "I'll need the both of you. My gout's fired up. Okay, grab the towels from the backseat and my cane, and let's go catch us an otter."

Rose turned around and reached behind her for a pile of faded beach towels sitting next to a cardboard box. Once she had them, she scooted around the side of the truck to hand May her cane, the towels slung over an arm.

"Hey, buddy," said May, leaning heavily on her cane and she limped toward Allan. "Take us to the critter."

"You up for this?" asked Allan, frowning.

"Sure am. You and Rose are gonna do the heavy lifting. I'm gonna boss you both around."

"Hey," said Allan, nodding to acknowledge Rose. Eyes averted. Voice tight.

"Hi," replied Rose. To keep her hands occupied, she tightened her ponytail and zipped her jacket. Now wasn't the time to apologize for the missed lunch.

"Allan, grab the bin, net, and bungee cords outta the back of the truck. That the shed?" Leaning on her cane, May pointed toward a building near the house covered in weathered cedar shingles.

"Yup," said Allan. "It's unlocked. Meet you there."

Rose walked in step with May, who was limping. After Allan joined them with the gear, they went inside.

"Pee-yoo," said May, pinching her nostrils with her fingers. "Smells like a rodent colony up and croaked in the walls."

To suppress her gag reflex, Rose reverted to mouth-breathing.

"Sorry, it's pretty rank," said Allan. "Uncle John doesn't come in here much anymore. He's crippled up with arthritis."

With the door closed securely behind them, May became all business.

"Right, here's what's gonna shake down. I can't crawl around on my hands and knees today, so I'll need the two of you to do that. Rose, you're on towel duty. Allan, take the net." May pointed at each of them in turn. "When we find him, you'll have to corner him. If he runs toward you, cuz, throw the towel over his head and hold him till Allan can put the net on him. If he comes at you, Allan, throw the net on him."

"How do you know it's a him?" Rose interrupted. "And why don't I get a net?"

"Him, her, whatever," said May abruptly. "You don't get a net because you don't know what you're doing, and he could be ornery. Towel is safest for you."

"There he is," said Allan, pointing. "Under the workbench."

Two beady black eyes crusted with pus peeked out at them.

"Oh, the poor thing," said Rose, her heart softening. "He looks like a baby."

"Yeah, he's a youngster. Plug up your bleedin' city-girl heart till we've got him. You guys ready? If he isn't compliant, I'll bonk him on the head with this." May lifted her cane off the ground.

"May!" Rose was horrified.

"Geez, relax, that's just a little animal-rescue humour," said May, chuckling. "We go dark sometimes to keep things light. Okay, Allan, you're up first."

For fifteen frustrating minutes, Allan and Rose took turns creeping up to Otto, as they dubbed him, throwing the towel or net, and missing their target. Whatever infection was raging through his system didn't seem to be slowing him down. May directed them from an old wooden chair in the corner.

Finally, Rose landed a towel toss over Otto's head. "Got him!" she cried triumphantly.

Allan approached with the net. When he put his hands over hers, an electric current spread from her fingertips to her shoulders. Then it travelled lower. To her pelvic chakra—home of desires—which Rob had awakened.

Maybe I should start practicing yoga again, she thought.

"You can let go, I've got him," said Allan tersely.

Rose slid her hands out, reluctant to release the otter, who had calmed down after an initial struggle. By now, they were all tired. Rose was also reluctant to release the feeling of Allan's hands on hers. And how different it felt when Rob had covered her hands just days earlier. His hands had been familiar. Comforting. Supportive. Allan's hands were—

May interrupted Rose's fantasy: "Nice work, kids! Rose, take the lid off the bin. Allan'll pop Otto in, then secure the bin with the bungee. These critters are escape artists."

When Allan had settled Otto on the backseat, next to the cardboard box, Rose and May climbed into the front. Rose noticed her cousin had trouble getting in. Frowning, she watched her pick up her left leg with both hands, then swing it into the cab after she was seated.

When May dropped the keys on the floor, Rose picked them up and handed them to her. After she returned to the condo, she planned to research gout. Something was not right.

May rolled her window down. "Thanks, Allan, you're a peach."

"Happy to help," said Allan, who still hadn't met Rose's guilt-ridden gaze. "And John says thanks."

"Tell him no problemo. Catch ya next time." May waved, rolled up the window, and started the engine.

Rose waved a timid goodbye.

As the truck reversed, Allan stuffed his hands in his jeans pockets.

He's sensitive, thought Rose sadly. *I hurt him.*

May interrupted Rose's epiphany.

"You did great, cuz! Did you have fun?"

"I kind of did," said Rose, surprising herself. "You're right, it is an adrenaline rush. And it feels good to know we're helping him. What's next?"

"Now we take ol' Otto here to the farm." May pressed the

gas pedal as she turned off the secondary road onto the main highway.

"Whose farm?"

"That's what we call the wildlife treatment and rehab centre," May explained. "It's about half an hour from here, in the middle of nowhere. They'll assess Otto and see if he's treatable."

Rose brushed boat-shed dirt off her knees. "Will he be okay?"

"Now, don't get too attached," said May sternly. "Critters will often hide an injury or illness until it's too late to do anything to save them. High mortality rate because of that. It's a downside of this work. But when we *can* help, the payoff is releasing them back into nature, where they belong."

Just then, Rose caught sight of two beady, pus-filled eyes peering at her in the rear-view mirror. Two tiny paws rested on the back of the seat.

"Jesus!" Rose shrieked.

"Christ!" May jumped. "You gave me a heart attack. What's wrong with you, woman?"

"Check the mirror and you'll find out."

May did. "Dammit, we'll have to pull over," she said, punching the four-ways.

Meanwhile, Otto appeared to be having the time of his life. When the truck was stopped on the side of the highway, Rose and May turned around to find him sitting on top of the cardboard box.

"Well, shit," said May, scratching her head.

"What's in the box?"

"A birthday cake. I'm taking it to a friend's party after this. Hope it isn't too squished."

Rose laughed so hard her abs started to hurt. "What do we do now?"

"In the glove compartment, there's a spray bottle with water in it. Squirt the sucker, but don't aim at his eyes. While he's stunned, throw a towel over him. Try to cover his head so he can't bite you."

"I don't think I'm up for this level of responsibility," said Rose with uncertainty. She was half terrified, half excited. "Should we call Allan?"

"Nope, you got this. Whatever happens, don't open the door or we'll lose him."

"What do I do if I catch him?"

"*When* you catch him, I'll get out, grab the net, and put him back in the bin. I'm not movin' too fast today, so you'll have to hang on tight while he wriggles. Once he's in the bin, I'll bungee the ever livin' daylights outta it and dig out the duct tape."

"Can he breathe in there?"

"Of course he can. We're rescuers, not assassins. We poke air holes in the bins."

Ten minutes later, Otto was wet, angry, and back in jail.

May inspected the cake before they hit the road. "Flowers'll need fluffing up. A few well-placed candles will hide the worst of it. We'll ply her with wine before she sees it. You wanna come?"

Rose smiled. "Thanks, but I've had enough excitement for one day. If you could drop me home after we take Otto to the farm, that would be great."

"Okey dokey. I'll have to do the intake paperwork when we get there, but that won't take long."

Rose was quiet as she looked out the window. Stands of evergreen trees, birches, and patches of ocean passed by in a blur. If Jim were alive, he'd bust a gut at her description of capturing Otto. City girl on her hands and knees in a dusty old boat shed rescuing a baby otter with infected eyes? Enjoying herself? Who would have thought? Not her.

She'd leave out the part about Allan's electrifying touch, of course.

Nineteen

SIX MONTHS TO THE DAY SINCE JIM'S DEATH, ROSE decided to head over to Hillcrest Cemetery. Margot had given her directions to Eric's headstone. Rose wanted to introduce herself to her neighbour's husband.

On Sundays from January through May, Fishnets & Fantasies was open from noon to five. Foot traffic was fairly quiet until tourist season kicked off in June. From then until the end of December, the hours were extended.

It was the second Sunday in May, and Wendy thought Rose could manage by herself at the shop that afternoon. She had arranged a death doula session with Margot, and Sonya had a writing deadline.

After a mid-morning walk with Molly and Relic along the waterfront boardwalk, Rose and her canine companions returned to the condo. The wind had made her eyes water, and her left eyelid was twitching. *My kingdom for a good night's sleep*, she thought for the umpteenth time. In the kitchen, Rose rinsed and refilled the dogs' water bowls, setting them back on their mats. Then she slung her knapsack over her shoulders.

"Back in a bit," she said, bending down to kiss both furry heads. As she locked the door behind her, she mused that Molly and Relic were doing well in their new environment. As long as she remained the centre of their universe, they were fine. She didn't think she could cope if anything bad happened to either of them. Yet she couldn't ignore that they weren't getting any younger.

The morning was cloudy and chilly, but dry. Rose was grateful for the wool hat and gloves she had bought at the farmers' market. Spring in Nova Scotia could be as unpredictable as a menopausal woman's moods: warm and calm one day, cold and cutting the next. It might even snow: one final, bracing bite on the bum by Old Man Winter. Poor man's fertilizer, the farmers called it. Dusting daffodils that were almost ready to reveal their sunny faces.

On the five-minute uphill climb to the cemetery, Rose spotted campaign signs for town councillor that had been hammered into the semi-frozen soil in front of brightly painted heritage houses. Booth King smiled charmingly at her from a few of them; the other candidates weren't familiar to her.

Arriving at Hillcrest, Rose jumped as church bells filled the air. Flashing her back to being in bed with Jim on vacations in the town. Tearing at her heartstrings.

Were the bells Anglican, Catholic, United, Baptist, Presbyterian, or Lutheran? For a small community, there was no shortage of places to worship. Rose belonged to none of them.

Wandering past the Academy and into the cemetery, Rose spied a headstone with *Betty Zinck* engraved on it. Wendy's best friend, who had died of lung cancer shortly before Fishnets & Fantasies opened. From the stories Wendy and Sonya had shared about Betty, Rose knew she had been quite the salty character.

Eric wasn't hard to locate. Margot had explained that he'd wanted to be buried close to the grave of a young woman named Sophie McLachlan. In 1879, when she was just fourteen years old, she was accused of stealing ten dollars from her employer. Back then, that was a lot of money. Everyone, including Sophie's mother, believed her accuser.

Sophie always maintained her innocence and suffered from terrible bouts of anxiety. Before she died, she wrote a letter citing biblical passages relating to unjust persecution and forgiveness.

And saying that she forgave her accusers. The teenager was believed to have died of a broken heart.

A few months later, the son of her employer confessed to the theft. There was a marker in front of her tombstone telling her story, along with a wrought-iron heart being torn in two by the chains attaching it to the short fence surrounding her plot.

Sophie's story had moved the blustery but tender-hearted Eric, whose final resting place was under a majestic chestnut tree. He had bought a plot near hers so those coming to pay their respects to him wouldn't forget her legacy: to not lose faith in your loved ones.

There was room in Eric's plot and on his headstone for Margot, when her time came. She had told Rose that while she wasn't in any hurry, neither was she afraid.

Shrugging off her knapsack, Rose set it on the ground. Reaching inside, she pulled out a blanket. Shaking out its folds, she spread it in front of Eric's headstone. Then she sat down, placing her knapsack next to her.

"Hi, Eric. I'm Rose, Margot's new neighbour. I've heard good things about you from her and Wendy." Rose looked up, peering at a crow perched on a tree branch above her. She gave him a stern stare. "Don't poop on my head, okay? I'm not in the mood. Even if it is supposed to bring good luck."

Back to the business at hand. "Margot told me you died of a heart attack. My husband, Jim, died suddenly, too. Six months ago today, actually." Lump in throat, she continued. "In fact, today is his forty-sixth birthday. So it's a really shitty day any way you look at it."

The crow cawed.

"Fuck off!" said Rose, glancing up. "Sorry, not you, Eric."

Rose's cellphone buzzed. Removing her glove, she pulled the phone from her coat pocket.

A text from Rima: *We've picked baby names!*

"You fuck off, too." Rose muted her phone and put it away. "Sorry, Eric, that was rude. I wasn't talking to you. I'm here because I wanted to introduce myself. And I brought a little something for the occasion."

Pulling her knapsack closer, Rose fished around inside, then took out a small bottle of rum she had bought at the distillery in town. Setting it on the blanket, she put both hands inside the knapsack, pulled something else out, and placed it in her lap.

"Eric, I'd like you to meet James Samuel Mercer, my husband of seventeen years. Together for twenty. He was a schoolteacher, then an advertising copywriter. Smart, nice guy. We met online. Do you know what that means?"

Rose decided the answer wasn't important. "Never mind, it doesn't matter. He lived in Vancouver, and I was in Toronto. We dated long-distance for a year before he moved to be with me. I'm from Nova Scotia, and we moved to Halifax ten years ago. Us in a nutshell."

The crow cawed again. Three times.

Rose tipped her chin up. "Shut *up*, you stupid bird! Can't you see we're having a moment?" Looking around for something to throw, she decided against killing a living creature on sacred ground. Though, if the creature wasn't on the actual ground, would it still be a sin?

I hope the churchies can't hear me talking to a dead man and screaming at a live bird. I can just hear them whispering, "There's the crazy widow. The one who bought the sex shop. Certifiable, she is. Better lock 'er up."

A thought suddenly occurred to Rose: what if the crow was Jim? Trying to send her a message? She fiddled with her wedding rings. Not ready to stop wearing them. Although she now knew her libido could still fire, she continued to feel fully married.

Picking up the bottle, Rose held it ceremoniously. "Eric, I'd like to propose a toast to Jim on his birthday and his six-month deathaversary. And to meeting you. I don't like rum—tastes like cough medicine—but Jim does, and Margot said you do. So...cheers."

Standing up, Rose opened the bottle, then poured the amber liquid slowly onto the ground next to Eric's headstone. As the last drop fell onto the earth, a deer with a majestic set of six-point antlers appeared in front of Sophie's grave.

Rose froze. Goosebumps pimpled her arms. The buck briefly made eye contact with her.

Is that you, Eric? Did all the spirits come out to play today?

What if the buck charged, impaling her with its antlers, tossing her around as effortlessly as a rag doll? She tried to push the gruesome image away. She imagined being gored to death would be a tragic way to go.

More tragic than being hit by a delivery van? Rose pushed that image from her mind. Recurring nightmares about the accident were more than enough.

Instead, the deer lowered his head to the ground, searching for something to nibble on. Then he wandered away, as quietly as he had arrived.

cℓℴ

As had become her Sunday work ritual, Rose had left Molly and Relic at home, since she would only be gone for a few hours. Margot had her spare key. Her neighbour enjoyed taking whichever of her six children, and many grandchildren and great-grandchildren, were visiting to pet the pups, give them treats, and let them out in the yard.

An hour into her afternoon at work, Rose had read all of the messages from customers asking her to order special products. That happened daily. Wendy had explained that when it did, if the request was reasonable, she'd order six of the items, figuring someone would buy the others.

Sometimes new, independent vendors approached Wendy. The previous December, for example, a local artisan had called to ask if she could drop off one of her product, to see if it would sell.

"What was it?" Rose had wondered.

"A beeswax candle in the shape of a penis," Wendy had replied. "It was massive! And her retail price was twenty-five dollars, so it wasn't cheap."

Rose had chuckled, picturing the penis drooping as the lit tip melted. "Did it sell?" she had asked skeptically.

"Within an hour!" Wendy had said. "I ordered six more, and they sold quickly, too. But that was all I stocked. As a rule, I don't order many seasonal novelty products because I don't want them hanging around afterward."

Rose also learned that penis-shaped cookies were popular at bachelorette parties. She made a note to place an order for more cookie cutters.

When the door opened Rose looked up, slack-jawed. Before her stood the older woman she'd caught peering in the front window. The clear plastic rain bonnet covering her curls was tied securely under her chin, even though, like before, there was no rain in the forecast.

Her Peeping Thomasina had arrived.

Pushing her paperwork aside, Rose greeted the woman as Wendy had instructed. "Hi, I'm Rose, the shop's new owner. Please feel free to browse and let me know if I can help you with anything."

"Thank you, dear, but I've been in here before. I'm Mrs. Jean Joudrey. From Blue Rocks. Not to be confused with Mrs. Jean Joudrey from Italy Cross. She's a Protestant and an alcoholic, but the Lord doesn't judge and neither do I. I've heard all about you. It's lovely to finally meet you. I hear you're from Toronto." It was a statement, not a question.

Rose wondered what else Mrs. Jean Joudrey had heard, wrongly or otherwise. Accepting the woman's extended right hand, she was surprised by the strength of her grip. She was mid-seventies, if a day.

"It's nice to meet you, too," said Rose politely. "Actually, I'm from Wolfville. But I went to university in Toronto, and I worked there for sixteen years. Then my husband and I moved to Halifax, where we lived until...I moved here." Rose hurried to change the subject. "Um...your hair looks nice."

Puffing up like a peacock at the praise, Mrs. Joudrey patted her bonnet proudly. "Now, isn't that sweet of you to say, dear. I just had it done yesterday in Bridgewater. I like it to look good for church. Which reminds me..." Rummaging around in her enormous handbag, Mrs. Joudrey pulled out a pamphlet. Waving it in the air, she exclaimed, "Found it!" Then she placed it on the counter. "I thought you might be interested in this," she said, pushing it toward Rose. Then she leaned in closer. "Goodness, dear, did you know your left eyelid has a terrible twitch?"

"Yes, I do, thanks." Gritting her teeth, Rose closed her left eye and placed a finger on the offending lid. Opening that eye and blinking rapidly to restore her vision, she picked up the pamphlet and read the front: *St. Norbert's Bereavement Support Group. All welcome.* Rose was fairly certain St. Norbert's was the town's Catholic church.

"I attend every month, and it's done me a world of good since my Tommy passed from this world to the heavenly one above, God rest his poor demented soul." Mrs. Joudrey quickly crossed herself. "Lost to Alzheimer's at the end, he was. You could tell him a parrot was prime minister and he'd nod, smile, and say he'd voted him in."

Rose had been prepared for Mrs. Joudrey to hint that she'd heard about a miraculous warming-gel "liniment" that relieved arthritis. Not be blindsided by a septuagenarian grief-support groupie. Taken off guard, she didn't have a clue how to respond. Her first weak attempt—"I'm not Catholic"—was brusquely brushed aside.

"Doesn't matter, dear, many of our members aren't." Mrs. Joudrey waved a hand in dismissal. "We gather in fellowship of the bereaved, although the Lord is always present, of course. St. Norbert's room-rental fee was cheaper than the other churches, is all. I'm a longstanding member of the Catholic Women's League, which has certain…perks…shall we say."

Attempting to steer the conversation away from herself, Rose said, "I'm sorry for your loss." It sounded like a platitude, but something had to be said. "When did your husband die?"

"Fourteen years ago next month. Not a day goes by that I don't have a little chat with him. You know, a *Good morning, my love* over my first cup of tea. *Isn't the weather frightful? You wouldn't put a cat out in it. Could you help me come up with this answer in the crossword?* Even if I know the answer." Mrs. Joudrey winked. "Makes him feel smart. I talk to him as though he's still with me."

Rose imagined that when Tommy Joudrey was alive, his wife had done most of the talking then, too.

"Well, thank you for…this," said Rose slowly. Remembering her manners. Trying not to look at the pamphlet like it was a cockroach that had crawled onto the counter. "It was kind of you to think of me. Could I interest you in something while you're here? One of Wendy's soaps, perhaps?" Soap was always a safe starting point.

"You know, just last week I finished one of her bars, so I'll take two more." Mrs. Joudrey fished around in her handbag for her wallet. "Smelled of cinnamon, it did. Like an apple pie baking. I've been using one of Tommy's old Irish Springs ever since. Practically fossilized after all this time, and such a strong scent. Land sakes! Don't know how I ever stood it. Lovely bright colour, though."

If I'm using Jim's dried-up soap in fourteen years, I hope someone locks me up and throws away the key, thought Rose as she walked over to the soap display.

"Anything else?" asked Rose sweetly.

"Come to think of it, now, there is," Mrs. Joudrey said coyly. "I heard from a…special friend…that you sell a liniment that works wonders on arthritis. My knees pain me something bad, and that Bengay doesn't do a blessed thing."

Might your special friend be Stanley Shupe? thought Rose, suppressing a smile. Wendy had told her the story to explain why she stocked so much of the warming liquid.

"I know exactly what you mean," said Rose, walking to the display and pointing them out. "I was a gymnast when I was young, so I have a touch of arthritis, too. How many tubes would you like?"

"You're still young, dear," said Mrs. Joudrey, patting Rose's arm. "Might as well give me two tubes, to save a trip. I don't get out as often as I used to."

"Sounds good. And remember, you can always phone in an order and we'll deliver it," said Rose. "Is that everything?"

Mrs. Joudrey was eyeing a vase filled with feather ticklers in various colours. Plucking out a purple one, she said, "This will be perfect for dusting my Royal Doulton figurines. I've got quite a collection. Worth a small fortune on the eBay, I daresay."

Rose smiled as she rang in the items, wrapped them in tissue, and placed them in a paper bag with a handle. *Arthritis and dust, my ass.*

Just then the door opened and four women in their late twenties walked in. Rose wondered if they were a bridal party. She reminded herself again about ordering more cookie cutters.

"Thanks, Mrs. Joudrey," said Rose, handing the bag over

the counter. "It was nice to meet you. Enjoy the rest of your day."

"You too, dear," said the older lady, absentmindedly patting her bonnet. "And don't forget about our little group. There'll be tea and cookies. Sometimes Mabel Knickle makes mocha cakes."

Rose's grandmothers had made mocha cakes. She wondered how old Mabel was. Or if there were any men in the group. Maybe that's where lonely elderly women around here connected. But she wasn't old yet, or lonely enough to join ranks with the likes of Mrs. Jean Joudrey.

As soon as the door closed behind her, Rose slipped the pamphlet into the recycling bin. Then she turned her attention to her customers.

"Hello, ladies!" said Rose with forced cheerfulness. "How may I help you?"

Twenty

EVERY JUNE IN NOVA SCOTIA, AS BILLOWING WAVES of purple, pink, and white lupins bloomed in ditches along the highways, there came a day when it stayed warm enough outdoors that it was safe to put away the flannel bedsheets. Leading up to this moment, people played a repetitive indoor game of heat on, heat off, heat on, heat off. You never knew in which week the warming trend would happen, but when it did, it was cause for celebration. So long, extra layers! People happily peeled heavy outerwear like layers of an onion.

At the same time, the grass grew and greened up, and the trees and shrubs that had shed their leaves in autumn began budding. Maples, oaks, chestnuts, birches. Rhodendrons, azaleas, spireas, honeysuckles, lilacs. All around, nature sprang to life in a canopy of colour.

That day had arrived in Lunenburg. After closing the shop on the second Friday in June, Rose and the dogs hightailed it to Daisy's house in Bedford to drop off her winter clothes and boots, pick up her spring and summer outfits, and hug her family. On Saturday, John and Joanne drove in from Wolfville to have lunch with everyone.

The entire nuclear family sat at the dining room table. Rose and her parents. Her sister, brother-in-law, three nieces, and nephew. Contributing to the conversation. Reaching for water glasses. Sipping. Chewing. Laughing. Molly and Relic were on the floor, patiently waiting for food to be slipped to them. It was familiar, comfortable chaos.

Everyone was there. Except for Jim.

But unbeknownst to his in-laws, Jim *was* in the house. In Daisy's basement. On Rose's bedside table. Next to their wedding photo. Rose felt less lonely when he was nearby. She had started thinking of the eco-friendly container as her *emotional support urn.*

Over vegetarian lasagna, John and Joanne listened raptly to Rose talk about the shop, peppering her with questions about cross-merchandising, bundled pricing, loss leaders, and flash sales.

"What kind of store is Fishnets & Fantasies?" interrupted thirteen-year-old Lulu.

Chatter ceased. Cutlery clinked as it fell onto plates. The two older girls giggled, then looked at their parents. Ryan's face flushed as he examined his hands.

Rose shot Daisy a *Didn't you tell her something age appropriate?* glance. In return, Daisy grimaced, replying silently with an *I asked Steve to* face.

Daisy and Rose both stared at Steve.

The man in question ducked down to slip a baby carrot from the crudités plate to Molly.

No-nonsense Joanne came to the rescue. "It's a shop for adults who want to buy products to help them enjoy sex more."

"Oh," said Lulu. "What kind of products?"

"You'll find out when you're thirty and not a second sooner," said Steve sternly. Rose knew he was only half-joking. Everyone laughed.

Lulu shrugged. "Whatever." At this stage of her life, she was more concerned with passing her next piano exam than daydreaming about romance.

The previous year, during Daisy's sex talk, Lulu had announced that boys held no romantic appeal for her whatsoever. And she was quite certain they never would. Everyone accepted her announcement as easily as though she had stated

"I prefer chocolate to chips." Including John and Joanne, who had been liberal-minded hippies once upon a time.

"You can visit the store sometime if you like," said Daisy.

"Am I allowed in?" asked Lulu, raising a forkful of lasagna to her mouth.

"Yes, with a parent," said Rose. Daisy raised her eyebrows in surprise.

Lulu shrugged again. "Yeah, maybe."

"I'll come!" said Ella, a grin spreading across her face.

"Me, too!" said Katie, digging an elbow into her mother's ribs.

"What do *you* think about my shop, Ryan?" Rose asked her painfully shy nephew.

The boy looked up from his plate, red-faced. "I wish it was a comic book store."

Rose laughed. "I don't blame you. If your friends ask, just tell them your aunt is an entrepreneur and leave it at that."

Ryan nodded. "May I please be excused?" As soon as Steve said yes, the boy bolted.

During this visit, Rose had chosen not to drive by Drummond Court. Doing so would serve no purpose, she felt. Steve reported that the tenants were great. That was one less thing to worry about. Because right now, several worries were bouncing around her brain like balls in a bingo spinner.

For example:

That she'd be alone for the rest of her life.

That she'd never fall in love again.

That she'd fall in love again and feel guilty about it for the rest of her life.

That she'd never have committed, monogamous sex again (the one-off with Rob didn't count).

That she'd have committed, monogamous sex again and feel guilty about it for the rest of her life.

Because ever since Allan Conrad had placed his hands over hers in the boat shed, she'd been daydreaming about having sex. With him. If they *did* have sex, which wasn't going to happen—it was clear she'd hurt him by not showing up for lunch—Daisy would go into hysterics.

No wonder she couldn't sleep.

For a few minutes each day, Rose allowed herself to fantasize about sex with Allan, trying to justify her lascivious longing so soon after becoming bereaved. The irony was not lost on her that she owned a sex shop but wasn't getting laid regularly.

Until Rose had slept with Rob, she'd felt...dead inside, sexually speaking. And she'd been concerned about that. Menopause had come and gone. Her thirties, when sex with Jim was an almost-daily event, were long behind her. She'd been sleeping with the same man for twenty years. The thought of having a new naked man's skin pressing against hers terrified Rose. And excited her. Those thoughts would cause her pelvic chakra to fire again.

The next day, Rose would attend her second social event since moving to Lunenburg: an afternoon celebration to mark Margot's ninetieth birthday at Central United Church's hall. There would be tea, sweets, and small talk. Rose wasn't sure she was up for it. But she also knew it wouldn't be healthy for her to hide in the shop and the condo forever.

She had written down in her journal her biggest concerns about going:

(1) *what to wear*
(2) *if Allan will be there*
(3) *if I'll be relieved, or disappointed, if Allan isn't there*
(4) *will Jim forgive me if I'm disappointed that Allan isn't there?*

Maybe I do need therapy, she worried.

When her suitcase was stuffed with her spring/summer wardrobe, Rose hugged each relative in turn, put her clothes and dogs into the wagon, and started the ninety-kilometre drive back to Lunenburg.

౭ఌఄఄ

When Rose awoke the next morning, still nestled in bed, the dogs in no hurry to rise, she greeted Jim out loud, as she always did.

"Good morning, honey. I love and miss you, but I'm thinking about having sex with another man. No, not Rob, that won't happen again, although it served its purpose. Someone else. Would you forgive me if I did? It won't be today. And maybe not at all. But I hope I'll have loving, regular sex again someday. I miss your touch. And...I'm lonely."

There. It was out. Rose waited for Jim to send a reply through the ether.

Silence. Sighing, she grabbed her journal and pen from the bedside table and wrote down her words while they, and her pain, were still fresh.

Why did other women's dead husbands "talk" to them, their spirits sending comforting signs? She supposed the deer in the cemetery could have been Jim's spirit, but she wasn't convinced. Her husband was decidedly tight-lipped. Rose realized with a start that it wasn't all that different to how he'd been when he was alive.

Rose checked her cellphone for texts from her inner circle. None. Busy with her new life, she'd been a terrible friend lately. Neglectful. Self-absorbed.

She should message Yuki. It was an hour earlier in Toronto, so she didn't expect to receive a reply right away.

How's your hedgehog? Things still hot and heavy?

Five minutes later, Yuki surprised her with a reply. Did people sleep with their phones under their pillows?

Like I haven't heard that before LOL. All good thx. I know it seems fast but we're talking about moving in together. Think he might be The One. Will keep you posted xo.

Rose smiled. Next on the catch-up list was Rima.

Hey lady, how are the baby plans progressing?

If her phone was nearby, Rima was a thirty-second responder.

If all goes well, Baby No. 1 will come home with us in Aug and Baby No. 2 will be born in Sept. It's gonna be busy! Morning sickness isn't much fun but it's soooo worth it. Can't wait for mat leave to start. Harry will try to take some time off. My mom will come help for a few weeks.

As annoying as Rima had been when Rose was riddled with motherhood indecision in her thirties, she was happy for her friend. And Harry was a good guy. They deserved to have their dream of expanding their family come true.

So happy for you! Take care. Hugs from the east coast. xo

Rose yawned. Stretching her arms above her head, she glanced at the alarm clock next to Jim. Eight-fifteen. Right on schedule, church bells chimed. Time to get up.

Rose dressed. Fed herself, Molly, and Relic, then walked them around the block. With their twelfth birthdays approaching, her dogs were tiring more quickly. Their muzzles were almost completely grey. Was it her imagination, or was Relic limping? Maybe she should take them to the vet for a physical exam and blood work. She wouldn't allow herself to wonder how much longer they'd be with her.

Back at the condo, Rose stood in front of the open bedroom closet, contemplating the clothes hanging inside. Margot's nine-tieth-birthday celebration called for something special. A dress, certainly. She flicked hangers from left to right. Inspecting each item. Frowning. Some would be too loose, given that she'd dropped ten pounds. One hundred and fifteen was too light for her five-foot-six frame. Once her appetite returned to full strength, she was sure the weight would pile back on.

When she reached the last hanger, Rose's fingers stopped flicking.

"This'll do," she said, nodding approvingly. The navy-blue dress with dainty white and yellow flowers and ruffled cap sleeves had been a bit tight when she'd bought it. Now it should fit perfectly. The boat-style neckline would hide her tattoo, which so far only Rob had admired. She added sandals and a yellow shawl. Sterling-silver earrings and a bracelet. Minimal makeup. A drop of lavender essential oil on each wrist.

Why did she feel like she was dressing up for a date?

Glancing at her left hand, her wedding rings were a stark reminder that she wasn't.

By the time Rose felt ready, it was one-thirty. The drop-in celebration was taking place from one to three. Margot tired easily, and her family—five devoted daughters and one son, plus their spouses, grandchildren, great-grandchildren, and great-great-grandchildren—didn't want her to be overcome with exhaustion.

When Rose walked into the church hall, it was jam-packed with at least one hundred people. She wasn't surprised. Margot had lived in Lunenburg her whole life and was sweeter than honey. Feeling lost and alone, Rose almost turned on her heel.

That's when she felt fingertips on the middle of her back.

"Come here often?" said a familiar voice.

Rose turned around and laughed, relieved to see Allan's face, green eyes glinting. Perhaps he had forgiven her? "Nope, first time. How's Taylor Swift?"

"Full of beans, as always." Allan paused, looking her up and down. "Not wearing your otter-rescuing outfit today?" His dimples flashed. Rose thought he looked dashing in dark denims, a blue-and-green-checkered shirt, and a sports coat.

"Ha, no. Hopefully May won't get an urgent text and want to drag me along. Is she here?" Rose scanned the crowd for her cousin.

"Yes, over there," said Allan, pointing to a corner. "Telling tall rescue tales, no doubt."

May was sitting with some seniors. Her mouth was moving a mile a minute. Her friends were laughing. A couple of canes leaned against their table, but Rose couldn't tell if one belonged to her cousin.

"Wow, she dressed up," said Rose, noting May's grey dress pants and yellow button-down shirt. "I'm going to say hi."

"I'll come with you," said Allan. "I'll introduce you to a few people on the way."

Rose barely heard him. Her attention was laser focused on the gentle pressure of his hand on her back. Slowly moving down her spine.

Her pelvic chakra was molten lava.

It took twenty minutes to reach May, with Allan guiding Rose through the throng. She was ever conscious of his touch. She met former mayor Mary Lohnes and her husband, Lorne Pictou, a retired bank manager. The animated middle-aged woman with a silver pixie cut and diamond nose stud was Cathy Young. Her husband, Derek, looking pale from his bout with Lyme disease, shook Rose's hand firmly.

Along the way, Mrs. Jean Joudrey (not the alcoholic Protestant) nodded a polite hello, with pinched lips, in Rose's direction. *She's probably pouting because I haven't shown up at her bereavement group*, thought Rose. *The judgmental old sourpuss. It isn't a popularity contest.*

As Rose and Allan inched their way across the crowded room, she said hello to Sonya and Booth. They were a handsome couple, standing head and shoulders above everyone else. Sonya's wrist had healed nicely. Booth's campaign for a council seat seemed to be going well.

They're so lucky to have each other, thought Rose. Even with all she knew about Sonya, and how imperfect her life had once been, she was jealous.

༄

From their seat near Margot's table, Wendy and Paul waved at Rose and Allan.

"They look cute together," said Wendy, nudging Paul's shoulder.

"Don't start matchmaking," warned Paul, popping the last bite of a lemon square in his mouth. "Best to mind your own business."

"Why not? It worked with Megan and Will." Wendy had introduced her independent contractors, then in their mid-forties, at a business meeting a few months before opening Fishnets & Fantasies. Within a year, they'd married and had twins.

"Do you think he's still hung up on Ellen?" asked Paul. There'd been a time when Wendy and Paul had hoped Allan would become their son-in-law.

Wendy knew that Allan would turn fifty in a couple of years. She wished he could find someone kind to settle down with.

"He can't possibly be," said Wendy. "It's been a decade, for Pete's sake."

"He hasn't had a girlfriend since," Paul pointed out.

"That we know of," said Wendy, dabbing the corners of her mouth with a napkin. "He's a private person."

Paul snorted. "This town is way too small to keep secrets— we'd have heard."

"Maybe," said Wendy, shrugging. "Anyway, I don't think he's ever fully recovered from that high school girlfriend of his—remember? His fiancée. She ran off with another man. Never showed her face in town again. Serves her right."

"That was rough," agreed Paul. "What was her name?"

Wendy furrowed her brow. "Can't remember. Her father owned the Foodland for a few years."

"Right," said Paul, picking a brownie off his wife's plate. "He was a dick, too."

Wendy wouldn't let it go. "At the very least, Rose could use a new friend. And it wouldn't hurt if it was a handsome single man around her age."

Paul rolled his eyes but kept quiet.

❧

The couple in question, who didn't realize they were being scrutinized from a distance, finally reached May.

"Would anyone like tea or coffee?" asked Allan.

"I know a saint when I see one! You're always serving, even on your day off," said May, holding out her empty teacup. "Fill 'er up, buddy!"

"I'll have tea, too, thanks," said Rose. "One milk, no sugar."

"I'll put some sweets on a plate, too," said Allan.

Rose sat on the empty chair next to her cousin. "You look nice."

"Thanks. This is my go-to outfit for special occasions. Birthdays, weddings, funerals. I don't socialize much, so it always feels new." May looked Rose up and down. "You clean up good, too."

"Thanks. How's Otto?" Rose hoped he'd made a full recovery.

May's face lit up. "That little firecracker? The folks at the farm took him over to Laura at the animal hospital. She fixed him right up with antibiotics. No charge, god love 'er. We released him back into the wild two weeks later. That's Laura over there with her hubby, Fred. Did you know he's Paul's son with another woman?"

"Yes, I did know that," said Rose. She followed May's finger to a pretty brunette standing next to a thin man with greying blond hair sticking up like Einstein's.

"Where's my manners at?" said May, shifting gears to introduce the woman and two men sitting with her. "These here are three of my fellow rescue volunteers. Couldn't do what I do without 'em. Everyone, this is my cousin Rose." The three seniors smiled and said hello.

Rose was surprised. The trio was old, in their seventies, at least. She now knew from first-hand experience that wildlife rescues were physically demanding. *I really need to stop stereotyping older people*, she chided herself. Working at Fishnets & Fantasies had taught her that lesson pretty fast.

Before Rose could reply, Allan returned balancing a full tray. Rose watched with concern as May clenched and unclenched her left hand several times before picking up her teacup. She hadn't realized her cousin was left-handed.

May didn't miss Rose's scrutiny. "Gee-dee gout," she said quickly, grimacing. "It's running rampant."

Conversation ceased as Margot's eldest daughter gave a brief, heartfelt toast to her mother over the microphone. Seated at a table with her immediate family at the front of the room, Margot looked happy but drained. Birthday cake was cut, plated in single servings, and passed around.

Thanks to everyone's body heat, the hall was hot. Also, Rose suspected the radiators were still turned on. She shrugged off her shawl and slung it over the back of her chair before she started sweating. Sitting beside her, Allan laid his sports coat on an empty chair.

In a split second, the calm turned to chaos.

One minute Margot was lifting a forkful of cake to her mouth; the next she had slumped onto the shoulder of the daughter sitting next to her.

"Mom! Help! Someone call 911!" Margot's daughter cried.

Paul leapt into action, his firefighter's first-aid training kicking in. Sonya was already speaking to the 911 dispatcher, explaining Margot's condition with clinical, professional detachment as Paul assessed her.

"Female, age ninety," said Sonya. "Unconscious. Breathing. Lips and fingertips appear blue. Airways open. Faint but regular pulse."

Six minutes of stunned and awkward silence later, an ambulance sped into the parking lot. Sonya led the paramedics to their patient. They easily lifted the petite Margot onto a stretcher. Her family surrounded their beloved matriarch and moved with her en masse, never taking their eyes off of her.

After the ambulance was gone, those remaining in the hall scattered, whispering their concerns and fears.

Did Margot overheat? Or was it a heart attack? That's what killed Eric, may he rest in peace.

The Catholics crossed themselves.

Rose had stayed rooted to her seat. Frozen in fear. Not ready to bear another loss. In the short time that she and Margot had been neighbours, she had grown very fond of her new friend.

Allan broke the tension. Addressing May and Rose, he said, "Why don't we go to the Banker for a drink?"

"I really should get back to the dogs," said Rose, who felt weak herself.

"You've been gone for half an hour," said May curtly. "The dogs are fine. After seeing poor Margot being taken away on a trolley, I could use something stronger than stewed church-lady tea." Pausing, May peered closely at Rose. "Are you okay? Your left eyelid's twitchin' up a storm."

Rose sighed, gently touching the fluttering lid so she wouldn't ruin her eyeshadow. "Yes, I know. I can feel it. I'm sure it's nothing to worry about."

Allan frowned, but said nothing.

"You should try to get more sleep," said May, who had bags under her own eyes. "All right, posse, this here train's leaving the station. Let's head for the saloon."

Too tired to protest, Rose reached over to pick up her shawl and purse. She was surprised to see Allan hold out a hand to May. Without a word, her cousin took it, using him as leverage to help her rise from her chair. As soon as she was standing firmly on both feet, she dropped his hand.

Something strange was going on with May, but Rose didn't know what. There were clues. Joint pain. Fatigue. Mobility and balance issues. Vitamin D and anti-inflammatories. Swimming. Appointments in Halifax.

Everything added up to more than gout, she was sure of it. At that moment, however, she didn't have the emotional capacity to try to figure it out.

Twenty-One

THERE WAS NO QUESTION THAT CLIMATE CHANGE was affecting the coast. South Shore summers used to boast moderate temperatures, with ocean breezes keeping things comfortable. Now, on certain July and August days, the heat waves oppressing Lunenburg made it feel more like Lagos.

In the town's churches, ceiling fans simply moved the hot air around. Congregants fanned themselves with bulletins. Men mopped perspiration-beaded bald heads with handkerchiefs. Locals and sightseers sought shade outside, wide-brimmed hats offering added protection. Sandy beaches were dotted with colourful umbrellas and tents. In close quarters at the shop, Rose had discovered, the scent of customers' sunscreen could be as cloying as cologne.

Rose was grateful that both her condo and Fishnets & Fantasies had air conditioning. And that she lived in Nova Scotia, not Nigeria. Given the choice, she'd choose minus twenty degrees Celsius with windchill over plus forty with humidity. You could always pile on more layers, but you could only peel off so much clothing in public.

Word had spread across town that Margot had been discharged from hospital two days after being admitted. And that she hadn't suffered a heart attack. For the time being, Rose's kind neighbour was staying with her son and daughter-in-law across town. Wendy had explained that her aunt needed additional tests done in Halifax to try to pinpoint the problem.

It was both a relief, and a worry, Rose thought.

❦

Once summer hit, Wendy warned Rose to brace herself for a crowded shop and brisk sales. All three staff members should be prepared to be run off their feet. In July and August, tourists descended on the UNESCO World Heritage Site in droves. Lunenburg's historic architecture, natural attractions, good food, and friendly community drew people from all over the world.

As Wendy had predicted, sales skyrocketed over the Canada Day long weekend. The shop was so busy that tensions ran high. Customers were demanding. Staff was exhausted. During the rush, Rose decided to leave Molly and Relic at the condo. She hired Allan's oldest niece, Jasmine, to walk them at lunchtime.

One Saturday afternoon, after Sonya had left and Rose had locked the door, she began closing the point-of-sale system on the payment terminal.

"I'll do that," said Wendy, moving behind the counter. Waiting impatiently for Rose to get out of her way.

"That's okay, I've got it," said Rose, not taking her eyes off the terminal screen. She didn't have the energy to cope with Wendy's bossiness today. "You can restock."

Wendy didn't move. "I'd like to review the day's sales," she said. "Why don't you restock?"

That didn't sound like question, thought Rose.

Carefully considering her next move, Rose decided to not beat around the bush.

"Who's in charge here?" she asked, meeting Wendy's gaze.

The older woman's face flushed. Rose watched as the muscles around her friend's mouth tightened.

"Wow, that was harsh," said Wendy, taking a couple of steps back.

"You didn't answer the question," said Rose. Hoping this wouldn't be their last conversation.

Wendy held out her hands, palms up. A dramatic gesture of resignation. "You are, *boss.*"

"Okay, then. I'll close up while you restock," said Rose, adding, "thank you."

If there was one thing Rose had learned about Wendy over the years, it was that she didn't give up easily. In the past, she had admired that tenacious quality. It's how she'd gotten Fishnets & Fantasies off the ground, after all.

Now, not so much.

"You're the new owner," said Wendy frostily, "but you're still learning. Today was a big sales day, and a lot can go wrong in the system. Three months in, and you think you know everything already?"

Now Rose's face turned crimson. "When you started working here, how did you learn?"

Wendy saw where Rose was heading. "From my mistakes," she admitted. "But you don't have to. I'm here to teach you to avoid the same mistakes I made. Trust me, it'll make your life easier."

Rose shook her head. "I have to make my own mistakes. And you have to let me, as hard as I know that is for you to do. You're used to being in charge. I get that. But if you can't let go of being the leader, then...maybe you should buy the business back."

Wendy looked as shocked as Rose felt. She hadn't meant to say that. The knee-jerk reaction had caught her off guard, while her defenses were down.

"Maybe I should," said Wendy slowly. "Maybe we should both think about that for a few days. Why don't you call Sonya to see if she can take my shifts next week while I think about *that.*"

Wendy had made her point.

Still in charge.

"No problem," said Rose, her stomach knotting. She knew from Wendy's stories about her fights with Paul that her friend would need time to cool off before she'd be able to listen to reason.

Wendy collected her purse from the storeroom and left without saying goodbye.

"What am I doing here?" Rose said out loud. "Maybe Daisy was right. Maybe I did run away."

In that moment, surrounded by boxes of lemon-flavoured lube, all Rose could think about was how much she wanted to go home.

The blowup with Wendy aside, work was a necessary distraction for Rose. Her eighteenth wedding anniversary loomed the next weekend. Saturday, July sixteenth. The first without Jim.

Their anniversary was the first thing on Rose's mind when she woke up that morning. After four hours of tossing, turning, and fretful dreams.

Eighteen years ago that day, Rose and Jim had planned an afternoon ceremony with a justice of the peace at the Old Orchard Inn, a short drive from Rose's childhood home in the Annapolis Valley. They had flown down from Toronto the weekend before to finalize the planning in person. Jim's parents had flown in from Vancouver and were staying for the week.

Rose and Jim had decided to book a room at the inn as well, instead of staying with her parents. For privacy purposes. And because Daisy and Steve had decided to bunk with the Ainsworths, as their family was expanding. Ella was toddling around at two, and Daisy was in her first trimester with Katie.

An only child of older parents, Jim's best man had been his brother-in-law, Steve. Daisy had been Rose's maid of honour. The sisters had booked massages, manicures, and pedicures at the inn's spa the day before.

Held in a rustic barn with high wooden ceiling beams, the ceremony had been followed by a banquet dinner for eighty guests, and a dance with a live band. Rose had worn an ivory lace sheath dress, with delicate cap sleeves and a V-neck. The garter gracing her left thigh had been blue. Her pearl drop earrings had belonged to Joanne's mother.

Jim had looked dashing in a three-piece, dark-grey suit and white shirt with French cuffs. At six foot two, he still stood several inches taller than Rose in her satin pumps. When they recited their vows, the bride had to tilt her head up to meet her groom's sparkling blue eyes.

Rose reached a hand from under the covers so she could lightly touch Jim's urn, tears slipping down her cheeks. "Happy anniversary, honey. This one is hard. I love you. I miss you. I haven't forgotten you."

Stretched out at the foot of the bed, Molly barked. As a rule, Rose's dogs didn't talk much. Molly stood up. Yawned. Stretched into downward dog. Then padded over to Rose and licked her salty cheek. His sister's bark had woken Relic up from his bed on the floor. Sensing that he was missing something important, he put his paws on the top of the mattress and woofed quietly. Rose reached over to help him up. The three of them settled in for a snuggle.

"I know you miss him, too," said Rose, feeling comforted by their warm bodies. "Eight months is a long time to not see someone you love." She patted them gently. "So is forever."

Soon, the three of them would get up to have breakfast and start their day. Putting one foot, and paw, in front of the other. Finding a way to carry on.

❦

Carrying on came in the form of getting up and going to work. The next day at the shop, in walked a tall, elegant, older woman with short, spiky, snow-white hair and tastefully applied makeup. Silver bracelets jangled on both wrists. Colourful statement rings adorned several fingers. Patchouli and pot permeated the air.

"Good morning. You must be Rose," said the woman. "I'm Jean Joudrey from Italy Cross. The watercolour artist. Not to be confused with the judgmental Jean Joudrey with the poodle perm and the perpetual pout." In case there was any lingering confusion, she added, "From Blue Rocks."

Then the glamorous woman threw her head back and laughed. "The old battleaxe is still pissed I slept with her husband. Once was more than enough, though, I can assure you. Good riddance."

Rose raised her eyebrows but said only, "It's nice to meet you, Mrs. Joudrey."

"Jesus, call me Jeannie. Mr. Joudrey is in Mexico sipping margaritas with his thirty-year-old mistress. I'm divorcing his philandering ass. I feel orgasmic just thinking about the alimony. His spineless brother was no better. Yes, I know, I'm one to talk. But my husband cheated first, then left the country and never came back. So my affair doesn't count."

Rose guessed it counted with Mrs. Jean Joudrey of Blue Rocks. And hang on a second...

"Did you say *brother*?" asked Rose. She was confused by the profusion of Joudreys performing in this small-town soap opera.

"That's right. Identical twin brothers married two Jeans. Hysterical, yes?" Jeannie threw her head back, shrieking with mirth.

"The good news is that I have a date, so I need a new body stocking. The last one got ripped to shreds."

Rose was speechless. She couldn't decide if she was impressed or in shock. Luckily, she found her customer-service voice. "The body stockings are over here," she said, walking to the rack.

Jeannie followed. "Also, I know you carry local artwork," she said, flipping through the garments to look for her size. "I thought I'd bring a few of my pieces in for your consideration. Wendy never took a shine to them."

"I'd be happy to look at them," said Rose. "You might want to call or message me first to make sure I'll be here." She suspected the woman's creations were more Georgia O'Keeffe than Maud Lewis, with a little Jackson Pollock thrown into the mix.

"Will do, darling," said Jeannie. Plucking a black body stocking from its hanger, she practically waltzed it to the counter. Rose rung it in, folded it, and wrapped it in tissue. With great care, she placed it in a bag with more tissue poking out of the top.

"Thanks ever so much, beautiful young Rosebud," said Jeannie, her bracelets clinking musically as she picked up the bag and her purse. "Tata for now!"

As Jeannie swept out of the shop with a flourish, Rose smiled and shook her head. No one had ever called her Rosebud. For some reason, she didn't mind when Jeannie Joudrey from Italy Cross did.

Rose couldn't recall the last time anyone had called her young. Or beautiful. But she knew it would have been Jim.

Twenty-Two

ONE MORNING, ROSE AWOKE WITH A DOG PRESSED so closely to her back that it felt as though she were being spooned. The sensation was warm and comforting, and strong enough to rouse her from a vivid dream. She and Jim had been strolling in a field of blooming lavender, holding hands. Turning to look at her, he'd smiled. Just as he opened his mouth to speak, she woke up.

Could it be that her nightmares were gone for good?

"Move over, you big bed hog," she said, nudging whichever furball was pushing against her.

Opening her eyes, Rose became instantly alert. Molly was sound asleep at her feet. Relic was snoozing on his bed on the floor.

Rose turned to look at Jim's urn. "It was *you*," she said softly. "What took you so long? And what were you trying to tell me?"

Rose would have to note in her journal that Jim had reached out to her for the first time from the beyond. Journalling wasn't an ideal substitute for therapy, but between that and the widows' books, she felt like she was finally processing her grief.

Because Rose had to get ready for work, she didn't have time to analyze her experience. But she was certain it was a sign. That Jim was letting her know he hadn't abandoned her.

The rest of the week, there were other signs that her husband's spirit was present. Twice when she turned on CBC Radio at the shop, his favourite song, "And if Venice Is Sinking" by Spirit of the West, was playing.

In her journal, Rose wrote:

Oh, how I miss you. Every second of every day. I miss your smile, you grabbing me for a hug, my head on your chest when we nap. I miss your voice. I miss cooking dinner together, having conversations with you over a meal. Sharing our day. I miss holding your hand and kissing your lips. I miss saying I love you, and hearing you say it back. How has it been nine months already? If I could go back in time to last November, I'd hold you tightly every day, knowing it was our final month together.

Dropping her pen and closing her journal, Rose sniffed the air. The faint scent of smoke wafted up her nose. She loved the smell of wood stoves in the fall, although this was more pungent. Then her thoughts turned to Wendy, and how she could repair their rift. And if she couldn't, how best to bow out of the business gracefully.

❧

Across town, Wendy was pulling weeds from her herb garden when her husband came running out from the garage, holding his pager.

"Electrical fire at the Lutheran church," said Paul, pulling his wife to her feet.

Wendy wrapped her arms around him. "I love you," she said. "Be safe."

It was important that she always spoke those words before he went on a call. Just in case. Like she had done every day he'd gone lobster fishing. Even if she was angry with him for some reason. Even a stupid reason.

"Love you too," said Paul, holding her tightly. "I'll call when I can."

Watching his truck pull out of the driveway, Wendy walked to the garage to fetch a spade. Her thoughts returned to the spot in the garden where goutweed had overtaken her herbs. She'd have to dig it out. Rain was forecast for that evening, and she wanted to get ahead of it.

Out of the blue, a shiver ran up her spine. Pushing away her recurring nightmare, she set off to tackle the invasive species.

☙

It took less than three minutes for Paul to drive from Oxner Drive to Medway Street. The cinder-block and brick fire hall was located near Burger King, and across from a daycare. Whenever the trucks peeled out of the front bays, lights and sirens flashing, the kids came out for a look. Some of them hung off the fence, mouths gaping open in awe at the action unfolding.

After parking to the left of the hall, Paul ran in the side door, passing the rescue boat on the way to his locker. Since he was first to arrive, he pressed a button that opened all five bays. The trucks sat gleaming. Ready for business. First engine out. Ladder truck second. Third was the rescue truck with the Jaws of Life, carrying four extra firefighters wearing breathing packs.

Stowing his things in his locker behind the ladder truck, Paul then turned to his gear. More firefighters streamed in, nodding to each other in greeting. They aimed for twenty on each call but usually ended up with fifteen, depending on who was available. There were almost fifty volunteers, every one of them as brave as the next.

Fire boots and pants with suspenders went on first. Jacket next. Stuffing gloves into his jacket pocket, Paul picked up his helmet. His breathing apparatus, which was hooked into the truck's seat, would go on at the scene. Helmet last. Full gear weighed fifty to fifty-five pounds. If he was carrying an axe to break a door or window, more.

It took all of two minutes for the trucks to arrive at the church. Reverend Lukas Kroll was standing outside. Pacing, and wringing his hands. His main concern was the whereabouts of Chester, the church's resident cat. Flames were leaping out of the large, multi-paned front window, broken by the force of the heat. "Be strong and courageous. Do not be afraid, do not be discouraged, for the Lord your God will be with you wherever you go," he could be heard praying.

"All right, let's do this," said Chief Rick Wentzel tersely. On command, his crew moved quickly and with purpose. They always entered in pairs. Because Paul stood over six feet tall in socks, his partner today, Larry Purcell, was well matched in height and heft. A thirty-year volunteer and full-time paramedic. Strong. Loyal. Brave, but not fearless.

Overhead, dark clouds threatened but refused to release the rain. Lightning sliced the sky, followed by a low rumble of distant thunder. After donning their breathing apparatus and helmets, Paul and Larry picked up a hose and made for the front door. Each had a thermal imaging camera that allowed them to see through the smoke when searching for people or animals. Lukas had been inside when the fire started, so the front door was closed but unlocked. Not needing to use a battering ram saved precious seconds.

Paul and Larry were the first to enter the building, with Paul slightly ahead. Once inside, they dropped to their hands and knees to begin crawling. It felt like being in the middle of a bonfire. Beautiful stained-glass windows were breaking all around them. Cameras out, they scanned for Chester but didn't expect to find him. Cats had a way of finding an escape route when danger loomed. If they had time.

Looking at Larry, Paul pointed to the ceiling. His partner nodded. Turning on the hose, Paul aimed it to cool the gasses there. He tried to slow his breathing. The heavier he inhaled and exhaled, the more air from the tank on his back he used. He had about thirty minutes' worth. When there was seven minutes left, an alarm would sound to alert him. He had plenty of time.

Seconds later, Paul heard a deafening crack. He looked up just as a fiery wooden beam broke away from the ceiling.

The next thing he knew, he was lying flat on his back. His helmet was on the floor a foot away. He turned his head painfully to the right, his eyes blurred by double vision. Barely able to make out the burning beam that had struck him, which now separated him from Larry.

Wendy and Ellen flashed before his eyes.

⁓

Ever since Paul had joined the fire service, Wendy had been trying to prepare herself. For the moment the doorbell rang while Paul was out on a call. When she would open the door, look at the chief's stricken, smoke-blackened face, and hear him say, "I'm so sorry."

When Wendy heard the doorbell's chime that day, she sat frozen in place on the living room sofa. Holding her breath. Heart pounding. Praying.

After a second unanswered ring, Rick opened the door. Called Wendy's name. Waited a few beats. Then walked inside.

Twenty-Three

WENDY'S WORLD TURNED UPSIDE DOWN.

For the foreseeable future, she wouldn't be able to help Rose at Fishnets & Fantasies. Buying it back, which she hadn't seriously considered once she'd calmed down, wasn't an option. Her long days were now spent at her husband's bedside in the intensive care unit at Fishermen's Memorial Hospital.

A week after the accident, Paul remained on life support. The Hebbs' death doula, Heather, dropped by regularly to get updates and to give Wendy a few moments of respite. Allan dropped off a card and flowers. Chief Wentzel stopped in when he could, to update Paul on what was happening at the fire hall. The doctors and nurses told Wendy that while coma patients might not be able to speak, it was possible they could hear.

A self-employed tech entrepreneur, Fred visited every evening, giving Wendy time every few days to drive home to shower, change clothes, and eat a little something, even though she had no appetite. Ellen was scrambling to take a leave of absence from teaching so she could fly home from Victoria. Fay's mother was recovering from a stroke in hospital there, so she couldn't join her.

Rose felt terrible for her friends. And guilty. And ashamed of herself. After their fight, she and Wendy hadn't patched things up properly. She was hearing the Hebbs' news secondhand, from Sonya or Cathy. Their argument seemed trivial now. She would find a way to apologize, even if it wasn't with words.

One thing was certain: Rose couldn't turn her back on Fishnets & Fantasies now.

Mostly, she couldn't bear the thought of Wendy joining her in widowhood. Still, there was a small space in her heart that yearned for a close friend who was going through the same thing in real time. Same loss. Same pain. Same loneliness. Her sense of alienation reminded her of how she'd felt in her late thirties, when she was riddled with indecision about motherhood. The odd woman out.

In the meantime, there was some good news in town. Margot's test results had come in: a heart murmur caused by iron-deficiency anemia. Her red blood cell count was dangerously low. The cardiologist deemed it an "innocent" heart murmur, one that occurs when blood flows more rapidly than normal through the heart.

Margot was ninety. At that age, Rose didn't think any type of heart murmur should be labelled *innocent*. Then again, she wasn't a medical expert. Margot would need several IV iron infusions before she started taking supplements.

Rose was relieved her neighbour hadn't suffered a heart attack, but she was still worried about her. The shop kept her mind busy during the day. Nights were another story. Tossing and turning, she doubled up on her sleeping pill dose. And kept talking to Jim.

୧ଛ୭

Summer's heat came to an end the first week of September, along with the busy tourist season. Rose was happy to bid both goodbye. Temperatures turned cooler and crisp, making dog walks more pleasant. Things were going smoothly without Wendy overseeing things...until they weren't.

Five months into her trial by fire, Rose was having a rough week. Several times over three days, customers had stopped by the shop, then left when they learned that Wendy or Sonya weren't in. *We'll come back another time*, they said with artificial sweetness before turning on their heels. All women. Around her age, or older.

It was odd. This had happened only rarely since Rose's first few weeks on the job. Younger customers didn't seem to care who was on hand to help them look for products or answer questions. *Have people heard that Wendy and I had a fight?* wondered Rose when the door swung shut behind the fourth turncoat.

Then there was Allan. Rose had called the Grand Banker to ask if he could recommend a plumber, since Paul was no longer available for handyman jobs. The tenant above the store had called to say the toilet was clogged and plunging wasn't working. It needed to be snaked, which was beyond her skill set.

Allan had offered to stop by to take a look. Brushing her hair in the bathroom and applying lip gloss, Rose was disappointed, then annoyed, when he failed to turn up. Had there been a crisis at the Banker? Or was he simply unreliable? She called Sonya, who gave her the number of their plumber.

At the same time, Daisy was getting on Rose's last nerve. In a recent phone conversation, her sister had casually mentioned that she was following Allan on Instagram. Rose was not. When they hung up, Rose scanned Allan's posts. The evidence appeared before her eyes: Daisy's comments peppered here and there. With smiley faces. And—seriously, big sister?—hearts.

Rose's blood boiled. It was just like in high school, when Daisy would try to steal Rose's boyfriends just to prove she could. Not that Allan was Rose's boyfriend. In fact, she couldn't even really call him a friend. They were friendly when they saw each other. And they had rescued an otter together.

Since moving to Lunenburg, Rose had laid emotional claim to the town, and everything—and everyone—in it. Daisy could fuck off and find her own new friends. Rose knew better than to address her feelings in a text. More than a decade ago, she had shared her conflicted emotions about motherhood with her childhood best friend, Sharon, in an email, shortly after Sharon had given birth to her first baby. She might have also mentioned that her friend's self-absorption throughout her pregnancy and new motherhood had been hurtful. Needless to say, that message didn't go over well with Sharon. After an explosive email exchange, they didn't speak again for a year.

Rose figured she had better press pause on messaging Daisy. For now. And while she admitted that her emotions could be compounded by grief, old insecurities were simmering.

Slipping her phone into a drawer behind the counter, Rose turned her attention to more practical matters, such as staffing. Sonya always took her vacation from the shop the last two weeks of September. During that time, the town held its annual three-day literary festival: *Get Lit in Lunenburg*, the T-shirts cheekily touted. Before Sonya published her first romance novel, she had joined the festival's volunteer committee. It was her attempt to establish new roots in her old hometown. Now, she was the group's president.

"You could ask Cathy if she'll sub for me," suggested Sonya, when she and Rose were scheduled together one Saturday. While they unpacked a box of books, Rose plugged in the kettle to make tea.

"The United Church minister?" asked Rose, eyebrows raised.

"Yes, she's very liberal. Once you get to know her a bit better, make sure you ask her about tarts and vicars," said Sonya, winking. "She's filled in for me before. Not for a while, though, since Derek got sick. But he's feeling better these days, so she might be up for it."

"I've never thought to ask Wendy why she doesn't hire millennials," mused Rose. "I mean, I'm the youngest of the three of us, and I'm no spring chicken."

"Most of the summer staff in town are students who don't stick around after August," explained Sonya. "She didn't want to deal with the turnover. Also, she figured that because a good chunk of her customer base is older, they'd be more comfortable interacting with someone closer to their age."

"She's so smart," said Rose, sighing.

"She is that," said Sonya, stirring sugar-free sweetener into her tea.

In a matter of minutes, Cathy had enthusiastically agreed to take a few part-time shifts while Sonya was off. "Is the Pope Catholic?" had been her reply. A spirited sixty-five, Cathy was nowhere near ready to be fully retired. Before her first shift, Rose would bring her in for a refresher.

"How are things going in the New Brunswick sugar bush these days?" Rose asked Sonya when she hung up with Cathy.

"First draft is done," said Sonya, giving a thumbs up. "That's always a weight off. I'll take a break during Lit Fest. Then, while I wait for my editor's comments, I'll start the next one."

"I'm in awe of how prolific you are," said Rose shyly.

"All you've got to do is start," said Sonya with a knowing smile. "I've been meaning to ask, how is your journalling coming along? And have you gotten in touch with Liz Penny?"

As the door opened, talk of writing ceased. Molly and Relic got up off their beds to greet their customers.

Twenty-Four

BY THE END OF THE FIRST WEEK OF SEPTEMBER, Ellen Hebb had joined her mother's daily vigil at Paul's hospital bedside. Her leave of absence had been approved for the fall semester. She was unwavering in her belief that her dad would wake up. Soon. And her mom would need her help during his recovery.

Ellen was grateful for Fred and Laura. It meant she and her mom wouldn't have to shoulder...*this*...alone. Neighbours, and a few of Paul's firefighter friends, were taking care of the Hebbs' home. Bringing in mail. Watering end-of-season pots of impatiens and the vegetable, herb, and flower gardens. Cutting the grass. Putting homemade meals and muffins in the freezer. All the small but meaningful ways a close-knit community comes together in a crisis.

The moment she arrived at the hospital, Ellen scanned her father's face for movement. "Any new signs?" she asked her mother. She had rented a car at the Halifax airport, barely keeping to the speed limit on her way home. Driving only just carefully enough so there wouldn't be two Hebbs in the hospital.

"Not yet," said Wendy, trying to sound hopeful as she rubbed moisturizer on Paul's hands and arms. "The doctor says he's still in the first stage."

Ellen had combed the internet for information. Stage one of a coma: unresponsiveness. Stage two: early responses, like opening and closing eyes. Stage three: agitated and confused, unaware of what happened. Stage four: higher-level responses, like picking up a cup with some difficulty.

The pair barely glanced away from Paul while they were in the room. Watching. Waiting. To see if his eyes opened, so he could move on to the next stage. They held his hands. Brushed his hair. Talked to him. About the weather. The blue jays and chickadees at the backyard feeders. The deer wandering along the trail next to their house. The last of the tomatoes ripening on the vines in their vegetable garden, and the spaghetti sauce Wendy would make with them. Paul's favourite meal.

"Mom, why don't you let me sleep here tonight," Ellen suggested on her second day home. Firmly. A small cot pushed against a wall had been Wendy's bed since Paul was admitted ten days ago.

"Thanks, honey, but you go on home. I'm okay."

"You need your rest," Ellen pushed gently. Knowing it was futile.

"I'm getting enough," said Wendy, trying to sound convincing. The dark circles beneath her brown eyes told a different story. "The nurses give me a sleeping pill."

"Mom, you can't go on like this indefinitely," said Ellen, her voice cracking. Tears filled her eyes. "You'll collapse."

"It won't *be* indefinitely," said Wendy firmly. Hugging her daughter, she added, "Dad is going to come out of this. He's too strong, and too much of a fighter, not to. And I know he isn't ready to leave us yet."

"How do you know?" asked Ellen, wiping her eyes.

"Because if there's one thing my training has taught me, it's that you shouldn't underestimate someone's will to live," said Wendy, brushing a strand of hair from her daughter's eyes. "When people are ready, they'll let go of life pretty quickly. Often with verbal permission from their loved ones. When they aren't, they'll cling to it. That's what your father is doing. While he's in the coma, his brain is resting and rebooting. We just have to be patient. And take it one day at a time."

"Like the alcoholics," said Ellen weakly. Dark humour was her cynical companion during tough times. Stress also caused her to bite her fingernails. Right now, they were so ragged they were raw.

Wendy smiled. "Do you know AA's serenity prayer?"

"Yeah, I think so, but I forget how it goes." Still suffering from jetlag from the four-hour time difference, and the sleepless nights leading up to it, Ellen failed to stifle a yawn.

"*God grant me the serenity to accept the things I cannot change, the courage to change the things I can, and the wisdom to know the difference,*" Wendy recited. "We can't change that Dad is in a coma. But we can accept that it's part of his journey back to us. And if it isn't, we'll help each other with acceptance and healing. There's no life without loss, kiddo."

Ellen picked up her knapsack. "Are you having a *Lion King* moment? Circle of life, and all that?"

Wendy smiled. "Maybe."

Ellen rolled her eyes. "Well, just don't *hakuna matata* me, because I *am* worried," she said wearily. Then she paused. "Mom, you know how you said some people die when they get verbal permission from their loved ones? Did you give that to Dad? Like you did to Betty before she died?"

A decade ago, when her best friend lay in the same hospital dying of cancer, Wendy had held her hand and said, "We're all here. Feel our love. Let go when you're ready." And Betty had.

Wendy held her daughter's gaze. "I did. The first night he was here. And he's still with us. I have faith in him. You should, too. Now go home and get some sleep, and I'll see you in the morning."

"All right. I'll bring you a change of clothes. But then I'm sending you home."

Wendy shook her head no.

Ellen persisted. "For an hour, to take a shower. You're pretty ripe, Ma."

Wendy swatted her daughter lightly on the bum. "Get going, you. I'm glad you're home. Dad is, too. Love you."

"Love you back." Ellen squeezed her father's hand and kissed his bruised cheek. Grateful that he was breathing on his own. Into his ear, she whispered, "Love you, too, Dad. Don't go yet. Goodnight."

In the hospital's darkened parking lot, Ellen lay her forehead on the rental car's cold steering wheel and cried.

Twenty-Five

WHILE PAUL REMAINED IN HOSPITAL OVER THE next two weeks, the Hebbs' normal lives ground to a halt. The rest of the town, however, carried on. Business as usual. The three-day Lit Fest was proceeding as planned the third week of September.

On the second day of the festival, Cathy joined Rose for a Friday-afternoon shift at Fishnets & Fantasies. The higher foot traffic in town meant more drop-ins.

"It feels great to be back in the sexual-pleasure saddle again," said Cathy, pinning her name tag onto her blouse.

Rose laughed, then grew serious. "Thanks again for stepping in. Poor Wendy and Paul. It's heartbreaking."

Cathy sighed, running her fingers through her hair—which, Rose noted with admiration, was as silver as a sterling tea service—until it stood on end. "Yeah, I really feel for them. Paul managed to survive forty years fishing lobster without serious injury, and now this."

Rose hesitated. "Do you think he'll recover?"

"*Jesus said all things are possible for one who believes,*" Cathy recited. "Mark 9:23."

"But people die," said Rose bluntly, pinning her own name tag to her blazer lapel. Avoiding eye contact.

"Well, yes, they do," said Cathy matter-of-factly. "I will one day, and so will you. How've you been holding up since Jim died? It's been how long, almost a year?"

Rose was taken aback by the direct question. Most people tiptoed around it. Or avoided it altogether. Afraid to mention

Jim's name, or the word *died*, for fear of…she wasn't exactly sure.

Uncertain of how to respond honestly, Rose trotted out the party lines. "I'm fine, thanks. Grateful to be busy. And to have the dogs." Rose cleared her throat. Shuffled some papers on the counter.

"Okay," said Cathy, nodding slowly. "You're fine. That's fan-fuckin'-tastic. Now why don't you tell me how you're *really* doing."

Rose exhaled slowly. And looked up to see gentle grey eyes gazing thoughtfully at her. With genuine care and concern.

"My heart hurts," said Rose, swallowing the lump in her throat. "Some days when I'm here alone, I run to the storeroom to cry. There are triggers. Certain songs. Milestones. Seeing a couple holding hands. Or, worse, hugging. Part of me is in pain. Another part is numb. I still can't believe he isn't coming back."

Cathy nodded knowingly. "I went through it when my parents died. To experience someone's death is to also experience grief and pain, and it's normal to fear these powerful emotions. Have you gone for counselling? And is your eyelid twitching because you aren't sleeping?"

Rose sighed, pressing a finger to calm the flutter. "No. And yes. I saw a psychologist when I lived in Toronto, but I never looked for one when I moved home. And I haven't slept through the night since Jim died. I have…nightmares, about the accident."

Cathy shook her head sympathetically. "You poor thing. Tell me, why did you stop seeing a therapist?"

Their conversation ceased as a millennial with a hipster beard and wearing a backwards ball cap walked in. Cathy helped him find the items on his wife's list: a lacy pink negligee, massage oil, and a gift card for fifty dollars. Punching a hole in his reward card and sending him on his way, she turned back to Rose.

"Want tea?"

Rose sighed. "Sure, thanks. Well, the short story is that I saw Charlotte in my mid-thirties, when I was trying to figure out if I wanted to have a baby. One year in particular was pretty rough. But before Jim and I moved to Halifax, I made my peace with the possibility that I might not become a mom. I guess I didn't see the need to continue therapy after that."

Crossing her legs on the sofa, Cathy nodded slowly. "Makes sense. You know, I went through something similar before I turned forty, so I get it. What about grief counselling?"

Rose couldn't help rolling her eyes. "You mean the St. Norbert's Bereavement Support Group? Mrs. Jean Joudrey— *not* the Protestant alcoholic—already tried to recruit me."

"Ha!" Cathy snorted, handing Rose a mug. "The old girl means well. But who knows? It might help to talk to others who are going through the same thing."

"I doubt it," said Rose skeptically. Although she liked Cathy, she was starting to feel defensive. "I mean, Mrs. Joudrey's a lot older than I am. They probably all are. I'd expect to be widowed at her age. Not at fifty." Rose sipped her tea. "Can I ask you a question?"

"Of course, I love a good question. Shoot."

"Any advice for how to get out of my own head?" Rose held her mug more firmly in anticipation.

Cathy tilted her head in thought. "Being of service to others always works for me."

Rose paused to ponder the point. "I guess that's what I'm doing here."

"In a way, yes...but this is work. I meant volunteering. Finding something that fills you up enough to help ease your heartache. There are plenty of opportunities around here."

Rose was silent, and she could see that Cathy sensed she'd better leave it at that. She had planted a seed. Now it was up to Rose to decide whether to water it or let it wither.

Getting up to pour more hot water into the teapot, Cathy changed the subject.

"Are you attending any of the Lit Fest events?" she asked casually.

"Yeah, I'm going to hear Sonya read at the School of the Arts tonight." Before the author had gone on vacation, she had mentioned that Liz Penny would be introducing her and the two other authors on the panel. Rose wanted to get a sense of the new publisher in town. If she had a good vibe and there was an opportunity—and she could summon her courage—maybe she'd approach her.

"Cool," said Cathy. When a customer walked through the door, she grinned. "Hey, look who it is! My favourite barkeep."

Rose blinked. And prayed her twitchy eyelid would behave.

Allan Conrad looked impossibly handsome. His dark, curly was still damp from the shower, the flecks of silver shining. He was wearing well-worn jeans and a green bomber jacket that made his eyes pop. Kneeling on the floor, he scratched Molly and Relic behind the ears and was rewarded with kisses.

Sensing that Rose was tongue-tied, Cathy jumped in. "How can we help you, young man?"

Allan's gaze landed briefly on Rose before moving to Cathy. "Stacy's birthday is coming up. Mom wants to get her something from here, but she doesn't know what. She sent me as her goodwill ambassador and personal courier."

Rose froze, frowning. Who was Stacy? His girlfriend? Not that it was any of her business.

"I've gotta visit the powder room, so Rose will help you," said Cathy, heading for the back. "Come get a treat, pups!" The dogs trotted obediently after her.

Alone with Allan, Rose gave herself a silent talking-to. *Put your big-girl businesswoman pants on.* This was challenging, given that she could practically reach out with her open palms to catch the pheromones Allan was emitting. Like iridescent liquid-soap bubbles. Slippery, and just out of reach.

Allan smelled nice, too. Like cinnamon or cloves. Had he showered with a bar of Wendy's soap?

Rose tried to stop herself from imagining Allan soaping himself in the shower.

Rose imagined Allan soaping himself in the shower.

Giving herself a mental shake, she asked, "What kind of things does Stacy like?" Afraid to hear his answer, if Stacy *was* his partner. Silk restraints? Fuzzy handcuffs? Satin blindfolds?

All of which were in stock.

Instead, Rose suggested a trifecta of the most modest products: "Soap? Massage oil? Lingerie?"

Allan scratched his head. "Damned if I know. I think it's best to keep out of my big sister's bedroom...sorry, that sounded creepy."

Rose laughed. Surprised at the relief rippling through her body. "Yeah, kinda." Now that she knew Stacy was Taylor Swift's human mom, she relaxed. "How old is she turning?"

Allan scratched his head again. "So many tough questions! I'm forty-eight, which means she'll be...let's see...fifty-two."

Fifteen minutes later—with Cathy not quite managing to mind her own business from the storeroom, where she'd cracked the door open to eavesdrop—Rose had pulled together a pretty gift basket filled with relatively tame products. Ones that a mother wouldn't feel too self-conscious giving her grown daughter.

While Rose rang in the purchases, Cathy returned bearing a box of scented candles.

"Are you going to the Lit Fest tonight, Allan?" she asked, batting her eyelashes innocently.

Rose blushed, busying herself with arranging tissue paper in the gift bag.

"No, I hadn't planned to. Why, who's reading?"

"Sonya, and two other local romance authors. Should be an interesting panel." Cathy ignored the dirty look her boss was shooting her way. *Pushing a romance-novel panel at Allan, for fuck's sake. Please stop!* Rose pleaded silently.

"Are you going?" Allan asked Cathy, swiping his credit card.

"No, I'll be home with Derek. He's much better, thank God, but he isn't one hundred per cent yet. Rose is going, though."

Jesus, Cathy! Rose shrieked silently. *I'll deal with you later.*

"Glad Derek is feeling better," said Allan, taking the receipt from Rose and tucking it into his wallet. "I won't be able to make it, though. I'm working the bar tonight."

He turned to Rose. "Feel free to drop by when it's over. A lot of the authors come for a drink after their events. Sonya usually does."

"Thanks, I might," said Rose, forcing a smile as the door closed behind him.

"I know Bessie Conrad, Allan's mom," Cathy said as soon as the door clicked shut. "She shops here all the time. You've probably seen her. Lovely woman. There's no way she'd send Allan to do her dirty work." She gave Rose a knowing look. "I think he may have volunteered for this particular mission all on his own."

Rose felt a familiar flutter, but she knew she wouldn't go to the Banker tonight. Her broken heart was being pulled in opposite directions.

That evening, shortly before the Lit Fest event was set to start, people were scrambling to find seats in the cozy upstairs room at the School of the Arts. Rose slipped into an empty chair near the back, placing her jacket on her lap and her purse between her feet. Glancing around, she noticed one of the local bookstores had set up a table to sell the authors' novels.

Just then, a short, plump, grey-ponytailed woman wearing a multicoloured caftan, black leggings, and well-worn Birkenstocks approached the podium. Liz Penny, the panel's moderator, looked like a friendly grandmother. Rose leaned forward to get a better look at Lunenburg's newest book publisher. She seemed at ease speaking in front of an audience. When she laughed, her head tipped back and her body shook pleasantly.

Maybe I'll say hi to her after, thought Rose, settling back in her chair. Then the butterflies started up in her stomach. *Or maybe not.*

An hour later, it was Sonya's turn to present.

"Some of you have heard this story before, so I'll keep it short," said Sonya. Looking poised behind the podium, she wasn't reading from notes. "I'm a retired physician, and my first romance novel was published ten years ago, when I was fifty-nine. I wrote it in secret—not even my husband knew!"

Sonya paused when a few audience members tittered, then continued. "My manuscript was rejected the first time I submitted it, but with helpful comments on how to improve it. I'm working on my tenth novel now." Appreciative murmurs rippled through the audience. "I'm a prime example that it's never too late to start—and that if you believe in your story, you shouldn't give up on it."

Sighing, Rose let her mind drift. Trying to imagine herself in Sonya's place behind the podium. Telling an audience about how when her husband died, she began journalling to process her grief, and how those journal entries laid the foundation for her award-winning memoir. *If I'm gonna dream, I might as well dream big*, she thought.

Applause filled the room as Sonya finished speaking. After Liz thanked everyone, the authors moved to chairs behind the table, where a lineup to buy signed books began forming.

Rose saw Liz chatting with an older couple. A few others hovered, wineglasses in hand, waiting their turn to speak with the publisher.

When the butterflies started up again, Rose bolted for the exit.

Twenty-Six

CATHY WAS FILLING IN FOR ROSE AT THE SEX SHOP. Her new boss was at home with a bad head cold, with clogged sinuses and nasal passages. A wastebasket full of crumpled tissues was on the floor next to the loveseat in Rose's condo, evidence that she had blown a layer of skin off her raw, stinging nostrils. With each swallow, her throat felt like she was ingesting shards of glass. No amount of lip balm could relieve her cracked, peeling lips.

It was the first time Rose had been sick since Jim died, and she was feeling sorry for herself. There was no one to make her chicken soup and chamomile tea with honey. To nip out to the pharmacy to buy cold medicine and cough drops. To walk the dogs. Sucking up self-pity, she summoned enough energy to take them out on their regular schedule.

Now, after a lunch of canned chicken-noodle soup and saltines that tasted of cardboard, she was stretched out on the loveseat under a soft Nova Scotia tartan blanket. A library book lay open on her chest. When she had finished all of the widowhood memoirs Daisy had given her, she had borrowed a psychological thriller. A feeble attempt at escapism. As far away from real life as she could run.

Normally, Rose loved the fall season, especially as a child growing up in the Valley's agricultural belt. Autumn in rural Nova Scotia brought colourful leaves. Apple picking in orchards. Pumpkin patches in farmers' fields. Bountiful fall vegetables at local markets—squash, brussels sprouts, broccoli, cauliflower, cabbage.

The days were shorter, the nights cooler. Perfect for fires in the wood stove and curling up on the couch with a cup of tea and a book. Lying limply on the loveseat, Rose couldn't stop thinking about her fiftieth-birthday party. How perfect it had been. She told herself she was reminiscing because she had time on her hands while having a rare Saturday off work. Even if she felt like crap.

On Monday, assuming she was feeling well enough to return to work, Rose would turn the animal-rescue calendar pinned to the storeroom bulletin board to October. Which, according to her library book, "was always the bleakest of months, full of shadows and ghosts."

The author has it wrong, thought Rose. She had always thought the bleakest month was November. Dark, angry skies. Relentless, bone-chilling cold rains. The first late-fall snowstorm, which wreaked havoc on the highways, thanks to the drivers who hadn't yet swapped out their tires. Out of control. Skidding into ditches and medians. Crashing into cars, pedestrians, and telephone poles.

This year, Rose knew, November would be bleak for more reasons than rotten weather and the wrong radials.

This year, her fifty-first birthday would be followed two weeks later by Jim's one-year deathaversary.

More miserable milestones. Which was why she was reading a novel about a thirty-year-old Houston dental hygienist pursued by two sexy men and a deranged kidnapper.

Rose blew her nose, then picked up her phone and scanned her texts. There were several, all waiting for her replies.

Rima: *Sorry it took so long to get back to you. Two new babies is a lot! Exhausted but happy. Harry says hi. More later.*

Yuki: *BEN AND I ELOPED!!! IN NIAGARA FALLS!!! FUCK YEAH!!!!*

May: *What's cookin' cousin! Don't be a stranger! Let's break bread soon!*

Her mother: *Haven't heard from you in ages. How's business? Love from J&J.*

Daisy: *Where are you??? Are you mad at me???*

Rose felt that Daisy's extra question marks were excessive. *Once an editor, always an editor*, she thought, sighing.

Putting her phone down, Rose rubbed her eyes and smiled. Yuki, married! Amazing. The last, and youngest, of her Toronto friends was finally hitched. Would a baby be next?

Shifting to a more comfortable position, Rose picked up her phone. Her fingers flew as she fired off short replies to everyone…except Daisy. She didn't have the energy to mend fences right now.

There was something else Rose kept meaning to do but was putting off.

Email Liz Penny.

At last month's romance-authors' panel, Rose had been too anxious to approach the publisher in person. *Coward*, she'd chided herself after she'd practically run from the room. Even though Liz seemed pleasant. An email introduction and inquiry would be safer. Also, she supposed she should have a writing sample, should she be asked to produce one.

Rose did not have a writing sample. Which is why she hadn't applied to Pitch the Publisher, even though Sonya had encouraged her.

The first sentence of her memoir kept turning around in her mind. Once she had massaged it mentally to the best of her ability, she'd be ready to write the rest of her story. Or so she hoped.

❧

Back at work on Monday, Rose had a surprise morning delivery. A courier handed her a massive bouquet of brightly coloured mums, zinnias, roses, and dahlias.

"Someone sure has taken a shine to you," said the friendly woman who placed the arrangement on the counter, admiring it as Rose signed for the delivery.

"It must be from my sister," said Rose, handing the slip back.

"Your sister, *sure*," the woman said, winking. "Wish I had a sister like that. Mine just calls to complain about her hot flashes."

The enormous arrangement must have cost a fortune. The business card taped to the paper read *Tulipwood Flowers*, the shop down the street. Carefully placing the heavy glass vase on the counter, Rose noticed a sealed envelope tucked between an orange rose and a red dahlia. Despite her first name, dahlias were her favourite flower.

"Did your Aunt Daisy send a peace offering?" Rose asked Molly and Relic. They cocked their heads at the question, tails thumping at the familiar name.

Rummaging in the drawer below the payment terminal, Rose found a letter opener. Sliding it beneath the envelope's seal, she pulled out the card. It was computer-generated. No handwriting that she could try to identify.

Congratulations on six months of shop ownership. Best wishes for your future success.

The card wasn't signed. Propping it next to the vase, Rose drummed her fingers on the counter, mulling over who might

183

have sent the flowers. Someone who knew her well enough to recognize that this was the half-year mark of her working at Fishnets & Fantasies.

Daisy was a good bet. It would be a smart suck-up strategy. But the sentiment didn't sound like her sister. Too formal. And why not sign it?

Her parents? Possible, but unlikely. Rose couldn't remember them ever sending her flowers. Not even when Jim died. Instead, they'd made a donation to the SPCA in his memory, as Jim would have wanted.

There was no way they were from Wendy, who was fully occupied tending to Paul. Nearly two months after his accident, he remained in a coma. Wendy and Ellen continued to take turns at his bedside. Talking to him. Holding his hand. Playing his favourite John Gorka and Joel Plaskett songs.

Rose scratched her head. Maybe a member of the local board of trade had sent them? To eliminate one suspect, Rose could have texted Daisy. But, fully knowing she was being petty, she held back.

Relic wandered over to the counter to look for a treat, with Molly a few steps behind him. After he sat and shook a paw, Rose gave him two biscuits for being such a good boy, then did the same with his sister. Absentmindedly rubbing the old gentleman's belly as he lay on the floor with his paws pointing toward the ceiling, Rose pursed her lips. Her hand passed over several small lumps she hadn't noticed before.

"Maybe it's time for you two to have a checkup," said Rose. Best guess, the dogs were now around twelve years old. Seniors. It made sense that they'd have developed some health problems, or they would soon. Good to get them examined. Having read about mass cell tumours in dogs, Rose prayed it wasn't cancer.

After googling the Lorne Street animal hospital, Rose made an appointment to take both dogs in for an exam the next morning. With Fred Hebb's wife, Laura Richardson. Rose was looking forward to meeting her. Sonya could handle the shop by herself.

Just then, the door opened. In walked the tightly permed Mrs. Jean Joudrey from Blue Rocks.

Rose pushed Relic's bumps, and the mysterious floral bandit, to the back of her mind. Pasting a smile on her face, she said, "Hi, Mrs. Joudrey. How are you today?"

"Well, now, not too poorly, dear, thanks for asking," said the older widow, adjusting her signature clear plastic bonnet, even though the sun was shining. "Although I do feel there's rain coming. It isn't what the meteorologists are saying, mind you, but they don't have the lick of sense God gave them. They just look out the window in the morning like the rest of us, give it their best guess, and then take that to the bank. I'm feeling an ache in my knees, as the Lord is my witness and saviour, and that spells rain."

Rose knew what was coming next. She decided to spare them both the verbal do-si-do.

"Do you need more warming gel, then?"

"Oh, yes, dear, that would be heavenly. You're an angel. Do you have a few tubes? I'll pick up some for my friends, too. And have you thought about bringing these sweet pups to a bereavement-support meeting? It'd be pet therapy for the rest of us."

Mrs. Joudrey opened her big purse, double chin tucked to her broad chest, frowning while fishing for her wallet. Pulling it out, she slipped another bereavement brochure onto the counter and pushed it toward Rose.

Rose ignored the pamphlet. As she walked to the shelf to pick up the warming gel, she let Mrs. Joudrey's last question slide.

What she couldn't have known then was the next day, only one of her beloved dogs would leave the animal hospital with a clean bill of health. And that for the first time, she would consider attending a gathering for the brokenhearted at St. Norbert's.

Twenty-Seven

THERE ARE TWO TYPES OF HOSPITAL VIGILS: ONE with a happy ending, and the other. Since Paul's accident in August, Wendy had barely left Paul's bedside.

Two months had felt like an eternity, with no change in Paul's condition. Every day, Wendy rubbed lotion into her husband's hands and feet. Talked to him. Played his favourite music. While the nursing staff admired her devotion, they were concerned about her. She only went home to shower and change her clothes when Fred or Ellen insisted. Tall and lean to begin with, her yoga pants were hanging off her bony frame. The dark circles under her eyes were moon craters.

Still sleeping on the cot in Paul's room most nights, Wendy woke one early October morning to the most beautiful sight she had ever seen in her sixty-nine years.

Her husband's blue-grey eyes—the same shade as a stormy sea—were focused on her.

Before she could react, Dr. Agbani walked in. Wendy appreciated the doctor's warm bedside manner and his ability to explain what was happening to Paul in plain language.

The two of them exchanged startled looks.

"Well, now, what is this?" Dr. Agbani's eyebrows were raised so high his forehead was a wave of wrinkles. Pulling a chair up next to Paul's bed, he covered his patient's hand with his own.

"How do you do, Mr. Hebb? I am Bisi Agbani, a doctor here at Fishermen's Memorial. It is an absolute pleasure to greet you this morning. You are here because you were hurt while putting out a fire at a church. You are a very brave man, sir. You have what is called a traumatic brain injury. You have been sleeping so your brain could heal, and we have been taking care of you during this time."

Wendy sat frozen on the cot. Afraid that if she moved, or spoke, the spell would be broken. That Paul would close his eyes, this time forever.

"I am going to ask you to do a few things for me, but only if you are able to," Dr. Agbani said to Paul. "Could you follow my finger with your eyes?"

Paul did.

The doctor smiled. "Very good. Now, this may sound silly, but could you stick out your tongue?"

Paul did.

The doctor chuckled softly. "Very good. If my children were here, they would stick their tongues out in return, but I am more polite. One last thing for now. I am going to hold your hand, and I would like you to squeeze it if you can."

Paul did. When he released his grip, the kind physician kept hold of his patient's hand.

"My friend, I am very pleased to tell you that you have just begun your journey to healing and recovery. We will travel this road together. Now, I am going to give the nurses this good news and consult with the rest of your care team. You rest now." Dr. Agbani patted Paul's hand once more, then smiled and winked at Wendy. Before leaving the room, he said, "You may kiss him, Mrs. Hebb."

Wendy slowly approached her husband of forty-seven years. Their eyes never left each other's. Leaning over the bed rail, she gently cupped his cheeks with her hands, then pressed her lips to his. Only when Paul returned the pressure did she allow her tears to flow.

෯

News travels fast in a small town. Bad news, especially. But good news, too. Sonya heard it from Ellen when she delivered a shepherd's pie to the Hebbs' bungalow. Cathy heard it from Sonya when she dropped by Fishnets & Fantasies on her way to physiotherapy. Mary Lohnes heard it from Cathy when she stopped in to buy a gift card for a friend. And so it went throughout the day, until almost everyone in town knew that Paul Hebb was conscious. Just in time for Thanksgiving. Something to be truly thankful for.

More good news was circulating around town: Booth King had won a seat on town council. Sonya had good news, too. *Love in the Sugar Bush* was scheduled to launch the following spring, and she was already several thousand words into her next book.

Two people in town had yet to hear the good news about Paul, however: Rose Ainsworth and Laura Richardson. The joyful texts were waiting for them, but they hadn't checked their phones. That's because they were standing close together in an exam room at the animal hospital. Where Laura was about to break good, and bad, news to Rose.

First, the good news: Relic's lumps were benign, and his blood work was fine. Rose breathed a sigh of relief.

And although both dogs had tested negative for Lyme disease, Molly's blood work was not fine.

"Chronic kidney disease?" Rose repeated blankly. "But she hasn't been sick. I thought Relic might be sick."

"The initial symptoms can be subtle, so it just shows up in routine blood work. Have you noticed increased drinking and urination?" As they talked, Laura kept running her hand along Molly's back. Relic was lying on the floor gnawing a dental stick.

Rose felt her stomach tighten. She thought long and hard. Had she? She'd been so busy, tired, and distracted, she might have missed something. "No, I don't think so. Maybe? I don't know." Tears pricked her eyes.

"Don't feel badly, it's common for the symptoms to be barely noticeable, especially in older dogs," Laura said reassuringly. "I'd like to do a few more tests to establish a better baseline."

"Okay," said Rose numbly. "Is she in pain? And is there any treatment?" Rose gave Molly another biscuit. "Good girl," she said, her voice breaking slightly. "My good girl."

"She won't be in pain, but as the disease progresses she'll feel nauseous and her stomach will be upset. We can put her on a medication to settle her tummy when that time comes. And we can start her on a special diet now that doesn't make her kidneys work as hard and will help keep her from feeling icky."

Laura paused, then put her hand on Rose's arm. "If I were you, I'd spoil her rotten. Trust me when I tell you that I know how difficult it is to make this decision. Our animals see us through so much, and they're there for so many milestones—the good *and* the bad."

Laura's eyes grew moist, and her voice wavered. "I've taken more time off work when my animals have died than I did when my mom died, and I loved her with all my heart. It's a completely different dynamic. Our animals are entirely dependent on us, for everything." Composing herself, she added, "This is a difficult decision you'll have to make, but I know you'll make it with Molly's best interests in mind."

Rose nodded, not trusting herself to speak. When she was able to, all she could muster was a wobbly "Thank you."

Back in the car with dogs, Rose decided she couldn't face going to the shop and putting on a brave face. She'd done enough of that over the past few months. In the parking lot, she texted Cathy to ask if she could work the full day. No explanation.

When Cathy said yes, no questions asked, she headed for the condo.

Then Rose changed her mind. Turning the Subaru around, she drove in the direction of Blue Rocks. Years ago, Wendy had told her that Paul always went there when he needed to clear his head.

The small fishing village was a six-minute drive from town. Rose turned right at The Lane, then slowed to a crawl to navigate the narrow, winding, pot-holed pavement. She passed by several stately summer homes that now outnumbered the modest original dwellings.

Reaching the harbour, Rose pulled off the road and parked facing the ocean. Scanning the blue slate rocks at the water's edge, she leaned her head back, closed her eyes, and let her thoughts float. For a second. And then Molly whined softly, a signal that she needed to pee. Rose clipped on their leashes, put on her gloves, and flipped up the hood of her jacket to stop her hair from whipping in the wind. Together, the family of three walked along the road.

Rose glanced at a handful of small houses, a roped-off dock, a kayak business, and general store closed for the season. But her mind wasn't on her surroundings. At that moment, there was one person she wanted to talk to about Molly, and one person only. Someone who wouldn't spout empty platitudes, or tell her to keep calm and carry on. Someone who would know this particular heartbreak intimately.

After Rose returned to the condo and got the dogs settled, she texted May.

⸙

Although Paul continued to show slow, steady signs of improvement, the Hebbs skipped making a big Thanksgiving meal on Oxner Drive. No one had the interest or energy to go through the motions for tradition's sake. Besides, the cozy bungalow wasn't where they wanted to be. Instead, Wendy, Ellen, Fred, and Laura packed themselves tightly into Paul's hospital room to eat the turkey sandwiches one of Margot's daughters had delivered. There were sandwiches for Dr. Agbani and the nurses, too.

In Victoria, Fay's mother was recovering from her stroke. "Things are moving in the right direction," her health-care team kept saying. Fay was also having a makeshift Thanksgiving meal in her mother's semi-private room at the rehab centre. Ellen's hope was to spend Christmas with her parents, then return to Victoria before New Year's to prepare for the spring semester.

In a text, Rose had politely turned down Daisy's offer to spend Thanksgiving with the Turners. Instead, she had picked up a pizza from the Salt Shaker Deli and watched an episode of *The Great British Baking Show* (it was Italian week). Although Rose still wasn't following Allan or the Grand Banker on social media, she couldn't resist checking now and then to see if Daisy had continued to comment on his posts. She was relieved to see that she hadn't. Maybe the flowers *had* been a peace offering. She'd text her sister soon.

⁓

Less than an hour after Rose had messaged May about Molly, her cousin's pickup truck squealed into the condo's parking lot. After wrapping Rose in a bear hug, she sat with her legs stretched out on the floor and said to Molly, "C'mon, girlie, give cousin May a kiss."

Molly obeyed, followed closely by her brother.

"You don't look like a sick pup at all! No, you don't! No, you don't!" said May in a sing-song tone, shaking her head and tickling Molly's tummy. "But Mama tells me you are, so we're gonna love on you even more. Yes, we are! Yes, we are!"

For the first time since Laura had given her the news, Rose burst into tears.

"That's right, let it all out," said May, struggling to stand up so she could go sit next to Rose on the loveseat. Her cane was where she'd dropped it near the door. "You've had a shitty year, cousin. Cry those tears. Feel your pain. It's real. And it's gonna get worse before it gets better. This right here is the Heartbreak Hotel."

When Rose stopped sobbing, she wiped her face and blew her nose. "I feel like I just lost five pounds," she said.

"You *did* get rid of a lot of snot," said May, nodding in agreement.

Rose laughed. "No, I mean I feel lighter emotionally."

"Well, sure you do," said May, patting her cousin's shoulder. "I like to say you might as well laugh as cry, but a good cry is chicken soup for the soul, too. Been there, done that many times myself."

Rose decided it was now or never.

"So listen—and yes, I'm changing the subject—but I did some research on gout, and it sounds to me like you have something more serious."

May held up her palm. "Hold up there, missy. I know what you're going to say, and you can just calm the frig down."

"I *am* calm," said Rose quickly, before May completely cut her off. "But I think you may have Lyme disease."

May's jaw dropped. Her hand floated down to her leg. "Say what?"

"Lyme disease. You have so many symptoms that—"

"I don't have Lyme disease."

"Have you been tested? You're in the woods all the time rescuing creatures infested with goodness knows what, and the South Shore is crawling with ticks."

"Cousin, don't worry," said May confidently. "I don't have Lyme disease."

"Then what *do* you have? Because I know it isn't gout, and that you're keeping the truth from me. I've just told you that my dog is dying, so if you can't be honest with me about what's going on, then...then I think you should leave."

There. Rose crossed her arms, having said her piece. Molly and Relic whined softly, not liking the distressed tone of their human's voice.

May whistled. "Lady, that took a lot of balls. I respect you for it. Yes, I do. Sometimes I need to be put in my place. You're right. I'm a big fat liar. But I felt that you had enough pain to shoulder, and I didn't want to burden you with mine."

"Spit it *out*," said Rose impatiently. "What's wrong with you?"

"Ha! That's a loaded question." May shook her head. "How much time ya got?" she continued, ticking points off on her fingers. "For starters, I like animals more than people. Haven't had a romantic relationship in twenty-five years. Can't stand my own kin. You're the closest I've had to a sister in a long time. In fact, I'm gonna call you my sister-cousin from now on."

May drew a deep breath in, then let it out slowly. "A year ago, I was diagnosed with something I like to call May Surrenders. Not as in gives up, because that's not May's way. As in, I've made my peace with it. My neurologist prefers to call MS by its clinical name."

Rose blinked. Blindsided.

"Multiple sclerosis?" She held her cousin's gaze.

"Yup. Primary progressive. Nerve damage is the main problem. My legs are weak and stiff, so I have trouble walking and with balance. Fatigue and pain. Brain fog. Sometimes I think of a word but can't spit it out."

May paused as Rose tried to absorb the news, and the shock.

"Treatments don't work too well, but I go to Halifax every six months to get a shot of meds," she continued. "I won't have any relapses or remissions. It'll just keep getting gradually worse over time. So I've decided that when it's my bus stop, I'll get off. For now, I swim. I do physio. And I care for animals, 'cause that's what keeps me going."

"I'm so sorry, May. Why didn't you tell me? Does everyone know? Does Dad know?" Although Rose hadn't been in her cousin's life for long, she felt hurt just the same.

"My parents are dead and my sisters don't know, so I doubt Uncle John does," said May, shrugging. "Yeah, people around here know. I asked them to keep it on the down-low where you were concerned. You're dealing with enough. And...I didn't want your pity."

Rose frowned. "Why'd you think I'd pity you? Do you pity *me*?"

"Well, yeah, 'cause you're pathetic," said May, holding a hand with the thumb and index finger in an L-shape on her forehead. "Big frickin' loser. But in spite of that, I like you. And I love your dogs."

Rose couldn't help laughing. "May, you're one of a kind. Good thing, too. How about this—we'll both be straight up with each other from now on. Deal?"

May spat on her right palm and extended it toward Rose. "Deal."

"Gross," said Rose. "I'm not shaking that until you wipe it off."

May swept the offending palm across her shirt front, then stuck it out again.

Rose clasped her cousin's hand.

"Okay, what's next on today's therapy agenda?" said May, leaning back against the sofa cushion.

"Hmmm, let's see," said Rose, tapping her index finger against her lips. "I'm turning fifty-one in two weeks, and two weeks after that is Jim's one-year deathaversary. You?"

"Jesus, I can't beat that," said May. "I've just got a slow-moving disease that'll eventually kill me. You win, sister-cousin. Boo-hoo, you!"

"It isn't a competition," said Rose primly.

"Everything's a competition," said May, grinning. "But enough about us. Great news about Paul Hebb, eh?"

Rose's face lit up. "It sure is."

"He hasn't spoken yet, but he's responsive. Allan told me that everything is moving in the right direction, as the docs like to say."

"That's the best news I've heard in ages," said Rose, shoulders relaxing as she exhaled. "Thanks for letting me know." She hesitated, then asked, "How is Allan?"

"Besides having a big, fat, middle-aged man-crush on a certain sister-cousin of mine who won't give him the time of day, he's dandy," said May, winking. "Crying tears in his beers behind the bar every night, but don't let that upset your apple cart. That said...don't be a dummy, either."

"I don't know what you're talking about," said Rose, picking a dog hair off her jeans.

"Come *on*. A guy doesn't send a gal flowers if he doesn't have a crush on her, is all I'm saying. But that's enough heart-to-heart for one day."

Allan had sent the flowers? Rose hadn't considered that. But why hadn't he signed the card? Why keep it a secret? Unless he *did* have a crush, and he was shy.

Impossible, thought Rose. *Someone that good looking can't be shy. And how does May know he sent the flowers?*

Before Rose could pepper her cousin with questions, May

looked down at her buzzing phone. "Gotta jet. Deer in a ditch on Heckman's Island. Get my cane, will ya?"

"Oh sure, now that your secret's out, you want me to wait on you hand and foot?" asked Rose, heading toward where May had dropped the cane on the floor.

"That's right," said May sweetly. "My wish is your command. If you're nice to me, maybe I'll leave you something in my will."

"I'm a rich widow, so don't knock yourself out," said Rose dryly.

"No shit, really?" May's eyebrows shot up. Then she grinned. "Can you loan me twenty bucks? And do you wanna come with me?"

"No, and no," said Rose, shaking her head.

"You're a wet blanket," May complained, taking the cane from Rose's outstretched hand.

"So I've been told," said Rose, shrugging.

"Maybe you should have a nap so your left eyelid'll stop twitching," said May, making her way toward the door. "That right there is sure to drive a dude in the opposite direction."

"You're impossible," said Rose, laughing. Then, looking at Molly asleep on the couch, she grew serious. "Thanks for coming. I appreciate your support. I think it's safe to say I'm going to need more of it soon."

"You're welcome," said May, leaning on her cane. "That's what sister-cousins are for."

May bent down to pat the dogs, then hugged Rose and went on her way.

Twenty-Eight

SINCE ROSE'S BUILDING WAS FULL OF SENIORS, THERE hadn't been many trick or treaters at Halloween. Margot had dropped by with her youngest great-grandchildren, who had come to show off their costumes and get mini chocolate bars. Rose was relieved that her friend had been well enough to move back into her place in September, with home care in place a few days a week. A rotating cast of family members stopped by regularly to fill in the gaps.

After the ghosts and goblins were gone, Rose had made tea for Margot. Sitting on the loveseat, with a dog asleep on either side of her, she looked frail but happy.

"It must be wonderful to have such a big family," said Rose. She placed Margot's mug on a coaster on the coffee table before settling into the armchair.

"I'm very blessed," said Margot. "I'm so proud of them, and I know Eric is, too."

"Do you mind if I ask how Eric died?" Rose didn't want to upset her friend with painful memories.

"Not at all, dear," said Margot, taking a sip of tea. "He had a heart attack. No warning, very sudden. Quite the shock, I must say."

Margot chose not to mention that her husband's heart had stopped beating while they were making love. Married for sixty-one years at the time, Eric had never been shy about publicly proclaiming his passion for his longtime bride. And showing how much he loved her in private.

Strangely, in the ten years that Wendy and Rose had known each other, that explicit detail hadn't been revealed. There were some small-town secrets that were too sacred to share with outsiders. Even if they were close friends.

"That was a decade ago, yes?" asked Rose. She smiled when Margot absentmindedly moved a hand to rub Molly's head.

"That's right," said Margot, nodding. "We'd just watched the ten o'clock news. I took a moment alone with him before I called for an ambulance, but I knew he was gone. In some way, it feels like it was yesterday. But also, a lifetime ago. Jim died suddenly, too, didn't he?"

Rose's heart always skipped a beat when someone spoke her husband's name.

"Yes. He was hit by a van while he was biking to work," said Rose, holding back tears. "So I wasn't with him when he died. That will always weigh on me...that he was alone, and he might have been scared. Or have suffered. Although the medical examiner's report said he died on impact." Those words sounded so clinical.

"That's tragic, dear." Margot's look was pure sympathy. Not pity. "With you both so young, and so much of life left to look forward to. You know, there's a good grief-support group over at St. Norbert's. Going there helped me when I was newly bereaved. Jean Joudrey can be a pill sometimes, but her heart's in the right place."

Rose resisted the urge to sigh. "Mrs. Joudrey has dropped by the shop a couple of times to give me a pamphlet about the group," she said. "She's persistent, I'll give her that."

Margot looked at Molly fondly as she stroked her ears. "I hear you've got a sick pup here, even though you'd never know it to look at her."

Rose explained Molly's diagnosis, and that Laura had told her that when she stopped eating and drinking, it would be time.

They weren't there yet.

"That's the problem with loving someone, isn't it?" said Margot with a ghost of a smile. "If you have a heartbeat, you're bound to get your heart broken. Not just once, but over and over again—whether it's a spouse, a child, a friend, or a pet. But the joy that happens in between the meetings and the partings makes it all worthwhile."

"I'm *done* with romantic love," said Rose, finishing her tea. "I'm too old to date. Who'd be interested in a childless middle-aged widow, anyway?"

"Nonsense!" said Margot with vigour. "My friends Sally and Peter just got married, and they're in their eighties. They played bridge together when their spouses were alive, so they had a shared history."

"Well, I don't have a shared history with anyone who might be eligible, so that's out even if I *was* interested." Her mind turned briefly to Rob. But, no. He had served his purpose.

"Promise me you won't stop yourself from loving again because you're afraid of more heartbreak," said Margot. "You're too young, and your heart is too generous. If love presents itself, please try to be open to it. Life is sweeter shared."

"Were you open to loving again after Eric died?" Rose was curious.

"No, dear, but I was almost eighty, and we'd been married for sixty-one years. He was my one true love. I knew I wouldn't be too far behind him, although I can't believe I've made it to ninety. I still feel twenty up here." Margot tapped her temple.

"I'm turning fifty-one tomorrow," said Rose, who had kept quiet about it. Wendy knew but was respecting Rose's request to not make a fuss.

"Happy birthday, dear. What are you doing to celebrate?"

Rose snorted. "Nothing. I'm not in a celebratory mood. The first anniversary of Jim's death is in two weeks. He held a surprise party for my fiftieth, so at least I had that." She tried to not sound as full of self-pity as she felt.

"Well, my dear, I'm feeling tired, so I must be off home," said Margot. "Thanks for the tea and the talk. I'll be thinking about you tomorrow and wishing you well. You're a lovely girl, and a good neighbour."

At the door, the two women hugged. "Goodnight, Margot, sleep well," said Rose.

After letting the dogs out in the backyard for their final pee, Rose got ready for bed. The sooner tomorrow was behind her, the better. That morning, she had woken up from an unsettling dream—what she was calling "the dream of the displaced." In it, she had been staying with old friends in Toronto and was out for the evening, but she'd forgotten to write down their address and couldn't remember how to get back to their house. Rose had awoken feeling disoriented. Lost. Her mouth had been open as though she were crying in frustration, but no sound had come out.

Clearly, her mental waters were muddied. Almost a full year after Jim's death, she doubted she'd find her North Star again.

ငၹၥ

Besides Wendy and Margot, one other person in town knew about Rose's birthday. Wendy had respected her friend's right to ignore it, but since Rose hadn't specifically asked her to keep it a secret, she had mentioned it in passing. To Allan.

Wendy knew that Allan had been busy working on the plot of waterfront land he owned on Hermans Island Road. There, he'd spent the last two years building a tiny house. From scratch. By himself. It was his passion project, something he picked away at as time and money became available. He had no plans to move there permanently from his Tupper Street bungalow in town, but he had long dreamed about spending weekends and holidays at a quiet escape on the ocean.

The tiny house was almost done. It just needed a few finishing touches on the interior. But that wasn't what Allan was toiling on today.

Even though it was early November, and overnight temperatures had been cool, the ground had yet to freeze. That made it easier for Allan to push his spade into the earth, over and over, until he was standing before six deep, evenly spaced holes.

Wendy had mentioned that Rose didn't want to celebrate her birthday. Knowing how generous he was, she guessed he'd find a way to do something special for her. His crush was currently the worst-kept secret in town. Only Rose seemed oblivious.

Stopping to wipe the sweat from his face and sip from a Thermos of coffee, Allan surveyed his efforts with satisfaction. His gaze landed on the six black buckets lined up along the side of the tiny house, their contents destined for each hole. The backbreaking work wasn't done yet, but it would be soon.

Allan sighed. From the moment he'd laid eyes on Rose Ainsworth at the Banker, he had wanted to know her. Not because she was beautiful, although she was definitely that. Auburn hair, with a touch of silver. Hazel eyes that assessed and absorbed. She hadn't had much of an appetite, but that was probably grief. That first day, he'd watched her pick at her salad. She seemed so sad, but Allan could tell she had substance, and soul.

One day at the Banker, Deb, a career server in her fifties, had caught him watching Rose, who was lunching with Cathy.

"You lovelorn, boss?" asked Deb, pushing an empty tray toward him. "That's Rose from the sex shop, ain't it? Seems like a nice young gal."

"She's not that young, only a couple of years older than me," replied Allan, shrugging. "She's nice enough, I suppose. I don't think she's done grieving her husband. She knows what she's doing with the shop, that's for sure."

"Well, that's all you need to know to be her friend," said Deb, picking up the tray he'd filled with drinks. Then she winked. "Maybe give her a broad shoulder to cry on, eh?"

Allan shook his head. "Back to work, or I'll dock your pay for insubordination."

Deb snorted. "Ooh, the boss used a big word. I'm quakin' in my boots."

Allan didn't believe in love at first sight. That was for romantic comedies. At forty-eight, he had sown more than his share of wild oats. Often with women he'd hooked up with after they'd met at the Banker. For one night, or two. Nothing more.

Ten years ago, Allan and Ellen Hebb had seen each other exclusively for a few months following a summer when Ellen had waitressed at the Banker. After their chemistry had cooled, they'd known there was an expiry date on their relationship. Ellen had wanderlust and wanted to move away to start her career. No one was surprised when she accepted a job offer clear across the country. A long-distance relationship was never discussed. She and Allan had parted on good terms.

Now and then, some well-meaning person would try to set Allan up with a mutual friend. He'd go along with it. What was the harm? But nothing had stuck. In the new year, he was planning to foster another one of May's rescues. Maybe this time it'd be a foster failure, and he'd keep the mutt.

The rosebushes were Allan's way of expressing his budding feelings for Rose. The question keeping him awake at night was whether she might feel something for him.

Twenty-Nine

WHEN ROSE WOKE UP ON THE FIFTEENTH OF November, her phone buzzed with messages from friends, family, and former co-workers so often she had to turn it off. She had decided to go to work as if it was any other day. Even though she was fully aware that it wasn't.

Messages had overwhelmed her on her birthday, too. She hadn't turtled then, although it had been tempting. But responding to them had been draining.

It was the one-year anniversary of Jim's death. The dreaded deathaversary.

In the morning, Rose had greeted Jim as usual. There had been no sign that he'd heard her. She hadn't wept. If anything, she felt numb. The dawning of what she thought would be a monumental "first" milestone felt...empty.

Maybe it was because Rose had something else on her mind. Over the last week, Molly had been eating less, and drinking and peeing more. Subtle signs that her kidney disease was progressing. She'd make an appointment to have more blood work done.

Not yet, not yet, not yet became her mantra.

Later that day, for the first time since Jim's death, Rose lost her cool. In public. At work. When she blew up all over Mrs. Jean Joudrey from Blue Rocks.

Mid-afternoon, while Rose was congratulating herself on getting through the day without falling apart, the nosy old bat with her rain bonnet tied tightly under her double chin walked in, said hello, and set another bereavement brochure on the counter.

"I know what day it is, dear," said Mrs. Joudrey, her mouth pursed in sympathy. Tapping the brochure, she added, "I wanted to remind you that our group is here for you whenever you're ready."

It was precisely that second when Rose lost her shit.

"For the love of god, I DO NOT need you!" she shouted. "You OR your stupid sad-sack group! I am PERFECTLY FINE. I am HANDLING THINGS on my own, thank you very much. Now would you please stop bothering me and take your crummy brochures"—Rose grabbed the offending pamphlet from the counter and threw it on the floor—"AND LEAVE ME ALONE!"

Pausing to catch her breath, Rose fully expected Mrs. Joudrey to turn on her heel and scurry away, muttering madly. When she got home, she'd call every member of the Catholic Women's League to let them know how unspeakably rude *that Rose Ainsworth from Toronto* had been.

That would be the end of Mrs. Jean Joudrey from Blue Rocks.

Good riddance.

Praise the Lord.

Hallelujah.

Amen.

Fuck 'em if they can't take a joke, thought Rose, waiting for her nemesis's dramatic exit.

Mrs. Joudrey did not exit, dramatically or otherwise. She bent over. Picked up the brochure. Placed it back on the counter. And smiled.

"Atta girl, I knew you could do it! Bet that felt good. I thought I might have to come back one more time. That's anger, the second stage of grief. You've got three more to go. Then you'll be sleeping through the night, and that eye tic will disappear. See you soon, dear."

As Mrs. Joudrey's hand touched the door handle, she paused and turned around. "I almost forgot. Mabel asked me to pass along that her mocha cakes are legendary in Lunenburg County. And that she rolls hers in crushed cornflakes, not peanuts. No one wants their throat closing up, now do they? Although we do have EpiPens in the first aid kit."

When the door closed, Rose stood slack-jawed behind the counter. The wily old bird had been baiting her—and she'd done a fine job of it, too. Shaking her head, she picked up the brochure and looked at it. Instead of putting it in the recycling bin, she slipped into the storeroom and tucked it in her purse.

⌒∞⌒

The following week, Rose was back in the animal hospital's exam room, awaiting Molly's blood work results. Relic was lying on the floor gnawing happily on a dental stick. Although Molly held one between her paws, she hadn't touched it.

Laura Richardson entered the room with a grim look on her face. She sat on the floor next to Molly so she could kiss her head. "I'm sorry, Rose. It's time. Things are going to get unpleasant for our friend very quickly, and we don't want her to suffer."

Rose wiped her nose and cheeks with the back of her hand. "Does it have to be right now?"

Laura stood up. "No," she said gently. "But in a day or two. Would you like me to come to your place, or have it done here?"

Rose thought about where she wanted her beloved Molly to take her last breath.

Drummond Court. Their real home. With Jim holding her hand, and Molly's paw. But that wasn't an option.

"Here, I guess," said Rose, sniffling.

Then she thought about who else could be there to comfort her. "Is it okay if I ask my cousin May to come?"

Laura smiled. "That's a wonderful idea. She'll be a great support. Although she'll probably cry harder than both of us combined. When it comes to animals, she wears her heart on her sleeve."

In spite of her heartache, Rose couldn't help but smile. "She sure does."

⚮

Two days later, Rose and May sat on either side of Molly, who was lying on her favourite dog bed in the same exam room. Rose had removed her collar with her ID tags and tucked them in her purse.

Each time she was kissed and stroked, Molly thumped her tail weakly, but she didn't have the strength to lift her head. Knowing this was Rose's first time putting a pet to sleep, Laura softly talked her through each step. It was a miracle, but May kept quiet.

Seconds after Laura injected an overdose of anesthetic into one of Molly's front legs, she fell into a deep sleep, snoring ever so softly. The next needle would stop her heart within a couple of minutes.

Then it was over.

The three women wept and embraced. *It isn't easier with goodbye closure*, thought Rose, wiping her eyes and blowing her nose. Composing herself enough to thank Laura for her kindness. The animal hospital would call when Molly's ashes were ready to be picked up.

May, who had been here in this room for this reason many times before, ushered Rose out the back door so she wouldn't have to face strangers in the waiting room. Her cane tapped along the polished floor. They had come in Rose's car, but May had driven so Rose could sit in the back holding Molly.

May spoke first. "Busts up my heart every time."

"Doesn't it get easier, after you know what to expect?" asked Rose, unlocking the car doors remotely, realizing she'd have to go through it all over again with Relic.

"Nope," said May, putting her cane in the backseat and climbing carefully into the driver's seat. "Every loss is a fresh heartbreak."

"Losing them didn't occur to Jim or me when we adopted them," said Rose as she climbed in, casting a glance at the now empty backseat.

"Of course it didn't," said May knowingly, starting the engine. "If it did, no one would ever choose to love an animal."

"How can people keep getting more, knowing how it's going to end?" asked Rose. "I don't think I could. It's too painful."

"Sure, you could. Bringing another one home is healing. You aren't replacing the one who died, your heart just finds space for the new one. Some people bring a new pup or kitty home the next week because their house feels too empty without one. Other folks wait a year or more, until the next critter finds them."

"I'm worried that Relic will be lonely without his sister," said Rose, her voice wavering.

"He will be, and so will you," said May. "But you'll miss the little lady together. And you'll have each other. And me."

∽

The next week, when Rose opened her eyes each morning, after snuggling with Relic in bed, she said good morning to Jim. And to Molly.

On her bedside table sat two biodegradable urns. A big hot apple pie package, and a small one. Next to each was a framed photograph.

Over the past year, Rose had realized time and again how short and precious life was. How important it was to leave this world with as few regrets as possible.

It was time to make her peace with Daisy.

Reaching for her phone, she composed a short, heartfelt text, then pressed send.

Thirty

PAUL HEBB'S HEALTH-CARE TEAM AT FISHERMEN'S Memorial—speech therapist, physiotherapist, occupational therapist—was pleased with his progress. He was doing so well, in fact, that Dr. Agbani and his colleagues decided he didn't need to be moved an hour away to the rehab centre in Halifax. That pronouncement came as a huge relief to Paul's family. The closer he was to home, the easier it would be on everyone. Ellen was still planning to return to Victoria after Christmas, but would spend stretches of time at home the following summer while she was off.

When it was clear that Paul was well on the road to recovery, Wendy dropped by Fishnets & Fantasies to talk to Rose about her return to the shop. After hugging each other wordlessly, for a few seconds longer than they normally would, the two women spoke simultaneously.

"Wendy, I'm so…" Rose began.

"I've been wanting to…" said Wendy.

Laughing, the old friends went to sit in their usual spots on the sofa. As they had done for a decade.

"May I go first?" asked Rose.

"Sure," said Wendy, crossing her legs.

"Okay, well, first I want to say that I'm so, so sorry for snapping at you the last time we worked together." Taking a shaky breath, she continued, "You were just trying to help, and I didn't react very well. I hope you'll forgive me."

Wendy reached over to hold her friend's hand. "Apology accepted, but unnecessary. I can be a real pain in the ass sometimes. In hindsight, you handled the situation well. You didn't lose your cool, and you set a healthy boundary. That's good management. So now I'd like to apologize for overstepping my role."

"Apology accepted, but also unnecessary," said Rose, awash in relief. "I guess we should have anticipated that our working together wouldn't be all unicorns and rainbows."

Wendy smiled. "I guess we should have."

"Second," Rose continued, recalling the words she had rehearsed, "I can't even begin to explain how worried I've been about Paul, and you and Ellen. I wanted to reach out but didn't know how, or if you'd want to hear from me. I don't think I could have borne it if he hadn't...turned a corner."

If he hadn't lived is what almost slipped out.

"I thought about you a lot," said Wendy, releasing Rose's hand and settling back against the cushion. "And about you losing Jim, especially the way it happened, so suddenly. Without a chance to say a mindful goodbye. If Paul had died, I'd been given that gift of time and preparation. It really opened my eyes to your pain. And to what you must have been feeling when Molly died."

"Thank you," Rose almost whispered. "So, are we good?"

"We're good," said Wendy, standing up. "Shall I make tea?"

"Tea would be great," said Rose, feeling lighter.

In the months before Paul had been admitted to hospital, Rose had learned a lot from her mentor. They decided that while Wendy would no longer be a physical presence at Fishnets & Fantasies, she'd be available to answer questions as needed. Sonya knew almost as much about running the business as Wendy, and Cathy was happy to take on more shifts. As soon as Wendy was able to, she planned to resume her death doula certification.

"My biggest concern is that some customers will still want to deal with you when they come in," said Rose, frowning.

"Is that still happening?" asked Wendy. Rose noticed that the dark circles beneath her friend's eyes were fading.

"Less than it used to," Rose admitted. "But some people have it stuck in their heads that I'm from Toronto, which I'm sure doesn't make me popular. I keep telling them I was born and raised in Nova Scotia, but it doesn't seem to matter."

Wendy shrugged her shoulders. "Whether they think you're from Toronto or Wolfville, to them it just means you weren't born and raised on the South Shore. You could live in Lunenburg for the next thirty years and they'd still feel that way about you. It isn't personal. It's a generational thing. I don't think you'll lose those customers for long. And you'll gain new ones who don't care where you're from—and those, my friend, are the customers worth keeping anyway."

Just then, the door opened. Allan walked in carrying a beautiful bouquet of flowers. Wendy saw Rose blush before she got up to meet him at the counter.

"May told me about Molly," said Allan quietly. "I'm sorry for your loss. She was a great girl."

Allan placed the flowers on the counter, along with a card in an envelope and a Ziploc baggie. Then he removed his gloves and toque. "The flowers are for you, and the biscuits are for Relic. I made them this morning. There's peanut butter in them, so I hope he isn't allergic. You can freeze them and take them out a few at a time."

"You baked dog biscuits?" Rose lightly touched the bag of bone-shaped treats.

Allan smiled. "I make them every Christmas for Taylor Swift. Huge hit. She eats them all in one sitting. But she's a lot bigger than Relic."

"Thank you," said Rose, her eyes growing moist. "The flowers are stunning."

Allan noticed Wendy on the couch. "How's Paul?"

"Everything is moving in the right direction, as the doctors keep saying." She smiled. "It's hard to be patient, because we want him to come home, but he's doing really well."

"That's great news," said Allan. "Please give him my best, and tell him I'm thinking about him."

"Thanks, I will," said Wendy, looking at her watch. "I'm actually heading there now."

"Give him a hug for me," said Rose, while Wendy put on her coat.

"Will do," said Wendy. The women embraced.

Then Rose and Allan were alone.

"She's had a rough time of it," said Allan. He hesitated. "You both have."

"That's life, I guess," said Rose, shrugging. "No one gets a free pass from suffering."

"I wondered..." Allan's voice trailed off. Rose waited. Not wanting to prompt or interrupt.

Allan cleared his throat. "I wondered if you and Relic would like to go for a drive on your next day off. I've been working a piece of land on Hermans Island. Real pretty spot, right on the water. Thought you might like to see it before it's covered in snow."

Rose hesitated. It wasn't that she didn't want to go for a drive with Allan. It was that she was afraid to. She had feelings for him, but they were muddied up by grief. And it was dawning on her that he had feelings for her. Which was terrifying.

"Allan, I..." Rose faltered.

"It's okay," he said quickly. "Doesn't have to be now. We could go in the spring."

The truth was, Rose wasn't so sure she would still be here in the spring.

She glanced at the flowers, at the dog biscuits. If she couldn't take a chance on Allan, could she ever take a chance on anyone again?

"No, I...*would* like to go. Could we do it on the weekend? I'm off on Sunday."

Allan beamed. "Sunday's good, as long as the weather co-operates. How about I pick you both up just after lunch? Would that work?"

"That would work," agreed Rose.

Although she and Daisy were communicating again, this was something she planned to keep to herself.

Thirty-One

THAT SATURDAY NIGHT, ROSE HAD AN ACTUAL DATE
lined up. She hadn't told anyone about it. Not even her family
or friends. In case there wasn't a second one. With Christmas
fast approaching, she hoped it would be a healthy distraction
from another bleak holiday.

Rose's date was with Margot. And a roomful of strangers.
The older woman had agreed to attend a bereavement support
group meeting with her. Rose drove the two of them to the
church hall for seven o'clock. Relic was in the backseat. His
human hoped the meeting would be helpful for him, too.

On the short drive to York Street, Margot briefed Rose on
who would be there. She had checked in with Mrs. Joudrey, the
group's facilitator. Members came and went, depending on their
needs and their schedules. Tonight's group would be small. Rose
listened closely as Margot described them:

*Jean Joudrey, seventy-four; husband Tommy died
fourteen years ago.*
*Mabel Knickle, eighty-one; husband John died of colon
cancer last year.*
*Lorne Pictou, seventy-three; wife Gwen died of ovarian
cancer eleven years ago.*
*Sam Purcell, thirty-six; daughter Jamie, age four, died
six months ago after choking on a grape.*

"Oh, gosh, the poor guy," said Rose. Her heart ached for him.

"Yes, it was a tragic accident, and neither parent is to blame," said Margot. "Sam's father is the firefighter who carried Paul out of the church, you know."

Rose hadn't known. She remembered Larry Purcell from his visit to the shop. When she'd met him, his granddaughter had been alive.

Sam is so young, the same age I was when I was trying to decide if I wanted to have a baby, thought Rose. *He didn't get goodbye closure, either. And I bet he feels incredibly guilty. At least I wasn't driving the van that hit Jim. I suppose I should be grateful for that.*

Rose pulled into an accessible spot in the parking lot near the door. When Eric died, Margot had given up their car. Because he had done all of the driving, she had lost her confidence for it, even though she'd always renewed her licence "just in case." She handed Rose the permit for the window that she used when her children or grandchildren took her to appointments. Walking long distances tired her, but she wasn't keen on a walker. Not yet.

"It's terribly sad," Margot continued. "A parent isn't supposed to bury their child. It isn't the natural order of things. Lorne is married to Mary Lohnes, our former mayor, and Sam's wife, Beth, is Mary's niece. Mary thought it would be good for Sam if Lorne came to the meetings with him."

"Does Beth come, too?" asked Rose.

"No, dear, she sees a grief counsellor," said Margot matter-of-factly. "And it's better for Sam to not have to be careful about what he says. Otherwise, he'd worry he might say something that would be hurtful for Beth. They're grieving together, of course, but they need to mourn separately, too."

As Rose unhooked her seat belt, something struck her as odd. Turning to look at Margot, she asked, "If Mrs. Joudrey's husband cheated on her, why would she start a bereavement support group?"

Margot paused. Never one to give in to gossip, she chose her words carefully. "Well, they were very young at the time, with three toddlers. Back then, Tommy was a bit too fond of the drink. It only happened the once, and he begged Jean's forgiveness, which she gave him. For the next forty years, he was devoted to her, until the day he died."

Rose shook her head. "How can she bear to live in the same place as her sister-in law? I get the sense that there's no love lost between those two."

Shrugging her slight shoulders, Margot smiled with the wisdom of a woman who has witnessed a great deal of life. "They've found their way. It's what you have to do in a small community, if you don't want your anger to eat you alive. Are the Jean Joudreys friends? No. But they've learned to tolerate each other."

Before Rose got out to clip on Relic's leash and tuck his bed under her arm, she looked at the white clapboard church with black trim. All of the churches in town were the same colour scheme, which Rose found confusing, given that they were different denominations. She had always wondered if there was a bylaw around that. Or if there had been a door-crasher deal on black and white paint at the hardware store.

With Relic in hand, Rose went around to Margot's door to help her out. She took the older woman's arm, and the three slowly made their way into the hall.

Inside, Rose easily identified the members based on Margot's description.

Except for one person she hadn't expected to see there, of all places.

In a long, flowing, multicoloured caftan, with her trademark jangly bracelets, Mrs. Jean Joudrey from Italy Cross sat next to Sam, sipping coffee, chatting, and sharing a plate of sweets.

"What's *she* doing here?" whispered Rose. "She isn't a widow."

Margot whispered back. "Well, she likes to say that her husband is dead to her. Divorce is *like* a death. The loss of a relationship in that way follows a similar pattern of grief." The older woman chuckled. "Also, she's social...that one would attend the opening of an envelope! And, she loves to irritate Jean. But Jean overlooks that because Jeannie's a crackerjack bridge player."

"Bridge?" said Rose, confused. Before she could probe further, Mrs. Joudrey from Blue Rocks—who for once was *not* wearing her rain bonnet—spotted them.

"Rose and Margot, hello! Everyone, this is Rose Ainsworth, first cousin of May Ainsworth." Rose felt herself blushing at the attention as polite smiles and greetings were offered from the group. "As most of you are aware, she took over Wendy Hebb's lovely little shop on Pelham Street. Everyone knows Margot, of course. Good to see you out and about, dear, and with a bit of colour in your cheeks. You gave us quite the scare in the summer. Cup of tea for the both of you? Rose, you really *must* try one of Mabel's mocha cakes, she made them especially for you."

Mabel, who was wearing what would be a strong contender in an ugly Christmas sweater contest, beamed.

When Rose was growing up, both of her grandmothers had made mocha cakes at Christmas. Like Mabel, they had rolled the small, cubed pieces of white pound cake with vanilla frosting on all sides in crushed cornflakes. As Rose got older, the bite-sized cakes showed up at the funeral receptions of elderly relatives, but the once-popular desserts were dying out with that generation. They were too weird for modern times, and too time-consuming to make. Yet Rose still found the contrast of their crunchy exterior and soft centre oddly appealing. And, for a moment, they took her back to her happy childhood.

Mrs. Joudrey made quick work of introducing the other members. Rose dropped Relic's leash and he happily made the rounds, greeting each person with tail wags. *He would have made a great pet therapy dog*, she thought. *Jim would be proud.*

"Rose, as our newest member, would you like to say something before we get started?" asked Mrs. Joudrey.

Sweat broke out on Rose's palms. As if on command, her left eyelid started twitching when everyone turned toward her. Clearing her throat, she said, "I'd like to introduce Relic, actually. His sister, Molly, died last week of kidney failure. We both miss her terribly."

The room erupted in sympathetic sounds.

"My darling cat, Moses, passed over the rainbow bridge in September, and I've been lost without him," said Mabel, wiping away a tear. "He was with me for twenty years. Your cousin May has been after me to foster a senior cat. I told her I'd pray on it over the holidays and get back to her with my decision in January."

Relic settled next to Sam, so Rose moved his bed there. It was as though the old boy could sense who needed him most.

Rose hesitated, wondering how much to reveal. They probably all knew, anyway.

"Relic and I also miss my husband, Jim. He died one year ago last month."

"I'm in my first year, too," said Sam softly, leaning over to rub Relic's head. "I'm finding the 'firsts' unbearable."

Rose didn't trust herself to speak without tearing up, so she just looked at him and nodded. All she wanted to do was wrap her arms around the shattered young man.

Maybe next time. Or maybe this wasn't a touchy-feely sort of group.

If there is a next time, thought Rose. Then she found herself speaking up.

"You expect the major milestones to hurt, but no one warns you how hard the small 'firsts' will be." Rose faltered, until Margot's hand gently covered hers. "The first time I had to take the car in to swap out the snow tires. Shovel the driveway. File my taxes. Jim took care of all of that. And when he did, he was taking care of me."

Mabel clucked like a mother hen soothing her chicks. "When John died, I was beside myself with bad nerves. Stayed in my housecoat and slippers for a month. Had the Foodland deliver my groceries, even though I could barely eat. Couldn't face church. Then Jean came over and had a little talk with me. I've been coming here ever since, and catering funeral receptions with the CWL. Being with people has done me a world of good, it surely has."

Jean, who was pretending to pick nonexistent lint off her spotless cardigan, looked pleased.

"It gets easier over time," said Lorne, shifting position on the wooden chair and crossing his long legs. Having grown up in the Acadia First Nation community in nearby Gold River, he had visited an Elder there after his wife died, to help process his loss.

"You never completely move on from grief, even though that's what people expect you to do," he added quietly. "It's more about moving forward. But the journey isn't linear. You'll take one step forward, then two steps back. Eventually, you discover a different relationship with your loved one based on precious memories, photos, and meaningful objects. I like to believe I'll see Gwen on the other side of the mountain. In the next life, wherever our spirits take us."

"That's a lovely sentiment, Lorne. I think we all hope for that, whatever our religious or spiritual beliefs," said Mrs. Jean Joudrey. Glancing at her watch, she saw it was time to get down to business. "Now, we only have an hour and a half, so Mabel can get home in time to watch *The Real Housewives of New Jersey*. Let's not waste it."

"I'm addicted," admitted Mabel guiltily, as though she was in the confessional. "Those gals are a trainwreck, and I just can't look away."

Mrs. Joudrey clapped her hands and pointed to a small table surrounded by four chairs. "Sam, Jeannie, Mabel, and Lorne, you're up. Margot, are you okay to sit this one out? I want to teach Rose how to play bridge. Sam caught on very quickly, and we always need a couple of spares."

"Not at all," said Margot. "I'm a little rusty myself."

"Nonsense, you're a shark. But thank you. I'll top up your tea."

Before whisking away Margot's empty mug, Mrs. Joudrey fished around in her voluminous purse, pulled out a pack of cards, and handed them to Mabel. The octogenarian in the Christmas sweater started shuffling the deck with the dexterity of a blackjack dealer at The Mirage.

Rose moved closer to Margot and said, "I'm confused. Is this a grief support group or a bridge club?"

Margot leaned toward her until their shoulders touched. "Bit of both, dear. We usually play cards when a new member shows up. It's an icebreaker. A full game takes three hours, so we won't finish. But that isn't the point."

"What *is* the point?" asked Rose, curious. This meeting wasn't at all what she had been expecting.

What *had* she been expecting?

Sad stories.

Tears.

Self-pity.

Platitudes.

Tepid tea.

Useless advice.

"The point is to get people out of the house and focusing on something else for an hour or so," said Margot. "This is most important for the newly bereaved, because we're all a bit blue at that stage. Doctors nowadays would call it depressed. I daresay I was pretty low right after Eric died. My children and grandkids couldn't fill the hole in my heart that was reserved just for him. Jean judges the mood of the members and decides who needs what on any given night. She's very good at it, actually. She managed to turn her grief into being of service to others."

Rose glanced at the bustling older woman wearing faux-fur-lined winter boots and a sensible skirt who was refilling their mugs. She was starting to see Mrs. Jean Joudrey from Blue Rocks in an entirely new light.

Soon, Relic was snoring softly beside Sam. Rose's heart softened each time the young man reached down to rub the old dog's head.

While Mabel deftly dealt thirteen cards to each player, Mrs. Joudrey explained the basics of bridge whist to Rose. Nibbling on a mocha cake and sipping hot, strong tea, the newest member of the St. Norbert's Bereavement Support Group began to relax.

"Your mocha cakes are delicious, Mabel," said Rose, finishing her third. "Thank you."

Mabel blushed fiercely. "Oh my, dear, that's very kind of you," she said, putting a hand over her heart as though to calm its fluttering. "I'm not one to boast, but they *are* quite popular in these parts. They're always the first to go at funeral receptions. I can barely keep up with the demand."

Until now, Jeannie had been quiet. Examining the cards she'd been dealt, she asked, "Did anyone hear about the excitement at the nursing home last night?"

When the group murmured no, Jean continued. "Apparently, Noreen Corkum got a get-out-of-jail day pass to visit her son in Blockhouse yesterday afternoon. She spotted a pan of brownies on the counter and packed a few to take back to share with her cellmates." Rearranging her cards, Jeannie threw her head back and howled. "Turns out happy hour was anything but! They were pot brownies. The residents who ate them thought they were having heart attacks. The staff called 911, and the paramedics came and eventually figured it out. Noreen's son had mixed half a pound of THC butter into the batter."

"What's THC?" asked Mabel, cocking her head. "Is it the TV channel? Or the girl band from the nineties?"

Jeannie was laughing so hard she couldn't correct her. Tears streamed down her cheeks. Then everyone was giggling, picturing walkers bumping into doorframes and cross-eyed seniors spotting Bing Crosby sitting on Santa's lap singing the Hawaiian Christmas Song.

When the mirth subsided, Lorne asked, "Are the residents okay now?"

"Oh sure, they're fine, although it's probably the first time some of them have ever been stoned," said Jeannie, dabbing her face with a tissue. "I can just imagine the paramedics reviewing their symptoms—confusion, memory problems, anxiety, paranoia, hallucinations. Half the residents have dementia, so you'd have to be a real detective. Guess the chocolate crumbs in the corners of their mouths gave it away."

"All right, that's enough chin-wagging," said Mrs. Joudrey, seating herself next to Rose. "And please, remember the golden rule."

"What's the golden rule?" asked Rose.

Mrs. Joudrey turned to face her newest recruit: "We can't change the cards we're dealt, just how we play the game."

Thirty-Two

WHEN ROSE GOT HOME FROM ST. NORBERT'S, SHE tuned in to *The Real Housewives of New Jersey*, imagining viewing it through Mabel's eyes. The celebrities' outrageous antics could be a source of small talk at the next meeting. *If she went back.*

As she put on her pajamas, she looked at the bottle of sleeping pills on her bedside table. Feeling as though a couple of ounces of weight had been lifted from her shoulders, she decided to take a half dose. Crawling into bed with Relic, she said to him, "Bridge isn't so bad, eh?" He thumped his tail on the bedspread in agreement.

When Rose next opened her eyes, the alarm clock said six. For the first time in more than a year, she had slept a solid seven hours.

Her left eyelid? Still.

Turning onto her back, Rose yawned and stretched. Snuggled up next to her, Relic did the same, pushing his front paws into her ribs.

"Good morning, Jim and Molly," said Rose, turning to look at their urns and photos. Relic thumped his tail at the familiar words.

It was Sunday. Rose's day off from the shop. Cathy had it covered.

Then it dawned on her. This afternoon, Allan was taking her for a drive.

Rose reached for her phone and started composing a text.

To the one person she knew who had only recently left the dating pool.

Hey, how's the old married lady? Still in the honeymoon phase, I'm sure. Quick Q: A handsome single man asked to take me for a drive this afternoon. I said yes. Relic is coming with us. Is it a date?

Rose wasted time online while waiting for Yuki's reply. Five minutes later, a buzz heralded its arrival.

Do you feel like barfing?

Rose smiled and typed one short word.

Yup.

Yuki's response came in seconds.

The answer is DUH. Yes, it's a date. Try to enjoy it. Don't smoke too much dope before it HAHAHA ya big square. And let me know how it goes xxoo

Rose smiled and sent her a thumbs up. Then she turned to a recent text from Daisy.

We love and miss you and Relic. All of us, Mom and Dad too. Please come for Christmas xo

Rose looked at Relic. "Would you like to go to Aunt Daisy's for Christmas?" At the sound of the familiar name, Relic's tail beat harder than a Phil Collins drum solo. She typed a short reply.

Thanks. We miss you too. We'll be there xx

After Rose had texted an apology for ghosting Daisy, her big sister had called with her own apology. And to confess that her menopausal mood swings had been causing her to act like a jealous teenager. For Rose, their conversation had been an eye-opener.

"Remember when I told you I was pregnant with Lulu?" said Daisy.

"Of course. I recall sobbing hysterically."

"Do you remember what I said?" prompted Daisy.

"No, that was thirteen years ago," said Rose. "I don't have to tell *you* that the over-fifty memory isn't reliable."

"I remember every word like it was yesterday, because I remember how I felt," said Daisy, her voice dropping to almost a whisper. "You were happy for me, but feeling sad for yourself because I was pregnant with my fourth child. Back then, you were struggling to decide whether you wanted children at all. You weren't sure, and Jim wasn't ready. I told you that you had the one thing I didn't that I often craved."

Rose had perked up then, as she did now. "Which was?"

"Freedom," said Daisy simply. "You weren't accountable to anyone but Jim, and he was an adult who could look after himself. I couldn't make a single decision for myself without considering how it would affect my children."

"Is there a point? What does this have to do with you crushing on Allan online?" asked Rose, sitting up straighter in the armchair.

Daisy sighed. "Not my proudest moment."

"Agreed," said Rose. She didn't want to make this *too* easy.

"And yes, there is a point, and I'm getting to it. I know this is going to sound strange, because I'm fully aware that your husband died and you miss him terribly," said Daisy, shifting to get more comfortable on her sofa. "But you've also got that freedom back. To look ahead to your future and design it in whatever way suits you best. I'm fifty-two. I've been married for three decades. I'm not an empty nester yet, and I won't be for years. I haven't felt truly free since before I met Steve."

"My kind of freedom is massively overrated," said Rose, her voice brittle. "I don't have a husband or kids. Who's going to visit me in the nursing home? Or put me in one? You don't know how lucky you are."

"Steve keeps saying he's going to die first, and our kids could end up scattered across the country, or around the world," Daisy pointed out. "Or—and I hate to say this, but you never know—I might outlive one of them. There are no guarantees I'll be taken care of in my old age just because my family is underfoot now."

"Your odds are better than mine," said Rose wearily.

"How about we agree to look after each other when the time comes?" asked Daisy gently.

Rose cut off their conversation by asking, "Do you still love Steve?" Although if her sister was considering divorce, she didn't really want to know. Rose loved Steve like a brother.

Daisy sighed. "Yes. But in my menopausal mania, I've been craving your freedom. And I decided to act on it in the safest way I could think of. On social media, with a handsome new man we had met together. Which was stupid, hurtful to you, and disrespectful to Steve. I get that now." She paused. "I'm sorry. And embarrassed."

Rose sighed. If her half-century on Earth had taught her anything, it was that life was a complex seesaw of delight and despair. Mountains and valleys. Mistakes and atonements.

"Apology accepted," said Rose. She'd never been able to hold a grudge after a heartfelt apology. Not even with Jim. She just wasn't wired that way.

"Do you *like* Allan?" asked Daisy tentatively.

"I don't really know how to answer that," said Rose

truthfully. "I mean, yes, I like him, superficially. But I don't really know him. He seems sweet, and everyone thinks highly of him. But am I ready for a serious relationship? No. Am I ready to go for a drive or for dinner with a new male friend? Yes. Or at least, I think so."

Rose didn't mention how physically attracted she was to him.

"Then you should go," said Daisy quickly. "I just want you to be happy."

Rose hesitated. "I'm worried that my future happiness with a new partner will be an insult to Jim's memory, and somehow diminish our love. I read something recently, can't remember where. But it went something like *I kept telling his memory to piss the fuck off, but it wouldn't. Grief is a bastard.* That sums up how I feel. Except I don't want to forget Jim."

"Oh, Rose," said Daisy, wishing her sister was within reach, so she could hug her. "Jim wouldn't want you to be lonely for the rest of your life. I'd like to think that your future happiness with someone new would honour your love for him."

Rose was silent. She wasn't sure she was ready for this conversation. "I'd like to think that, too," she said, "but I'm not sure that's how it works. Could we change the subject?"

"You got it, sis. How's our kooky cousin?"

Rose bristled, but she couldn't scold. Only a few months ago, she'd thought the same thing about May. "She isn't kooky, she's compassionate. She's been a great support to Relic and me. And...she has MS. I'm her only family, Daisy. Her folks are dead, and she doesn't speak to her sisters."

"Oh, no, I'm so sorry to hear that. Everyone is struggling with something, aren't they?"

"That's what I'm finding out," said Rose.

"Hold on—do you think she'd come for Christmas dinner?"

Rose chuckled. "You never know with May. I'll ask her."

᧙ᨌᨉ

Rose didn't overthink what to wear on the drive with Allan, who had warned her the ground might be muddy. It was relatively mild for mid-December, so she chose a black turtleneck, jeans, and hiking boots. Her outerwear consisted of a short down-filled coat, a wool toque, and mittens.

When Allan texted from the parking lot, Rose and Relic were ready. Rose buzzed him in, and the trio met in the lobby. Allan's curls were covered by a green toque.

Without thinking, Rose said, "That hat makes your eyes pop." Then she blushed.

"Thanks," said Allan, laughing. "My sister keeps buying me green hats and shirts, hoping the ladies will be dazzled by my irises. Shall I tell her it's working?"

Rose smiled. "You can tell her she has good taste."

Allan reached for Relic's leash, leading him and Rose to a silver SUV.

"Nice wheels," said Rose. "Are you sure you want dog hair on everything?"

"No offense to my buddy here, but in terms of fur, he's got nothing on Taylor Swift," Allan said, opening Rose's door.

"No offense taken," said Rose. "Goldens are notorious for shedding."

Allan walked around back with Relic, lifted the hatchback, picked the old dog up easily, and set him on a blanket. A car barrier would help keep him safely in place.

"Christmas carols or Blue Rodeo?" asked Allan, starting the engine. "And how do you feel about a heated seat?"

"Blue Rodeo, please, and I'm a big fan of hot backsides."
Jesus, did I just say that out loud?

Allan laughed. "So am I."

Are we flirting? She couldn't be sure. Rose hadn't teased a handsome single man in more than twenty years. She'd text Yuki later.

Glancing over her shoulder to check that Relic was settled, Rose leaned into her seat and let Jim Cuddy serenade her. The silence between her and Allan felt surprisingly comfortable. The heat at her back was relaxing, as was Allan's humming. If they were dating, she'd have put her hand on his thigh.

Rose stopped herself from putting her hand on his thigh.

Ten minutes later, Allan pulled into a rough, unpaved driveway on Hermans Island Road.

Rose turned to look at him. "You aren't planning to chop me up into little pieces and bury me in the woods, are you?"

Allan laughed and shook his head. "Nah, the ground is too hard at this time of year. I'd have to dump you in the ocean."

Rose laughed, touching the cellphone in her coat pocket. Fully charged. Just in case...

After Allan parked, he got out, walked around to Rose's door to open it, then retrieved Relic.

Rose was keenly aware that he was being a gentleman.

"The best view is just a short walk around that stand of spruce trees," said Allan, leading the way. Relic trotted happily next to him, while Rose followed behind.

"Mind your step here, it's a bit rootbound," said Allan, turning around and holding out a hand.

Even through thick mittens and gloves, his touch fanned a flame within Rose. If it hadn't been so cold, she might have thrown him on the ground and had her way with him.

"Here we are," said Allan, dropping her hand to point out the vista.

Before them lay a beautiful sandy beach, leading to water as far as the eye could see. The ocean was flanked by a mix of evergreen and deciduous trees.

"It's an oasis. You're so lucky," said Rose, walking toward the water. Then she looked left. "Oh my god, is that what I think it is?"

"Yeah," said Allan, beaming. "I've been working on it for a couple of years."

Before them stood a tiny house on wheels. It boasted cedar shingles, several small windows, a copper metal roof with a chimney pipe, and a wood-panelled door. A set of four wooden steps led to the entrance.

Rose looked at him in awe. "You're building it yourself?"

Allan's cheeks turned pink, and not just from the cold. "Yup. It's almost done. Want to see inside?"

Rose nodded.

"Come on, old boy," said Allan to Relic. He handed the leash to Rose so he could take off his gloves and dig the key out of his coat pocket.

Because the space was compact, the tour didn't take long. It was the coziest place Rose had ever been. Everything was miniature. Sink, counter, and two-burner stove. Composting toilet and shower. Sofa that turned into a bed over a table. Cupboards and shelves. Wood stove. No space was wasted.

Closing her eyes, Rose indulged in a daydream of the three of them spending a weekend here. Quickly opening them, she peered out a window, taking in the expanse of forest and sea. "I'm so impressed you did all of this yourself," she said. "I can barely hang a picture frame."

"I'm sure you have other skills," said Allan. Rose blushed; Allan did too. "Let's, uh, go back outside," he said, heading for the door. "There's something else I want to show you."

Walking around to the other end of the house, Allan pointed to six small plants spaced a few feet apart. It was clear they'd been put in the ground recently.

"What are they?" asked Rose.

231

"Rosebushes," Allan said with a nervous crack in his voice. He cleared his throat. "They're called *Braveheart*. They'll be a deep royal red, with double blooms."

In that moment, surrounded by nature and a kindhearted friend, a speck of Rose's sorrow floated away like dandelion fluff on the breeze.

"Allan…" Rose stopped, wanting to choose her words carefully.

"It's okay." Allan spoke quickly, facing Rose and taking her hand. "You don't have to say anything. I just wanted to share this with you. Maybe we could have a picnic here sometime… if you want to."

Rose squeezed his hand. "I'd like that. Thank you."

"You're welcome." Allan looked at the bushes. "I'm not much of a gardener, so I don't know if they'll make it through the winter."

"I'll help take care of them," said Rose. Voice wavering, she added, "Maybe we could bury Molly next to one of them. I can't think of a prettier spot."

Allan put his arms around Rose and pulled her close. Leaning into his chest, she wrapped her arms around his waist. They stood silently for a minute. Until Relic pushed his head against their legs, reminding them that he needed attention, too.

Allan released Rose, crouched down, and scratched behind the old dog's ears. "You're a good boy, old fella." Relic licked Allan's chilled cheek.

Watching them together, Rose wiped her eyes. "Daisy's going to lose her mind."

Allan looked surprised. "Why?"

"She thinks you're—and I quote—*a tall drink of water*."

Allan laughed. "And what do you think?"

Rose hesitated, but only for a second. "I think she's right." Only then did she lightly brush his cheek with her lips.

Thirty-Three

THE THIRD WEEK OF DECEMBER, THE FIRST significant snowfall of the season blanketed Lunenburg County with fluffy white powder. The afternoon of that first snowfall, Paul Hebb was discharged from Fishermen's Memorial Hospital. He sat dressed on the side of the bed, duffel bag by his side. Although he could now walk short distances unsupported, he tired easily. Thirty pounds had fallen away from his normally fit frame.

Ellen had gone to find a wheelchair.

Wendy couldn't stop smiling.

Dr. Agbani shook Paul's hand. "Mr. Hebb, you have been a model patient, and while I am sorry to see you go, I am also *not* sorry to see you go," he said, grinning. "I trust that you will continue to work hard in your outpatient rehabilitation. You must remember to be patient. Your recovery will be a marathon, not a sprint."

Paul grasped the kind doctor's hand with both of his before releasing it.

"Thank you," he said. "For everything."

Wendy hugged the doctor as Ellen returned with the wheelchair. Then the Hebbs headed home. To a driveway plowed of snow by a fellow firefighter. Path and front steps shovelled by Fred, who was dropping by later with Laura. And a fridge and freezer filled by neighbours and friends.

The Hebbs were home. And their Oxner Drive bungalow was bursting with gratitude and love.

As Wendy unlocked the door, Paul looked at the stained-glass *Welcome to Our Happy Home* sign hanging inside its window. A tidal wave of memory washed over him. Recalling the fight they'd had over a decade ago, about Wendy opening the sex shop. Slamming the door as she'd rushed from the house in anger, the sign had fallen to the floor, smashing into pieces. In secret, Paul had painstakingly glued it back together. Waiting for the right moment to put it back in its proper place.

Later that evening, Paul sat in his favourite recliner. A quilt kept his thin legs warm. Across from him on the couch, Ellen looked up from the text she was composing to Fay.

"Dad, did you hear Mom and me talking to you while you were...asleep?" She couldn't seem to bring herself to say *in a coma*.

Paul looked unsure. "I don't know. I do have a fuzzy memory of dreaming that I met John Gorka at the bandstand."

Putting down her phone, Ellen went to wrap her arms around her father and kiss his cheek.

∽

With only one week of shopping left before Christmas, business at Fishnets & Fantasies was brisk. Throughout the day, the door opened and closed constantly with customers coming and going. Cathy, Sonya, and Rose were run off their feet. But it had been a while since someone had asked for Wendy specifically. And Rose had started to recognize her regular customers, and even had a few favourites.

With the holidays fast approaching, no one could have been more surprised than Rose when Mrs. Jean Joudrey from Blue Rocks walked into the shop one morning.

Without her rain bonnet.

Wearing soft-pink lipstick. A spot of rouge on each cheek.

With retired postal worker Stanley Shupe following close behind her.

"Good morning, Mrs. Joudrey," said Rose, trying her best to sound normal.

"It is a fine morning, my dear," said Mrs. Joudrey. "Will we see you at St. Norbert's this Saturday?"

"I wouldn't miss a chance to take everyone's hard-earned cash away from them," said Rose, winking. Turned out she was a crackerjack bridge player. And she had decided that the group's members were her tribe.

"Now, dear, you know that bridge is an excellent activity to stave off dementia," said the older woman, pursing her lips. "And there's no gambling in the Catholic Church."

"What about bingo?" Rose couldn't help tease.

"That isn't gambling, that's fundraising," said Mrs. Joudrey piously. "Now, Mr. Shupe and I are here to get more of that warming gel. Our arthritis is awful bad in the winter."

"Awful bad," Stanley parroted, while turning up his hearing aid.

As the two women chatted, the elderly man looked perplexed as he picked up a penis-shaped candle. "G-golly," Rose overheard him whisper.

Mrs. Joudrey leaned closer to Rose. A whiff of what smelled like her late grandmother's Avon perfume nearly caused her to choke.

"I think *he* thinks it's a date," Mrs. Joudrey whispered confidentially.

Rose's eyebrows arched. "Is it?"

Mrs. Joudrey provocatively patted her tightly coiffed curls. "I think it might be."

Rose's feet were killing her. She was looking forward to closing the shop at noon on Christmas Eve and giving herself a few days of rest. Wendy had told her that in the days following the holidays, business was typically quiet: customers would be playing with their new products at home. In early January, however, those who had received gift cards would start dropping by to redeem them.

With five minutes to closing the day before Christmas Eve, Allan slipped into the shop. Relic greeted him like a long-lost friend.

"Some last-minute shopping?" asked Rose, wondering who was on his list.

Since their drive to Hermans Island, Allan had taken Rose to some of his favourite spots on the South Shore. Gaff Point. Hirtle's Beach. A section of the Bay to Bay Trail.

Never unchaperoned: Relic was always with them.

Although they hugged hello and goodbye, Rose hadn't kissed him again. Not even another chaste peck on the cheek.

"Ha, no, all done," said Allan. "I actually need you to come with me when you're finished here. Just for twenty minutes or so."

Rose raised her eyebrows. "What for? Can Relic come, too?"

"It's a surprise—and of course. I'll put him in the car now, and we'll wait for you there. I'm parked out front." As Rose passed the leash to Allan, he said to Relic, "Ready, buddy?"

Relic didn't need to be told twice. He liked this human.

While Rose locked the shop, Allan was waiting to open her door, closing it after she had buckled her seat belt. As he started the engine, she said, "Is there any point in asking where we're going?"

"Nope, but we'll be there in the blink of an eye," said Allan, turning on the radio to Band Aid singing "Do They Know It's Christmas?" Humming along. In harmony.

"I love this song," said Rose. "You have a nice voice."

Allan glanced at her. "Thanks. I sang baritone in my church's youth choir."

Rose giggled. "You did not!"

"Did too. You can ask my mother."

Is he hinting that he wants me to meet his mother?

A few minutes later, Allan pulled into the driveway of a modest two-storey farmhouse on Masons Beach Road, not far from the golf course.

"Let's go, troops," said Allan. By now, Rose knew to wait for him to open her door. That had taken some getting used to, but she'd discovered that she liked it.

Jim hadn't done that for her.

Rose tried her best not to make comparisons, but found it was impossible to avoid.

As the trio approached the house, the front door opened. The familiar face standing there split into a grin.

"Relic, come!" said May, patting her hands on her thighs.

Allan dropped the leash so Relic could trot toward his pal.

"What are *you* doing here?" asked Rose, confused. Although she had never been to May's house, she knew her cousin lived near Martins River. Not here.

A woman who looked to be in her early sixties joined May in the doorway.

"This here's my friend Louise," said May. "We help each other out on rescues. And we got one we want you to meet."

"Come on in," said Louise warmly.

After Allan and Rose took off their boots and coats in the entryway, they were led into the living room. Where Relic was sniffing another dog.

A beagle mix.

"This here's Lily," said May, watching the two dogs get to know each other. "Sweet as pie and good as gold. Six years old.

Surrendered because her human had to move into the nursing home and couldn't take her." May choked up, pounding a palm on her chest. "Broke his heart."

Lily picked up a rope toy and placed it in front of Relic. In seconds, the two were playing tug-of-war. Tails wagging wildly.

May looked at Rose. "Lily needs a home. Relic needs a friend. And Allan says he'll help you with both of them."

Rose looked at her cousin. Then at Allan, who nodded. Then at the two dogs playing.

Shaking her head, Rose said, "I don't know…"

"What don't you know?" asked May, eager to seal the deal.

"If I'm ready," said Rose, lowering her voice.

"Aw, we're never really ready, are we?" said May. "Sometimes ya just gotta take a chance."

Louise joined in. "I've had her for two weeks, to see what she's like with my dog. My wife has Max out on a walk now, so these two could meet in private. Lily and Max have been getting along great."

"Why don't you keep her, then?" asked Rose.

Louise smiled. "Because then we couldn't help other fosters who need us."

Rose sighed. Looking at May, she said, "This isn't my Christmas present, is it?"

"Seriously, sister-cousin?" said May, horrified. "Everyone knows you don't give animals for Christmas. The time of year is a total coinkeydink."

Coincidence or not, as Rose watched the two dogs play, her heart expanded.

Rose remembered what Mabel had said she'd told May about fostering a cat. "Can I think about it over the holidays?"

"Okay," said May, shrugging. "Just don't *overthink* it."

Lily followed everyone back to the front door. Kneeling

with her bum on her heels, Rose held out her hand. Walking up to her with all the trust in the world, Lily licked Rose's palm.

"Good girl," said Rose softly, scratching behind her ears. Standing up, she said, "Nice to meet you, Louise."

Moving to the doorway, Rose said to May, "Now I have a proposal for *you*. Daisy would like you to come for Christmas dinner."

May cocked her head. "Will you be there?"

"Yes, for one night," said Rose. "Up Christmas Eve morning, back Christmas day after an early afternoon dinner."

"I don't eat turkey," said May. "I make a mean nut loaf with mushroom gravy, though. And I'd just come for the meal."

"Great," said Rose, smiling. "Everyone will be happy to see you. And two of Daisy's kids are vegetarians, so you won't starve."

Rose knew that Taylor Swift would be sitting under Allan's chair at his sister's house on Christmas day, waiting to be slipped bits of food. Rose had accepted Allan's invitation to have hot chocolate with him in the tiny house on Boxing Day.

Saying one last goodbye, the threesome got into the SUV. As Allan headed toward Rose's place, he said, "Lily's a love bug. What do you think?"

Rose sighed. "She's adorable. And Relic certainly likes her. But I don't know if I want the responsibility of two dogs again. I have to admit, as a single person, it's much easier with one."

"I'll help you," said Allan quickly. "I was going to foster a dog over the winter, anyway. If you're feeling overwhelmed, I'll take her for a while. Or both of them."

Rose hesitated. "That sounds great, in theory. But...what if I'm not here next spring? Then I've got two dogs, whether I want to or not."

Rose noticed Allan's grip tighten on the wheel. They hadn't discussed what her plans would be when Werner returned to his condo in April.

"Are you planning to move back to Halifax, then?" asked Allan.

Rose ran her fingers through her hair. "I haven't decided. I like living here. I like running the shop. Honestly, I try not to think about what would have become of me if I'd kept working at home this past year. I know I'd have been isolated and depressed."

"I hear a big *but* coming," said Allan, passing the Knot Pub. Festive patrons spilled out onto the sidewalk.

"Yes, *but*," said Rose, sighing. "My goal is to get through Christmas, then see where I land."

"For what it's worth, people here like you, Rose." Allan paused. "I don't think it's a secret that I like you. I know I don't get a vote, but I hope you'll stay."

To lighten the mood, Rose teased, "Not a secret? Then why didn't you sign the card that came with the flowers? They were beautiful. I've never thanked you for those. That was so thoughtful."

Allan looked confused. "But I did sign it! It was an online order, so maybe my name got cut off. What, did you think you had a secret admirer?"

"No, I just assumed Daisy sent them," said Rose, laughing. "May told me later they were from you."

Allan chuckled as he pulled into the condo's parking lot. When he turned off the ignition, he turned to Rose. "There's something you should know about me...and women...or, more specifically, relationships..."

Thanks to May's loose lips, Rose already knew about Allan's broken engagement. Still, she didn't interrupt him.

Struggling to find the right words, Allan carried on awkwardly. "It's just that I've always been the one to be...left behind."

Rose smiled sadly. "I've been left behind, too."

Shaking his head, Allan said, "It's not the same. I'm just... not very good at...*you know.*"

"The outcome is the same," said Rose simply. "We're both single."

Single sounded strange to Rose. Different than *widowed*. She wondered which box she'd choose to tick on future application forms.

"Anyway...I hope you'll stay," he said again, looking her in the eye. Then he opened his door. Rose waited for him to help Relic and her out.

"Would you like to come up and see the place?" she asked, titling her head up to meet Allan's eyes.

"Thanks, but I'll take a raincheck," he said, zipping up his jacket. "I'm heading to the Banker to go over the schedule with my staff for New Year's Eve. I'll be tending bar that night. It'd be nice if you dropped by for a drink. Oh, and feel free to bring your wingman."

Rose punched his arm, exasperated. "May is *not* my wingman!"

Allan grinned. "That's not what she says."

Reaching out to touch his arm where she'd punched it, Rose smiled and said, "Thanks, that sounds nice. But I have to warn you, I probably won't make it to midnight."

Allan laughed. "I'm asleep by eleven most nights. I'll have to nap that afternoon."

Keeping her hand on his arm, Rose held his gaze. "Thank you," she said.

Allan looked confused. "For what?"

"For...everything," Rose replied. She hesitated. "For the record, I like you, too. But...I just don't feel right dating anyone while I'm still wearing these." Holding up her left hand, she added, "And I'm not ready to take them off yet."

"Understood," said Allan, looking at Rose's wedding rings. "I'm not going anywhere."

But I might be, Rose thought.

Taking Relic's leash, Rose and her loyal canine companion walked toward the condo. When they were in the lobby, she turned around and waved goodbye.

Epilogue

THE END OF MARCH FELT FULL OF PROMISE, AS spring began to poke its sleepy head from beneath the frozen ground. Hardy snowdrops and winter aconites pushing through the last of the snow would soon be followed by a brilliant display of crocuses, daffodils, and tulips.

On April first, the lease on the condo would be up. Werner had emailed from Berlin to arrange the key return. Rose was looking forward to meeting him and hearing about his family visits in Germany before she and Relic moved out. The day before they left, she'd leave Relic with May overnight so a professional cleaner could vacuum the dog hair.

While Rose packed her winter clothes in a suitcase, she realized that she'd been marking time in milestones in her journal.

Sixteen months ago, Jim had died.

Eleven months ago, she had moved to Lunenburg.

Four months ago, Molly had gone over the rainbow bridge.

Two months ago, she had adopted Lily.

Three weeks ago, she had removed her wedding rings.

Last night, she had kissed Allan again. This time, on the lips.

It was a lot of change to process. And Jim had been with her through all of it.

In *The Year of Magical Thinking*, Joan Didion had written that she knew why we try to keep the dead alive. It's to keep them with us, she explained.

That isn't a revelation, thought Rose wryly.

Joan's husband had also died suddenly. At the end of her first year of widowhood, Joan realized that if people were to continue to live after their loved one was gone, there came a point where they had to let them go. To let them be the "photograph on the table."

After almost a year and a half of rolling along like a grieving tumbleweed, Rose was ready to put down new roots. In Lunenburg. She would always love and miss Jim and do her best to honour his memory. But it was time to start her second chapter.

It was time to let Jim become the photograph on the table.

It was time to choose a resting place for his urn.

It was time to find a therapist.

It was time to say goodbye to Drummond Court, and hello to the bungalow she had bought on Linden Avenue. Next door to where Eric and Margot had raised a large, loving family, and where one of their granddaughters was now raising hers.

It was time to start writing her memoir.

Sitting at the dining room table, a smile played on Rose's lips as she glanced at the book that had arrived in yesterday's mail. It was from Daisy. The new collection of essays by David Sedaris.

Rose opened her laptop and looked at the screen. Created a new Word document. Placed her fingers on the keyboard. Closed her eyes, inhaled deeply, then slowly exhaled.

She felt light. At peace. Ready to start her story.

Opening her eyes, she typed the first sentence.

Shortly after my fiftieth birthday everything went to shit.

Acknowledgements

THE FINGERPRINTS OF FREELANCE EDITOR extraordinaire Elizabeth Eve and my magnificent Vagrant Press editor, Whitney Moran, are all over these pages, and I wouldn't have it any other way. Thanks also to the entire team at Vagrant Press, including the hardest-working publicist on the planet, Kate Watson, and mega-talented designer Jenn Embree.

Some of the characters in this book have returned from my novels *The Pregnant Pause* and *Fishnets & Fantasies*, but there are a few new ones, too. My second cousin Amy Pulsifer ("Our grandmothers were sisters") wanted me to create a quirky cousin, and thus May Ainsworth was born. Shirley Gordon's wildlife-rescue stories infused May with colour and compassion, as did Hina Ansari's inspiring personal journey with multiple sclerosis. Many thanks to these women for helping me bring May to life. Rest assured, however, that May's personality is entirely her own!

A deep debt of gratitude goes to Lunenburg and District Fire Department chief Darren Romkey for walking me through the firefighting scenes and patiently answering my fire-related questions. You and your fellow volunteer firefighters, and all first responders, are brave beyond measure.

I've never owned and operated an adult emporium, or any kind of retail business. Maria Deveau, the owner of Maria's Pleasure Chest in Yarmouth, Nova Scotia, took the time to explain to me what it's like to run a sex shop in a small town.

Kelly McInnis, one of the late, great Hobo Doucet's veterinarians, helped me give the right words to Dr. Laura Richardson in a pivotal passage. Dawn Carson's work as a death doula was integral to shaping Wendy Hebb's story. And Theresa Greer, retired executive director of Heart House Hospice, kindly reviewed the grief support group scene.

Although I'm a proud Acadian, I'm not bilingual. *Je remercie mon cousin Wade LeBlanc pour son aide avec la traduction française* (and thank you to Elizabeth Eve for helping me translate that!).

A big thank you to the first readers who were generous with both their time and praise for this book (in alphabetical order by last name, so there's no fighting)—Ali Bryan, Bobbi French, Amy Jones, Bette MacDonald, James Mullinger, and Debbie Weiss—all of whom are talented, funny writers themselves.

Marilyn Smulders recently retired from her role as executive director of the Writers' Federation of Nova Scotia. Her efforts to offer superior programming to writers in the province, and to unite members in myriad wonderful ways, will be missed beyond measure, as will she.

To the booksellers, book reviewers, book bloggers, and librarians who tirelessly promote Canadian authors, to each of you I say: Thank you, thank you, THANK YOU! Among those who go above and beyond the call of duty in my area are Sue Slade at Dartmouth Book Exchange in Cole Harbour; Allison Murray at Carrefour Atlantic Emporium in Halifax; Mike Hamm at Bookmark in Halifax; and Cheryl Marshall at Chapters in Dartmouth.

Finally, eternal thanks to the readers who first met Rose Ainsworth in *The Pregnant Pause* in 2017 and asked for a sequel. Back then, I had nothing more to say about Rose or her journey. It just goes to show that you never know where stories will take you, or when, or even how. Until you do. And then if you're lucky, you'll get a chance to share them.

JANE DOUCET is a journalist whose articles have appeared in myriad national magazines, including *Chatelaine* and *Canadian Living*. In 2017, she self-published her debut novel, *The Pregnant Pause*, which was shortlisted for a 2018 Whistler Independent Book Award. Jane is thrilled that Vagrant Press has re-released *The Pregnant Pause* with a fresh new cover. In 2021, Vagrant published her second novel, *Fishnets & Fantasies*. Her third novel, *Lost & Found in Lunenburg*, published in 2023, combines characters from her first two novels. Jane lives in Halifax, Nova Scotia, with her husband. To learn more, visit *janedoucet.com*.